A PROM to REMEMBER

A Prom to Remember

Sandy Hall

SQUARE
FISH

Swoon Reads

New York

SQUARE
FISH

An imprint of Macmillan Publishing Group, LLC
175 Fifth Avenue, New York, NY 10010
fiercereads.com
swoonreads.com

Square Fish and the Square Fish logo are trademarks of Macmillan and are
used by Swoon Reads under license from Macmillan.

Our books may be purchased in bulk for promotional, educational, or business
use. Please contact your local bookseller or the Macmillan Corporate and
Premium Sales Department at (800) 221-7945 ext. 5442 or by email
at MacmillanSpecialMarkets@macmillan.com.

Library of Congress Cataloging-in-Publication Data

Names: Hall, Sandy (Librarian), author.
Title: A prom to remember / Sandy Hall.
Description: New York : Swoon Reads, 2018. | Summary: From seven
viewpoints, relates the events of Senior Prom at Roosevelt High School.
Identifiers: LCCN 2017041901 | ISBN 978-1-250-30920-4 (paperback) |
978-1-250-11913-1 (ebook)
Subjects: | CYAC: Proms—Fiction. | High schools—Fiction. | Schools—
Fiction. | Dating (Social customs)—Fiction. | Friendship—Fiction.
Classification: LCC PZ7.H14844 Pro 2018 | DDC [Fic]—dc23
LC record available at https://lccn.loc.gov/2017041901

Originally published in the United States by Swoon Reads
First Square Fish edition, 2019
Book designed by Sophie Erb
Square Fish logo designed by Filomena Tuosto

1 3 5 7 9 10 8 6 4 2

LEXILE: HL730L

For Lauren Velella, who reads every draft.
Even the bad ones.

A PROM to REMEMBER

Chapter 1

Cora

In general, prom committee meetings bred their own special kind of suffering.

The decision over where and when to hold the prom took a year. The menu planning nearly ended some friendships. The debate over the prom song brought the committee to a grinding halt for a full month. Each time there were tears, storm outs, and once even some bloodshed.

To be fair, the bloodshed was technically a paper cut.

So maybe it wasn't all that dramatic. But it felt that dramatic to Cora Wilson. Being in charge was not all it was cracked up to be.

As she sat at the front of the classroom and called the meeting to order, she held back a yawn until her eyes started to water. She just didn't have the energy today. It was bad enough coming back to school after April break, but it was even worse to have a prom committee meeting first thing in the morning before school even started.

Rows of exhausted faces stared back at Cora, until Luke Martinez yawned and she couldn't hold hers back even one more minute.

"Are we boring you?" Amelia Vaughn asked from her spot in the third row. "I thought we had something serious to discuss."

Cora shook her head and got back to the task at hand. "The biggest thing we need to do today is decide how we want to deal with prom king and queen."

There was a groan from the group, and Cora couldn't be sure, but she thought their advisor, Ms. Huang, perhaps groaned the loudest.

Amelia stood, blond hair gleaming even in the unforgiving fluorescent lights, and her sycophants grinned up at her. "I think we need to keep the tradition of king and queen alive. I think it would be ridiculous to throw away this long-held practice simply because, well, you know."

She looked around the room hopefully, as if someone would read her mind and fill in the rest of the sentence.

"Fine. I'll say it, because I know everyone is thinking it." She paused dramatically. "Our class just doesn't have an obvious prom king."

Cora massaged her temples. "I don't think anyone wants to throw away the tradition completely, but it's sort of old-fashioned, don't you think? Since the beginning of the year we've discussed the possibility of not doing a king and queen vote but changing it to a merit-based prom court honoring the students who have helped so much this year and in previous years with class projects."

Amelia rolled her eyes and sat down. Cora counted it as a win.

Kelsey Anderson raised her hand. "I think there are plenty of guys who would make a great king, and I think maybe we should consider a new way of doing things without completely getting rid of the old idea."

"Okay," Cora said. Kelsey always had an opinion, but they weren't always particularly helpful.

"Like who would make a good king?" Amelia asked. "Our whole class is a bunch of beta males."

The room fell silent.

"Like maybe, um, Henry Lai," Paisley said, chiming in from the back of the room, surprising everyone. By the look on her face, she had even surprised herself. Paisley made no secret of the fact that she was only on prom committee to fill a void in her extracurricular activities.

"Just because you're dating him or whatever," Amelia started.

"He's not my boyfriend," Paisley interrupted with an eye roll.

"That's why I said 'whatever.' I'm sure it's some hippie-dippie, undefined thing."

"It's really not," Paisley said with a sigh.

Cora jotted the name down, wanting to keep track of any possibilities. Even though in Cora's eyes it was a weird and antiquated concept, especially for young, progressive teens, there might be a point to be made that Cora hadn't considered. She liked to keep an open mind for her classmates.

It might be nicer and easier if the class could unite behind tradition and elect a king and queen. But a small voice in the back of her head told her it was not a good idea to always take the nice-and-easy way out.

At least everyone had finally stopped complaining about the theme. "A Prom to Remember" had been the prom theme at Roosevelt High for the past twenty years. The prom advisor to the class of 1998 had gotten an incredible deal on five thousand plastic champagne flutes with the phrase "A Prom to Remember" etched into them. Since then the administration had insisted that be the theme so the keepsake flutes didn't go to waste.

Amelia had tried hard to argue the theme, along with several others on the prom committees, but there was no way of changing it at this point. Cora was a little jealous of future seniors who would get to pick their own theme. Not that she would ever say it out loud.

"And what about Jamie," Teagan said while Cora was busy flipping through her notes from past discussions about prom court.

"What about Jamie?" Cora asked, her ears perking up at the mention of her boyfriend's name.

"Well, he'd make a great prom king. He's a great boyfriend, you know it, I know it, the freaking custodial staff knows that Jamie Fitzpatrick is the perfect boyfriend and he would make a perfect prom king," Josie said.

Cora hesitated before jotting his name down, too.

"What about queens?" Cora asked. She glanced around the room. Luke Martinez jumped up.

"Okay," Luke said. "This is why the idea of a court is so much better. A queen and a king are totally unnecessary in the scheme of things. Like Otis and I should be able to participate in this stuff as a couple."

"And I get that," Amelia said. "But, ugh. You guys are going to make me say it out loud." Amelia's use of the dramatic pause was off the charts that morning. "I want to be prom queen! Is that such a bad thing?"

Cora caught Teagan's eye. They were definitely both internally cringing. This was such an Amelia thing, but before Cora could say a word, Luke continued.

"I mean, I'm sorry if it ruins your chances of living out your dream of prom queen, but it's so heteronormative," Luke said.

Amelia opened her mouth, but before she could argue, Teagan stood up and said, "I agree with Luke, and I think it's time to move on to something less traditional and keeping more in the spirit of our changing world."

Luke, who had remained standing the whole time, high-fived Teagan. "Down with heteronormative bullshit!" Luke cried.

"Hey, hey," Ms. Huang said, finally interjecting. "I understand that this is something we're all passionate about, but let's watch the language."

Luke grinned and cast his eyes down sheepishly. "I'm sorry. I get swear-y when I'm passionate."

"Makes sense to me," Ms. Huang said, looking at the clock. "How about we table this decision for now and get back to it next week?"

Everyone nodded.

"In the meantime," Cora said. "Prom tickets go on sale today."

"It's about time," Amelia said.

"This is perfectly on schedule. You know prom tickets

never go on sale until after April vacation. Once the whole promposal trend caught on, the school wanted a way to keep those disruptions to a minimum."

Amelia huffed out a breath. "And what are we supposed to say when people ask us about prom king and queen nominations?"

"Just tell them the truth. We're still figuring it out."

Amelia flounced out of the room flanked by her two lackeys.

Cora collected her things and waved as Teagan and her other best friend, Josie, left the room.

"Do you have a second to discuss prom court?" Ms. Huang asked Cora.

Cora glanced at the clock, calculating how long she had.

"I know, you're a busy girl," Ms. Huang said. "But maybe you could come to class a minute early today and we could talk quickly?"

"Yeah, sure," Cora said over her shoulder as she trailed her friends out of the room. "I would stay now, but I just have to go make copies of the agenda for the student council meeting."

"A million things to do, huh? Just another day in the life of Cora Wilson," Ms. Huang said with a knowing smile.

Cora made it out into the hallway where Jamie was waiting for her.

"Hey, babe," Jamie said, threading his arm around her waist.

"Please don't call me babe," she said offhandedly. Sometimes she felt more like an exasperated sibling than his girlfriend.

"Where are you off to?" he asked. "You gonna walk me to homeroom today? Carry my books?"

She grinned. She couldn't help herself. He was adorable in his own Jamie way. "Sadly I cannot. I need to make some photocopies."

"I'll walk with you, then, and hold your books."

"Fine, but we have to keep moving," she said as the warning bell rang, tugging on his hand as he walked past a couple of baseball dudes and high-fived or fist-bumped each of them. "Or you could just go hang out with your friends."

"I think I'm just gonna hang out with them, babe," he said, kissing the side of her head and spinning backward toward his friends.

Cora kept on moving down the hallway without further comment. She had bigger things to deal with.

Paisley

Paisley Turner followed Cora Wilson down the hall like a jungle cat stalking her prey.

She didn't want to interrupt whatever conversational foreplay Cora and her boyfriend were engaged in, but didn't they realize that Paisley had to get Henry's name off that prom king list? She had only put his name out there hypothetically. Panic set in when she saw Cora jot it down. The conversation had taken off after that, and Paisley couldn't get a word in edgewise, so it seemed like a better idea to wait until after the meeting. But Cora was basically ignoring her. Or maybe she didn't even realize Paisley was there.

The fact of the matter was that Henry was Paisley's best friend. She was way too aware of his neuroses, and he would disown her if he got nominated for prom king. It was the opposite of anything he wanted in this world. And she knew that. She could already imagine the face he would make, staring at her with his dark-brown-eye death glare. Angry Henry was a rarity, and Paisley was not prepared to deal with him. She shouldn't have opened her mouth.

However, there was little that annoyed Paisley quite so much as the sanctimony of Amelia Vaughn. And in the face of sanctimony, Paisley had put her best friend in a situation he would hate. But Amelia needed a talking-to, and while in her head Paisley was always giving Amelia talking-tos, she didn't quite have the balls to do it in person. Quite frankly, Amelia scared her.

However, she was happy to passive-aggressively nominate her best friend for prom king if it meant shutting Amelia up.

All the boys in their class might have been "beta males," to use Amelia's term, but that didn't make them terrible guys. *Sorry they don't live up to your high standards, Amelia.*

What irked Paisley the most was that she had somehow ended up arguing to keep the whole prom-king-and-queen dumpster fire even though she didn't care about it at *all*. She would have totally fought against the ridiculous tradition, except that she wanted desperately to prove Amelia wrong. The guys in their class were great! Just because they weren't the usual variety of jockish Sasquatches that Amelia had dated all through high school didn't mean they were second-class citizens.

And yet Paisley was definitely disappointed in herself. She was supposed to be fighting the patriarchy. "Nevertheless, she persisted," and all that good stuff. But there she was, supporting a victory for heteronormative bullshit, as Luke had so eloquently put it.

If she wanted to get to the heart of the matter, what really annoyed Paisley was that she was on prom committee in the first place. Unfortunately her advisor had insisted at the beginning of the year that Paisley put something else on her college applications besides "Mall-food-court potato technician," and prom committee just happened to fit in her schedule.

Also she heard there'd be free food at every meeting.

She had been lied to.

She could have, and probably should have, quit. But at this point in the school year it was easier just to ride it out and avoid confrontation. Especially since sometimes the drama within the committee was entertaining. Being involved in the drama was less entertaining.

The warning bell rang, and Paisley had no choice but to stop following the happy couple and head for her locker. She promised herself that she would track Cora down later and ask her to take Henry's name off the list. Henry would never be the wiser.

As Paisley made her way down the hall, passing through a sea of students and long rows of lockers, there was a certain buzz in the air.

Ah yes, the buzz of prom tickets being on sale and the flood of promposals happening everywhere she turned.

Given that tickets had only gone on sale like fourteen seconds ago, these weren't the elaborate sort of promposals that you see on the local news (barf) but the kind of spontaneous promposals that you might find in a teen rom com. You know, the kind where a boy was literally kneeling down in the middle of the hallway to ask a girl to the prom.

Barf, barf, barf.

Paisley huffed out an irritated breath as she spun her combination lock and started digging through the detritus that lived in the bottom of her locker.

Finding what she needed by touch, she slammed the door shut at the same moment there was a shriek at the end of the hallway where some girl was a little too excited about getting invited to the prom. To each his or her or their own, but this whole situation was definitely not for Paisley.

Paisley fished her phone out of her pocket and shot a quick text to Henry.

Paisley:

I will kill you if you ask me to prom.

Henry:

I will cancel the fourteen dozen roses that I sent to your house.

She slid into her seat in homeroom.

Paisley:

Leave the roses. I'll burn them in my backyard. I'm sure I could find some kind of cleansing ritual on Pinterest.

Henry:

I thought we weren't allowed to text each other while we were in the same room.

10

She turned around and gave Henry the finger.

He put his hands up in defense. "Hey, it's your rule."

"Rules were meant to be broken," Paisley said in a threatening-action-hero voice as their homeroom teacher wandered in and got their attention. Paisley turned back around and did her best to hide her grin.

Chapter 2

Jacinta

Homeroom was probably the number-one thing on "Jacinta Ramos's List of Things She Would Not Miss About High School."

It went like this:

1. Homeroom.
2. That certain smell in the cafeteria.
3. That certain smell in the girls' locker room. (She assumed the boys' locker room was likely even worse but, having no personal experience with it, decided to limit it to a smell she knew all too well.)
4. How long it took to get out of the parking lot after school while everyone else on earth was trying to leave at the same exact moment.
5. Feeling like a background character in her own life.

Number five was something that haunted her on a daily basis. But she wasn't going to let it get the better of her.

Jacinta wanted desperately to be seen as more than just a background character; she wanted to have one iconic high school moment.

And The Prom would be her moment.

The Prom was the hill she was going to die on. She had even made it her New Year's resolution. At the stroke of midnight, she whispered, "I will go to The Prom, and I will not be a background character for one whole night."

With prom tickets having gone on sale yesterday, it was finally time to make good on her promise to herself. She needed a date, she needed a dress, and she needed a huge dose of courage.

As she jogged toward her locker after homeroom to grab her sociology textbook, she found a couple standing in front of it with a bouquet of at least ten helium-filled balloons. When the girl said yes, a hasty celebratory make-out session started and Jacinta could not find a way in to her locker through the balloons.

How was it that Jacinta had gone through four years of high school without having even one boy hang around her locker? Isn't that what was supposed to happen in high school? Locker lingering? Wasn't that supposed to be how high school students found love?

At least that's what every teen romantic comedy movie that Jacinta had ever watched made her believe.

But Jacinta wasn't even lucky enough to be the romantic b-plot in the movie of her own life. She was shoved deep down in the credits and would be billed as "Unnamed Nerd Girl #3" somewhere near the bottom of the list. Her best friend, Kelsey, would at least be "Head Nerd Girl in Charge," and Kelsey's ex-boyfriend, Landon, who inexplicably still hung around them all the time would of course be "Head Nerd Boy in Charge."

Even if they were unnamed characters, at least Kelsey and Landon were in charge.

Jacinta had almost nothing to show for her four years of high school except for being Kelsey's sidekick.

She had about a million things she'd wanted to say in the prom committee meeting yesterday. First of all, she had wanted to tell Cora Wilson that she was doing an awesome job and not to listen to anything Amelia Vaughn had to say. Amelia was a total butt. Not even a butthead, just a butt.

But Jacinta had to agree with Luke Martinez on his point. The concept of having a prom king and queen was an outdated tradition and one she didn't want any part of. It was as good a year as any to get rid of it.

And maybe future senior classes would want to elect kings and queens and dukes and duchesses and whatever the hell else. But it didn't mean they had to. Maybe it was about time the class of 2018 put an end to things they weren't interested in.

Onward and upward, as they say.

The post-promposal make-out session came to an end, so Jacinta slipped in and got what she needed from her locker before setting off in the direction of her sociology class.

On her way there it was hard not to notice all the flowers and balloons and signs spelling out *Prom?* It had been like this every spring in high school. She wasn't sure when promposals became such a trend, but she couldn't deny that she kind of wished someone would prompose to her.

She sleepwalked through the rest of her morning, daydreaming about a faceless boy asking her to prom and trying not to feel too pathetic about this self-insert fan fiction she was writing in her head.

When she finally got to lunch later that day, Kelsey was sitting at their usual table holding court with Landon.

"I hate to say it, but I think I agree with Amelia. I think the class as a whole could do with some regular old, traditional prom stuff. I think it would be fun to do the whole king-and-queen thing," Kelsey said as Jacinta slid into a seat.

"I have to agree," Landon said.

He always had to agree with Kelsey. It was probably the only way they continued to get along after breaking up junior year.

"I don't," Jacinta said, setting her lunch on the table and taking a seat.

They both looked at her like she had desecrated some expensive piece of art.

"I don't think it's that big of a deal, but I definitely don't think we need to have a king and a queen. I think it's sort of ridiculous."

Kelsey audibly gasped.

"What do you think we should do?" Landon asked.

"I agree with Luke and them. We could do a court and recognize lots of other people. Don't you guys want to get recognized for all the work you've done? Neither one of you is going to be king or queen, no offense." Where this bold moment had come from was anyone's guess, but Jacinta felt a warm rush of pride for saying what she was thinking for once.

Kelsey and Landon blinked at each other and then blinked

at Jacinta. It was like they hadn't even considered their part in all of this.

"We have done a lot for the class," Kelsey said.

"We have," Landon agreed.

"Maybe it is time that we as a collective move away from weird old traditions like king and queen," Kelsey said.

Jacinta smiled. They were listening to her. They were *actually* listening to her. Maybe this was the first step toward a starring role, to not just being a side character.

"Well, I know how I'm voting next week," Landon said.

"Me too," Kelsey said. "I'm glad Cora gave us some time to think about this stuff. I would have hated to make a snap judgment."

Jacinta barely contained an eye roll at Landon's brown-nosing head nod.

Cameron

Cameron Wyatt was totally and completely over high school, and he couldn't help assuming everyone else was, too.

But then prom tickets went on sale, and it was like everyone started clawing out their own eyes to get a date.

Even if Cameron had been in the mood for prom, he didn't have anyone he wanted to invite. Well, he sort of did, but they had never met and had only spoken through messages sent via a shared laptop in English class. And the mere thought of inviting her made his face blush approximately the same color as his hair. It wasn't a good look and should be avoided at all costs.

Whenever there was computer work to be done, Ms. Huang would haul in the laptop cart and Cameron would make a grab for laptop 19. He would open it up and wait for the ancient machine to load the desktop where he would dig through the "secret" file that Laptop Girl had set up for them.

Though they had exchanged messages on nearly a daily basis for the past couple of months, they never exchanged names. Cameron didn't really want her to know who he was, and the only time she had asked, she seemed cool with keeping their messages anonymous.

The only reason he even knew she was a girl was because she made a comment about being her "mother's daughter."

It had all started in the beginning of the year when he grabbed a laptop off the cart and someone had changed the background to a picture of dancing cats with the caption "But consider this: the Great CATS-by." It wasn't the best joke ever, but it made him laugh.

He made the background a picture of cats marching and changed the caption to "What About Brave New Cats?" He put an asterisk next to the question mark with a note that said, "Please check for my disclaimer in the document called 'Bad Jokes.'"

The document when opened contained only the word SORRY written in 72-point bold font.

But apparently his bad jokes didn't stop her from continuing to engage with him. In that same document, she deleted his 72-point SORRY and started writing in normal-size font. She left a note on the desktop telling him to check the doc. (He wondered more than once if someone else was following their messages, but no one ever spoke up. Maybe they were the only two people who habitually used laptop 19.)

The first message had started with:

So I'm bored. I'm going to ask you a million questions (or maybe just five) on the off chance you'll answer them and then I'll have something fun to read. Please respond in complete sentences. The five questions are as follows:

- What's your favorite color?
- Can you use chopsticks?
- What's your first memory?
- What do you want to be when you grow up?
- Do you have a name?

He happily responded to all her questions.

My favorite color is green. But like LIME GREEN. A green that can be seen from outer space. A green so green you can practically taste it.

I cannot use chopsticks.

Number three is a difficult question. Because memory is a weird thing, isn't it? Do I really remember a certain moment, or is it because I've seen pictures of it and heard the story a million times? I would say that probably my first memory is being in a minor car accident with my mom when I was four or five. I know there are no photographs of this moment slipped into family scrapbooks. No one was hurt, it was only a small fender bender, but it's a pretty traumatic event for a kid. Also, I was really into police cars, so I remember when they arrived on the scene very distinctly.

Oh man. I have no clue what I want to be when I grow up. I had no idea that I'd be quizzed on this today, and I have no answer. "Something that's not terrible" is about as specific as I can get.

As for your last query, yes, I do have a name. But if it's all the same to you, I'd prefer not to share it. It's kind of fun being anonymous.

And I ask you the same million (or five) questions.

When he got the laptop the next time, Laptop Girl had answered and he had to work pretty hard not to laugh too much at her responses.

My favorite color is now lime green. You've convinced me. A green so green that you can almost taste it.

I am surprisingly good at chopsticks. I got a little obsessed with them after my aunt took me out to hibachi for my sixth birthday. I wanted desperately to be able to use them, so she took her time to show me, and after dropping several pieces of chicken on the floor, I managed to get one in my mouth.

Funny enough, I'm pretty sure that my birthday hibachi dinner is also my first real memory. There are other moments, but they're more like images than memories, like a trip to the zoo and getting a new couch. I really REMEMBER the restaurant and the onion volcano.

I don't know what I want to be when I grow up. I was hoping that you'd have an idea and I could steal it, much like your favorite color.

I, too, have a name, but I won't be sharing because you're right, anonymity is fun.

Every time the laptop cart was in the room, Cameron knew he had a treat waiting for him. It made English, and everything else about his senior year, a lot more bearable.

Cameron and Laptop Girl somehow remained anonymous even while sharing personal details. It worked for them. They

19

both agreed several times that it was nice to have someone to spill secrets to and to talk to without having to worry about anyone finding out.

> Unless you decide to print this out and start plastering it around the school.

she joked in one message. Then followed it up with:

> Please don't do that.

He reread their most recent exchange and grinned.

For a second, he wished that they could meet in real life. But that opened a whole kettle of fish that he wasn't prepared to deal with. Instead, he started a new message.

Chapter 3

Henry

Henry Lai liked to play a game in the long crowded hallways at school. It was called "How far can I go without touching anyone AND without anyone touching me."

The good news was that it was a pretty challenging game, good for his reflexes.

The bad news was that he never got very far. Henry felt like his classmates had little interest in personal boundaries. It was a shame to say the least.

The even worse news was that since prom tickets had gone on sale earlier in the week the traffic in the hallways had grown to a near standstill. Henry was at his wit's end just trying to get through the day.

He made it to his locker relatively unscathed Wednesday afternoon and checked his phone. He had a text from his best friend, Paisley.

> **Paisley:**
> Remind me that I have something to tell
> you later that I keep forgetting to tell you.

Why couldn't she tell him now? He hated waiting for stuff like that. All it was going to do to him was make him think and worry and wonder what she could be talking about.

> **Henry:**
> Why can't you tell me now?

> **Paisley:**
> I would, but I feel like I can explain
> things better to you in person.

> **Henry:**
> Oh well, that's not ominous or terrible in any
> way. I'm sure I'll have a lovely afternoon
> wondering about this. I won't be anxious at all.
> I won't be slowly driven mad by this thought.

> **Paisley:**
> Stop being so dramatic and
> go to baseball practice.

> **Henry:**
> Guess I'll stop being so dramatic
> and go to baseball practice.

He took a screenshot of these texts. Sometimes he did that with Paisley. Not because he wanted to preserve these conversations forever, but because if someone were to ever challenge him on his friendship with Paisley, these were the kind of things he liked to keep as proof. Also it was never a bad idea to keep receipts.

There was something about the way she talked to him, so no-nonsense, that no one else in his life had quite figured out.

Henry walked out of school with his backpack over his shoulder and his baseball glove in hand. He'd turned in the direction of the baseball field when he saw it.

The most terrible thing.

A promposal of epic proportions. This was no little moment in the hall that could be skirted around. This was happening in the front of the school at the end of the day.

He burned with the shame of secondhand embarrassment as a girl asked a boy to the prom right there in the middle of the school lawn. In front of God and parents picking up freshmen and students exiting the building and EVERYONE.

He was never sure if what he experienced in these moments was an overload of empathy or an overload of sympathy. Whatever it was, it was nearly crushing him. He couldn't move as he watched Margie Showalter hold up her hand-lettered and glittered sign that read STEWART SMITH—WILL YOU GO TO PROM WITH ME?

She was smiling broadly and obviously trying to hold the sign steady in the breeze.

Henry could see little flecks of glitter fluttering off into the air and blowing around. He imagined where those pieces of glitter might end up. A bird's nest, someone's unsuspecting ice cream cone, the sewer.

And then the worst thing happened. The absolutely worst thing imaginable.

Stewart Smith said no.

Henry saw him shake his head. His smile was apologetic.

He said a few things, but the words were obscured by the wind that was now kicking up even more glitter.

Things were falling apart in slow motion in the middle of the school parking lot. Henry didn't know how to deal with this horrible tableau that was happening in front of him. He had the distinct urge to run away and never, ever look back.

That's exactly what Margie was doing.

She wasn't running, though, just walking away dejectedly, and dragging her poster along behind her.

Henry accidentally made eye contact with her for a split second. His regret was swift and immense. She looked like someone had run over her dog.

"I thought he liked me," Margie said to no one in particular.

Henry's eyes went wide, and he knew he did not have the bandwidth for her sad state of rejection. He backed away from her, going off the path down to the field instead and winding his way across the lawn, trying to avoid the goose crap that was everywhere. For some reason, geese from a nearby pond liked to come up to the grass in front of the school and basically shit everywhere. It was an issue that the administration hadn't figured out a way to deal with yet, even though it'd been literally happening for years. Something about the new dam that had been built by the brook. It was a serious environmental issue.

Jamie Fitzpatrick materialized next to him, his long legs falling into rhythm next to Henry, barely managing to miss what could only be described as goose diarrhea.

"Oh gross," is all Jamie said as he sidestepped around it.

"Hey," Henry said, keeping his eyes on the ground.

"Why are you walking through this field of sorrow and goose shit?"

"Oh man, I just watched this really terrible promposal go down. Margie Showalter asked Stewart Smith, and the dude said no."

"That's awful. Why would you make such a big show if you weren't guaranteed a yes, you know?"

"I have no idea," Henry said. "I was just so embarrassed for Margie. I mean, I'd be embarrassed for anyone getting rejected, but there was something about this moment. I wished the ground would swallow me up on her behalf."

"How could the ground swallowing you up even help her?" Jamie asked.

Jamie was not the brightest bulb in the box. "It wouldn't. I'm just explaining to you that it was that embarrassing."

"Oh, I get you." Jamie bobbed his head. Henry had a feeling that Jamie did not get him but that he mostly wanted to stop talking about this. They were at the field house now where all the guys changed for practice. "I'm so freaking relieved that I have a girlfriend and don't have to deal with shit like that. You know, like rejection. When I ask Cora I know she'll say yes."

"You haven't asked her yet?" Henry asked.

"Nah, I'm waiting a couple days, until she'll be surprised and I know she'd kill me if I made a big deal about it."

Henry chewed his lip.

"What about you?" Jamie asked. "You gonna ask someone?"

Henry wrinkled his nose. "I'm not really interested in prom."

"Oh, come on, man. It's one of those things." Jamie paused and snapped his fingers, searching for the words. "You know. Like a thing."

"Tradition?"

"Well that, too, but like . . . Oh man, I'm so annoyed I can't think of this."

Henry shrugged.

"A rite of passage!" Jamie said, smacking Henry hard on the shoulder.

"I'm sure I'll live," Henry muttered, rubbing the point of impact. He wasn't in the mood to explain to Jamie Fitzpatrick that the anxiety of even considering the prom wasn't worth Henry's time.

He had a feeling Jamie wouldn't understand that sentiment, so he kept it to himself.

Lizzie

It was Friday night and the mall was hopping.

The parking lot was full, the stores were packed, and there were lines at every eatery in the food court. Except for Hot Potato. No one ever lined up for Hot Potato. It was always a last resort.

But the unpopularity of their workplace left Paisley and Lizzie with plenty of time to talk.

Lizzie leaned her hip on the counter by the register, looking alert in case a customer came up, while Paisley picked pieces of chive out of the adjacent container of shredded cheddar using the world's smallest tongs. They might actually have qualified as tweezers, and Lizzie had to wonder where Paisley even found them.

"So are you super psyched about prom?" Lizzie asked in a voice dripping with fake enthusiasm.

"Totally!" Paisley said with an eye roll of her green eyes and a rock-and-roll hand gesture. Her brown hair was cut into a floppy, growing-out pixie cut that really helped sell her whole vibe, Lizzie thought.

Lizzie attempted the same gesture back.

"I'm pretty sure you said 'I love you' in sign language," Paisley said.

"Oh, oops," Lizzie said.

Paisley could always pull off stuff like that. Lizzie just wasn't cool enough, particularly in comparison to Paisley. Lizzie was chubby to Paisley's waifishness, and her hair was frizzy instead of straight. Lizzie told herself over and over that it did no good to compare herself to other people, especially other girls, but there was something about Paisley she wished she could emulate.

"Anyway, I've been trying to figure out what exactly is so thrilling about going to prom," Lizzie said, changing the topic and attempting to cover her embarrassment. "Is it all the money you spend? Or stressing out over having the same dress as someone else?"

Paisley stood up, having finished her chive scavenger hunt, and brushed any errant chives she left behind off the work area. "If I had to guess, I would say it's the cummerbunds."

"Or the, you know, the sex thing," Lizzie mumbled.

Paisley thought about that for a second. "What?"

"You know. Our classmates are horndogs, in general, and there's an inherent sex vibe surrounding the whole thing, you know? Like all those prom movies about having sex for the first time, feeding the teenagers of America big dreams for loss of virginity."

"I don't have the proper sexy radar," Paisley said with a shrug.

A customer came up then, interrupting their conversation. As Paisley walked him through selecting his toppings and explained for the millionth time that yes, they only have potatoes, and no, they don't have any burgers, Lizzie thought about the prom. She definitely never wanted to go before. There was nothing about it that enticed her; she hadn't been lying to Paisley a few minutes ago.

But there was one thing that had been nagging at the back of her mind.

She rang up the customer, and he walked off in search of a burger to go with his chili cheese potato. It seemed like overkill to Lizzie, but she tried not to think too hard about it.

She turned to Paisley. "Do you think you'll ever regret not going?"

"Um, no," Paisley said, checking herself out in the reflective paper towel dispenser and fixing her visor. She turned to Lizzie.

"Aren't you on the prom committee? Isn't it your duty to go?"

"I'm only there for something to put on my college applications. Do you think you'll go?"

Lizzie's shoulders fell. "Never in my life have I ever wanted to go to prom. I didn't understand the romance of it, or what the point was in general. But now, it's like something has changed."

Paisley gave her a knowing look. "I'm going to assume this is about Mystery Boy."

Lizzie buried her face in her hands. "Yes," she said, her voice muffled.

"It's nothing to be embarrassed about," Paisley said.

"It's not?" Lizzie asked, peeking out from behind her hands.

"Of course not. Just because I'm dead inside doesn't mean that everyone has to be."

"You're not dead inside."

"Fine, I'm not dead inside, but sometimes I feel dead inside. Like I never have the *feelings* that other people do," Paisley said.

Lizzie stood up straight, preparing to defend her friend from herself, which was a confusing situation but one Lizzie felt quite strongly about.

"You are totally awesome," Lizzie said.

"Oh, I am. But I'm pretty sure that's what my problem is with all of this. I don't get it, you know?" Paisley said.

Lizzie shrugged. "I don't get it, either. I'm sure we don't *get* it in different ways, but that doesn't make you an emotionless robot."

"I mean, I might be an emotionless robot. I don't even feel anything about graduating from high school. Like, nothing."

At that moment, someone cleared their throat from the other side of the cash register.

Lizzie turned around, plastering her best Hot Potato smile on.

"Oh, it's you," Lizzie said when she saw her friend Madison standing there.

"Damn, I can't believe how fast your customer service smile faded when you saw me," Madison said.

"It didn't fade, it was overtaken with relief that I didn't have to stop being lazy and actually help a customer."

Madison looked over to Paisley, who nodded. "It's true. We've had a quiet evening, so it would suck to have to, you know, do our jobs."

"What if I actually wanted a potato?" Madison asked.

"Do you want a potato?"

"Nah, I had dinner," Madison said as she slid across the counter. "So what did I miss with you two?" She sat on the little stool in the corner out of the line of vision of anyone passing. Someday Paisley and Lizzie would get in trouble for letting their friend go behind the counter, but hopefully tonight was not that night.

"Lizzie's in love with Mystery Boy," Paisley said.

"Paisley's an emotionless robot," Lizzie answered as Paisley threw a piece of bacon at her and missed.

"Don't waste that!" Madison said. "Bacon is delicious and shouldn't be wasted. Also Paisley's not an emotionless robot. But Lizzie is totally in love with Mystery Boy."

"Aw, thanks, Madison," Paisley said as Lizzie hit her square in the face with a limp piece of broccoli.

Chapter 4

Otis

Otis Sorenson was doing his calc homework Sunday afternoon. At least, his calc homework was open on his desk in front of him. If you wanted to get technical about it, he was paying far more attention to the conversation he was having via text with his friend Tag.

Tag was having girl trouble. Or "women problems" as Tag liked to say.

Tag:

So I thought everything was fine. We definitely hooked up in the back seat of my car.

Otis:

What does "hooking up" even entail? It's such a vague concept. Like, I don't need the play-by-play. But I never know what people mean when they use that phrase. Sex? Everything but sex? Heavy petting?

Tag:

Heavy petting? What is this, the '50s?

Otis:

Fine, I meant necking. Did you neck with her in the back seat of your '57 Chevy at the drive-in after the sock hop?

Before Tag's answer came through, Otis heard a few strains of music. He checked the volume on his computer, but it seemed like the noise was actually coming from outside.

Otis might not have even bothered to check, but it was a really familiar song. A song he couldn't quite put his finger on. At least not until he looked outside.

Otis's bedroom window faced onto the street, and standing outside, leaning against his car, was his boyfriend, Luke, holding up his iPhone that was hooked to his car's speakers and blasting Peter Gabriel's seminal classic, "In Your Eyes."

Otis couldn't help but laugh as he opened his window, stuck his head out, and looked down at his dark-eyed, smooth-skinned, awesome-haired boyfriend. "Like a young Ricky Martin," Otis's mom once said in passing. So Otis then googled young Ricky Martin and was not disappointed.

Luke had used what Otis hoped was masking tape to spell out the word *PROM* on the roof of his car. If it was not masking tape and it took the paint off, then Luke was definitely going to be in trouble. His parents were sticklers about that car. They were better than Otis's parents, though, because Otis didn't even have a car and instead was forced to share with his older sister whenever she deigned to come home from college for the weekend.

Otis leaned his elbows on the windowsill and smiled down at Luke, who grinned up at him.

"Have you ever even seen *Say Anything*?" Otis asked, knowing full well that the answer was no.

"No, but I know an iconic romantic scene when I see it, even if it's only a GIF on Tumblr. And I know you love this no matter how much you want to pretend that you don't."

Otis's smile only grew, like he couldn't even contain it on his face. He'd had braces for a ridiculously long time, and his teeth were incredibly straight thanks to that, but when he smiled, he still had a tendency to keep his lips pressed firmly together. But right now, even after seven years of braces and being embarrassed about how terrible they looked, he smiled so wide, he had no choice but to open his mouth.

"I wasn't expecting this," he called out to Luke while waving at a neighbor walking his dog. "It's completely awesome."

"Good, I'm glad you think so," Luke said. They'd been together for about six months now but had been friends much longer. Back in middle school they were on the same baseball team and they hung out sometimes. But in high school Otis got super into baseball and Luke drifted toward the theater kids. They didn't spend much time together in high school. At least not until they were at a party junior year and Luke drunkenly told Otis that he was gay.

Otis, at that point, had no idea he himself was gay. But when he realized he was into guys last fall, the first person he wanted to tell was Luke. They've been together ever since. Sort of.

It took Luke a few tries to crack Otis. Not so much because Otis didn't like him but because even though Otis was out, he wasn't sure how out he wanted to be. It took him a little while to find a balance. And once Otis went looking for the balance, he found a lot of support.

It helped that there was some other major high school drama going on around the time Otis and Luke started dating publicly. (The vice principal resigned out of nowhere, and there were tons of rumors swirling around about the cause.) By the time everyone got around to noticing Luke and Otis, it didn't feel like a big deal.

All of Otis's worries were for nothing. There wasn't any hate or homophobia to be found. Not within the senior class, at least. There were some underclassmen who seemed intent on making Luke's life a bit of a nightmare, but a few well-placed words and some intimidation from the guys on the baseball team fixed it right up. Otis wasn't sure how he got so lucky.

Luke and Otis were, for all intents and purposes, a happy couple. Both content to go on dates and hold hands at school, to text for hours or just watch TV together. It was a low-maintenance relationship.

What Otis worried about in the dark corners of the night when he woke up suddenly and couldn't fall back to sleep was what if all they had in common was an appreciation for cheesy movies and, you know, being gay. Because while Otis knew he liked Luke a lot, he had a feeling Luke might be in love with him. And Otis wasn't sure if he was there yet.

He worried a lot about the day that Luke would tell Otis he loved him and Otis would say something terrible like "Thank you" or "I'm quite fond of you, also." It would be embarrassing and so disappointing for Luke.

But it was easy to forget worries like that when Luke

showed up on a sunny spring evening to make a grand romantic gesture.

And pretty much all of Luke's gestures were grand and romantic. Otis tried to keep up, but he often felt like he fell a little short. Though he would make up for that on Monday morning when Luke opened his locker for his own promposal.

Otis was still smiling when he said, "Come on. My mom owns *Say Anything* on DVD. You should get indoctrinated."

"I'm going to assume that's a yes to prom, then?" Luke asked.

Otis picked up his notebook and scrawled the word YES across one of the pages in big bold letters, and showed it to Luke, before he closed his window and raced down the stairs.

Otis met Luke on the front porch, kissing him long and slow, before pausing to smile at him, just because he felt like smiling.

"I don't think I've ever seen so many teeth in your mouth. I had no idea you had this many teeth," Luke said, threading his arms around Otis's waist and kissing him some more.

Jacinta

Sometimes being the youngest of five meant that Jacinta's life was a circus. People coming in and out at all hours, loud noises, booming voices, other people's agendas. She learned at a very young age that she was definitely not the center of the universe.

Other times, being the youngest was strangely quiet. Because of all those people having their own agendas, it often meant that Jacinta was left in the dust.

For example, one Sunday night in mid-April it was only Jacinta and her mom eating dinner together since the rest of the family was off living their lives. Technically, they were all running late for dinner.

"I thought they'd be home by now," Jacinta's mom said as she took the chicken out of the oven. "We're going to eat without them because I don't want the food to get cold."

When they sat down at the table, it was no shock to Jacinta that she was in her mother's crosshairs. There were no other children to pester.

"What's going on at school lately?" her mom asked.

"Pretty much the usual," Jacinta said. "The other day in prom committee we decided to have a prom court along with electing a prom king and queen." It had been a pretty good discussion for once. No arguments or tears or bloodshed. Everyone, even Amelia Vaughn, seemed happy with the compromise.

"Oh, prom," her mom said with a big grin.

"Yes, prom," Jacinta said.

"Is there anyone you want to go with?"

Jacinta glanced up from her plate where she had been concentrating on chasing a piece of corn around with her fork. It did not want to be eaten. She almost admired its will to survive, and then remembered that it was literally just a piece of corn.

"There is not," Jacinta said.

"Oh, there must be someone. I know you have lots of eligible boys in your class."

Why her mother knew anything about the boys in her class

was a mystery to Jacinta, considering *she* didn't even know about the eligible boys in her class.

"So when is it exactly?" her mom asked, unperturbed by Jacinta's reticence on the subject. This was not her first trip to the rodeo with children who didn't want to talk about something. And while Jacinta was in fact quite excited about the prom, there was something leading about her mom's questions that made her hesitate to give too much information.

"It's June first."

"And where is it?"

Jacinta put her fork down and took a sip of her water. "Mom, I told you all about this months ago. I've been working on the prom since sophomore year. I helped them pick out the venue and the date and all of that right from the start."

"I can't always keep track of everything!" her mom insisted.

"I know, but this is old news. It's at the Sheraton, the first Friday in June."

"Oh, that's a beautiful venue. Your cousin Elena got married there. Remember?"

"Yes. I remember."

"Why didn't you tell me when tickets went on sale?"

Jacinta blinked at her mother. "I had no idea you were this interested in the prom." She decided to turn the tables on her. "Why are you so interested in prom all of a sudden?"

"I guess I was worried that you weren't talking about things because you felt neglected in the face of Flora's wedding. She's kind of taking over. I know she is, and I don't mean for you to get lost in the middle of everything."

"Oh. I appreciate that," Jacinta said, going back to her food.

"Do you need money? For anything? A dress or a limo with your friends? Did you buy a ticket?"

This was far more attention than Jacinta had received in years, or at least that's how it felt.

"I don't need money. I didn't buy a ticket. I'll let you know when and if I do. I don't really have anyone to go with at the moment."

"I was thinking," her mom said, placing her fork down on her plate. "I bet Henry Lai doesn't have a date. He flies under the radar like you do. You could go with him. I could talk to his mom about it at work tomorrow."

"Oh my god, Mother," Jacinta said. But before she could argue the point further, the front and back doors opened simultaneously and most of her immediate family poured in, including her dad, her sister, her sister's fiancé, and two of her brothers.

Her conversation with her mother was definitely over.

Her family was loud, and Jacinta had never learned to be loud enough to be heard over everyone else's din. She never minded getting talked over, but she hated trying to compete for her mother's attention. She'd rather not even try than to lose out to her older siblings, which was pretty much what always happened.

Jacinta took the opportunity to slip out of her mother's focus and let the rest of her family take over the spotlight. It was in fact one of her greatest talents.

The next morning in school she approached Henry at his locker.

Henry Lai was an interesting person, in Jacinta's mind, made less interesting by the fact that their moms seemed to constantly want to push them together. When they were kids their moms wanted them to be friends and as teenagers it had been implied on more than one occasion that they should date.

It left things between Jacinta and Henry awkward and weird.

Not to mention that he'd had a surge in popularity during their senior year that made Jacinta feel like he was out of her league.

"Hey," Jacinta said as she got close to him.

Henry looked up and smiled when he saw her. "Morning," he said.

"Um, so I think you need to be aware that my mother is likely going to talk to your mother about the prom today at work."

"Oh god, it's so embarrassing when this happens," he said, squeezing the bridge of his nose like this whole concept gave him an instant ice-cream headache.

"This is completely my fault. I take full responsibility this time," Jacinta said.

He put his hand on her shoulder. "You really don't have to. It's our meddling moms' fault."

"All I did was say the word *prom*, and she was offering to set us up." Jacinta bit her lip and looked down. "But listen, just in case this, you know, keeps going on with our moms, I was thinking I should have your number. I could have texted you last night to warn you."

"Good idea," Henry said, pulling his phone out of his backpack.

They exchanged numbers and set off in the direction of homeroom

"It's actually so weird that I don't have your number,"

Henry said. "We could have been presenting a more united front against our moms for all these years."

"At least we finally came to our senses," Jacinta said as she turned to go into her homeroom.

"Yeah, it was about time. See you later," Henry said with a grin as he continued on down the hall.

"See you," Jacinta said.

Maybe Henry wouldn't be a terrible prom date, Jacinta thought as she walked away. But if she ended up at the prom with him, she would do it on her own terms and not her mother's.

It was definitely worth considering.

Chapter 5

Otis

Otis bounced on his toes as he and Luke walked into school Monday morning, that's how excited he was for Luke to get to his locker.

He could barely speak for fear that he'd give away the surprise he'd left for his boyfriend on Friday. He'd worried that after Luke's promposal that all the fun would have gone out of his own gesture, but now he couldn't wait for Luke to see it.

"I'll meet you back here after homeroom," Luke said, pausing to give Otis a quick kiss on the cheek, but he came up with nothing but air because Otis had continued on in the direction of Luke's locker.

"Nah," Otis said casually as he kept going.

"Are you being weird?" Luke asked, catching up with him. "I feel like you're being weird."

Otis shrugged and did a little shoulder shimmy when they got to Luke's locker.

"Okay, I've never seen you do anything like that before. You're being totally weird, and I am totally weirded out by your weird," Luke said with a hand on his hip.

Otis gestured toward Luke's locker.

"What?"

He gestured more emphatically.

"I guess I should open my locker?" Luke asked.

Luke took his time going through his combination as if he knew every second Otis had to wait was pure torture. When he finally popped it open, several containers of orange Tic Tacs popped out and an avalanche of them waited inside Luke's locker.

Luke picked one of the containers up off the ground. It said on the side, "You + Me = Prom?"

Luke laughed so loud he shocked the freshman girl who was passing at that moment.

"Oh my god," Luke said. "Did you *Juno* me?"

Otis smiled.

"Ugh, I'm so mad at you for doing this."

"I put them in on Friday after baseball, but then you scooped me with the invite yesterday. I figured there was no reason to come get them all out of your locker early this morning, though. It would have been such a waste. Also because Madison would have killed me since she's the one who helped me write on all of them." Otis knew he was babbling, but Luke wasn't saying enough so he needed to fill the void.

Luke stared at one of the containers and grinned. "This is really so fantastic."

"Thanks," Otis said, feeling a little shy. "I figured I owed you since up until now my grandest gesture was surprising you with your favorite Slurpee."

"A Slurpee I cherished," Luke said, putting his hand on Otis's arm. "And mango isn't always available in this area of New Jersey, so it was extra thoughtful."

Otis shrugged, still sheepish.

"Although you realize I'm going to have to eat all of these myself, right? Because if I give them to people they're going to think I'm asking them to prom."

"You definitely have to eat every single one yourself," Otis said. "It's like a demonstration of your commitment to us."

Luke studied his locker, counting the containers with his eyes. "My god, how much did you spend on these? I mean really, except I don't mean that at all and please don't tell me."

"You can buy them in bulk on the Internet. It wasn't too much, I promise."

"But still! There's like a hundred boxes."

"A hundred and twenty, technically."

It was Otis's turn to laugh loudly. "I'm glad we're going to prom."

"Me too," Luke said.

"I just really appreciate you."

"Aw, I love it when you're sincere." Luke closed his locker. "We should probably go get your stuff now."

Otis nodded as they turned to walk down the hall. He made quick work of grabbing what he needed for his morning classes, and soon they were off to homeroom. "We should go on a date soon. Like a good date," he said.

"I am always up for a good date," Luke said, waving at someone as he passed. "Or a bad date, even. Let's go to McDonald's."

"That sounds like the perfect plan," Otis said, threading his arm through Luke's as they continued on their way.

"Or, you know, I was going to surprise you, but I talked to

my cousin and he works at the Holiday Inn Express. And he said he could get us a room for prom night." Luke raised his eyebrows and grinned.

"Wow," was all Otis managed to say as the shock of the statement settled in.

A hotel room.

With Luke.

On prom night.

He had to think about each of these concepts individually before he could handle considering them together.

"Should be awesome," Luke said, squeezing his arm in a wordless goodbye as Luke entered his homeroom.

Should be awesome, Otis thought to himself, standing in the hallway stunned. But there was also something vaguely terrifying about the idea.

He continued on to homeroom by himself, thinking about what a hotel room, one with Luke, on prom night entailed.

He should be totally psyched, right?

Someone would need to tell that to the pit of anxiety that was growing in his stomach.

Cora

Tuesday night and Cora was doing her best to avoid her homework. At this point in her senior year, was there really any reason to do it?

The answer was of course yes, but that didn't exactly motivate her to get her work done. When her phone chimed from her bed she leaped for it, as gracefully as one can leap from sitting cross-legged on the floor up and onto a bed.

Jamie:

You busy? Come over.

Cora:

I think I can manage it, as long as I'm not gone too long.

Jamie:

Cool, see you in a few. ☺ ☺ ☺ ☺

Technically Cora wasn't allowed out after dinner on school nights unless it was for a school-related event or responsibility. But maybe if she spun a quick little lie and breezed out the door before her parents caught on she might be able to make a run for her car. She grabbed her keys and shoved her wallet in her backpack along with a random book that she could use as a cover story.

Her mom and dad were in the living room watching the news.

"I need to run over to Jamie's for a second. We accidentally switched textbooks at lunch," she said, patting her backpack for extra emphasis.

Her dad's eyebrows knitted together, and Cora could tell he was about to say no, but her mom pressed a hand to his chest.

"You have an hour on the dot, and you better be careful driving my car," she said.

Cora grinned and raced out of the house before her dad could start lining up his arguments. As Cora had recently pointed out to them, sooner than later they were going to have to get used to the idea that she was an autonomous person. That she certainly wasn't going to be calling them from college to ask about going out.

She dropped into the driver's seat of her mom's sedan, and put on her seat belt before carefully pulling out of the driveway. She couldn't see her parents watching, but she could feel them, so it was worth it to be on her best behavior behind the wheel.

She pulled onto the main street and realized that this was kind of an odd request from Jamie. There was a spontaneity to the situation that should excite her.

But it didn't.

And she couldn't put her finger on why.

They weren't exactly a booty call couple, and definitely not on a Tuesday night. Normally she would have just said no, she wasn't allowed out, but that was how bored she was with her AP Spanish homework. He probably needed help with his trig and was trying to be coy about it. That had to be why she wasn't excited. He was so predictable.

For a long minute at a stoplight, Cora considered blowing Jamie off and texting Teagan and Josie to meet her at Starbucks. It was a feeling she was experiencing more and more lately. Unfortunately, she rarely had time to examine feelings like that.

Cora pulled up in front of Jamie's house and sent out a quick "I'm here" text. She was surprised when she got an immediate response telling her to go around to the backyard, only making her more curious. Homework alfresco? That didn't sound like Jamie.

When she walked around back, Jamie was standing on the edge of the deck. The sun was starting to set, and he had lit what looked like at least twenty or thirty votive candles and lined the ledge of the deck with them.

"Hey," he said with a grin.

"Hey," she replied. "What's going on?"

"Come on up," he said, gesturing with the grace of a game show host.

Cora slowly walked up the stairs, taking in the whole scene. The word *PROM* was spelled out in roses on the picnic table, and Cora couldn't help shaking her head.

"You're sort of ridiculous, you know that, right?" she said.

"Oh, totally. I have no qualms about my ridiculousness," he agreed. "But I also knew you would yell at me if I dared to pull something like this at school."

"Well, yes. And all these candles would definitely be frowned upon."

He nodded, running a hand over his short dirty-blond hair. "So what do you say, Cora?"

"Oh," she breathed out.

In that moment Cora saw the boy who she'd loved for almost as long as she could remember. Cute and perfect Jamie, who did everything so cutely and perfectly.

She and Jamie had been dating for over three years. It would have been longer than that if they started counting from when they first held hands at the planetarium on their seventh-grade field trip.

The two thirteen-year-olds would have definitely declared their undying love to each other then and there, like a contemporary Romeo and Juliet minus the suicide, but Cora's parents were strict with their rule about not letting her date until she was fifteen. So, instead, they counted from Cora's fifteenth birthday.

"Will you go with me?" he asked, his expression uncertain due to the length of her silence and probably the look on her face.

"Of course I'll go with you, you big goof," she said. He pulled her close and kissed her. She cut the kiss off quickly, telling herself his mom was probably watching from the sliding door in the family room.

"You really didn't have to do all of this," Cora said. She looked down at their intertwined hands, his light fingers woven through her darker ones.

"I didn't?" he asked. "Oh snap. Then I take it back. I was going to ask Teagan to the prom, so I guess I'll do that."

"You're completely ridiculous, you know that, right?" Cora asked.

"I am, but you like that about me, right?" he asked. She threaded her arms around his waist, and he pulled her in close. He was a few inches taller than she was these days. It was pretty funny to think that back in seventh grade when she first kissed his cheek while standing in the gift shop at that same planetarium, mere minutes after they'd first held hands, she'd had a solid two inches on him. But he caught up, as boys tend to do.

"I do like that about you," she said.

"Good," he said, squeezing her close.

Cora closed her eyes and pretended she felt safe and happy instead of a little bit claustrophobic. If she ignored the feeling maybe it would go away, particularly since they'd made their college plans together. In the fall, they'd both be going to Boston

University. Jamie had decided to go there since it was Cora's dream school.

The future was set for them. She had to hope she'd get past whatever this feeling was in her gut.

"And did you notice I haven't called you babe once?" he asked.

She was thankful that her face was still pressed up against him so he couldn't see her expression.

Chapter 6

Lizzie

Lizzie let out one short sigh of disappointment on Wednesday afternoon when the laptop cart was nowhere to be found in the English classroom.

But there was no time to wallow. As soon as the bell rang, Ms. Huang told the class to break into pairs and work on the discussion questions that she was passing out.

Jacinta and Lizzie looked at each other knowingly and pushed their desks together as fast as they could. They had a silent agreement that anytime there was group work they would pair up, in part because they knew they could trust each other to hold up their side of the bargain. The rest of the class, not so much.

Having a similar work ethic, both girls opened to clean pages in their notebooks and got right to work while the rest of the class meandered around, trying to find partners and pens that weren't completely out of ink.

Lizzie and Jacinta were already moving on to question two when Ms. Huang got called into the hallway for a moment. The class had been unsettled before that, but as soon as the door closed, they were even less settled.

Lizzie leaned back in her chair and rubbed her eyes. Jacinta propped her elbow on her desk and turned to Lizzie.

"So are you going to the prom?" she asked.

"Ugh," Lizzie said.

"Does that mean yes or no?" Jacinta asked.

"The prom and I have a complicated relationship at the moment."

"Is it really cheesy that I want to go?" Jacinta asked.

Lizzie smiled and sat up, not wanting Jacinta to think she was judging her. "Not at all. It's more common than not wanting to go."

Jacinta nodded. "It's just that my three brothers and my sister went to their proms and it always seemed so glamorous to me. Like the height of what it meant to be eighteen and graduating from high school, as if you were finally sophisticated enough to own a really pretty dress and have a boy in a tuxedo whisk you away in a limo."

Lizzie nodded.

"It's just super corny, right?"

"No, honestly, I do feel a little more inspired to go. Because you're right. There's something like closure that comes along with going to the prom. It's like a rite of passage in our society."

"Exactly! So tell me about your complicated relationship with prom." Then Jacinta's eyes lit up. "I forgot about Mystery Boy. You should totally ask Mystery Boy!"

"I know." Lizzie grinned. Jacinta had caught part of their conversation one day when Lizzie had left it up on the screen. "It's a little weird and a little complicated, but I really want to ask him."

"I love weird and complicated stuff. What's weird and complicated about it?"

"I need to figure out how to even approach this idea," Lizzie said. "How do you ask someone to meet you somewhere when you've never met them? When you don't know what they look like, and they don't know what you look like? How do you find each other in a crowd?"

"Maybe you should see if he says yes before getting too bogged down by the logistical details."

"But logistical details are all I have to hang onto right now," Lizzie said. "Otherwise I fall apart imagining meeting him. Maybe he's only good on paper. Maybe I won't like him in person."

"Do not fall apart. We have this under control," Jacinta said, flipping to a clean page in her notebook.

"What about the assignment?"

"We could do that in our sleep!" Jacinta said. "We only have two more questions to answer. You need help more than we need to answer those questions."

"Thanks, Jacinta."

"Now we just need to figure out what to say," Jacinta said, tapping her bottom lip with her pen.

By the end of the period, Lizzie had a short message written out that she could type up quickly the next time she had an opportunity to use laptop 19.

Luckily the next day the laptop cart was in the English

room. Lizzie wasted no time typing up her prom invite to Mystery Boy.

So, I was wondering. If maybe perhaps. She paused. She wanted desperately to delete what she had just typed. It's a good thing she had a rough draft to go by, because this was harder than she expected.

I'm going to leave that stuff there so you can see that I'm a little nervous about this. But I wanted to ask you to the prom. Or at least ask you to meet me at the prom. I want to meet you, and I feel like prom is the perfect time to do that. I don't know who you're attracted to, maybe you're not into girls and that's cool. But I wanted to at least ask. So, thank you and please consider meeting me. If not at the prom, if that doesn't feel right, then some other time? Maybe? I don't want this friendship to end.

Lizzie quickly saved the message and then closed the document before she could talk herself out of it or add more awkward rambling.

Jacinta looked over at her and raised her eyebrows in an unspoken question. Lizzie gave her a thumbs-up.

Her heart was beating a mile a minute.

Paisley

During Paisley's tenure as a potato technician in the mall food court, she had learned many things. One was that people talked a lot in the food court, and, because of her uniform and visor, Paisley was nearly invisible to them. Customers would continue talking to their friend or on the phone about personal things even while Paisley stood there waiting for their order. On top of that, due to a fluke in the food court's architecture, she could also hear conversations from several yards away in a nearby alcove.

She'd heard way too many stories to keep them all to herself. She'd often text Henry the best of them during her shifts.

For example, she had heard quite a few terrible stories about sex over the past few months. At the moment there was a group of college-aged girls sitting in the magical acoustic alcove talking about STDs.

She was frantically typing their conversation to Henry.

Paisley:

> Okay, so there are three girls. I will refer to them as G1, G2, and G3 from here on out.

Henry rarely even responded to these texts, but that didn't stop Paisley from sending them.

Paisley:

> G1: Ha, that guy is such a douche canoe. You know who he is, right?

> G2 & G3: Noooooo.

> G1: He's the one who gave me the raging case of the herp!

> G3: Why do you sound so proud of that?

G1: What? The herp is totally treatable and he's hot!

G2: He is hot.

G3: Even if he is a douche canoe.

Paisley paused in her transcription to look over at the table and get a better look at each of the girls. Was this what she had to look forward to in college?

Her phone lit up and got her attention.

Henry:
I don't believe they're talking about this.

Paisley:
I swear on a stack of bibles. I only took minor liberties and poetic license.

Henry:
Why do people talk about this stuff in front of you?

Paisley:
These girls definitely don't know I can hear them.

Henry:
Why do people talk about this stuff in public?

Paisley considered this for a moment.

Paisley stacked napkins and refilled the utensils so that her boss wouldn't have anything to say when he came in to help with the dinner rush. Even though what Hot Potato experienced during dinnertime could hardly be considered a rush. Paisley was happily surprised when Lizzie came in at five thirty.

"Hey," Paisley said. "I wasn't expecting to see you tonight."

"John needed to switch, and when he told me you were working I jumped at it."

Paisley grinned. "Well, you're in luck because it's been a super quiet afternoon and it's sure to be a super quiet evening."

As if on cue, three people got in line for potatoes. It was in fact the rushiest rush that Paisley had ever seen at Hot Potato.

After the girls finished helping the customers, there was a lull.

"That was more people than I've ever seen here," Lizzie said.

"I was thinking the same thing."

Lizzie was quiet for a beat. "I asked Mystery Boy to the prom."

Paisley whipped her head around to look at her from her place at the fixin's bar. "You what?!"

"I asked him to the prom," Lizzie said, obviously trying to hold back a grin.

56

"Oh my god, Liz," Paisley said. "I could tell you really wanted to go."

Lizzie shrugged. "We'll see if he says yes. I don't think he will, and then it'll be a moot point."

"But if he says yes, you'll have to actually go to the prom."

"I know. It could be fun. Jacinta Ramos kind of talked me into it."

Paisley shook her head and wiped up around the melted cheese container. At that moment, Amelia Vaughn and her lackeys took a seat in the area with the acoustical flaw.

"Well, well, well," Paisley said. "Look who's here."

Lizzie rolled her eyes. She knew all about Paisley's personal vendetta against Amelia. "Hopefully she says something truly damning this time and not that she doesn't like brussels sprouts."

Paisley narrowed her eyes at Lizzie. "I love brussels sprouts. And that Amelia hates them just goes to show that we are perfect enemies. Now shh, I need to watch my programs." Paisley pulled the stool up to the counter and chewed her lip. Lizzie stood next to her.

Amelia was saying something about prom, of course.

"Oh man," Lizzie whispered. "I can't believe Drew broke up with her."

"Yeah, they were a match made in high school," Paisley said with an eye roll.

"If only they could have been together forever," Lizzie said mockingly.

When talk turned to Amelia asking Henry to the prom, Paisley's ears perked up. "No," she hissed. "That's a terrible idea."

"Because you want to go to the prom with Henry?" Lizzie asked.

"You know I don't," Paisley said. "I just don't want Henry to get stuck with her. Like she's just not his kind of . . . person."

Lizzie nodded.

Amelia and her friends left soon after that. Paisley debated texting Henry what she had overheard, but knowing Henry it would keep him up all night and it really might be nothing. Best to err on the side of caution for now.

But Paisley would be sure to monitor the situation closely.

Chapter 7

Henry

Henry had been tiptoeing around his house since he got home from baseball practice an hour ago. So far this week, his mom had yet to bring up the topic of prom or Jacinta Ramos.

But as soon as he sat down for dinner Thursday night he knew his mom had an agenda. The whole family, his mom, dad, and younger brother, Deacon, were all present and accounted for.

She smiled over at him, and he knew his luck was up.

"So, Henry, I hear the prom is coming up," his mom said.

He silently thanked Jacinta for warning him about this moment. Otherwise he wasn't sure what he would have said in the face of this type of mom-vaguery. At least he knew where she was probably going with this topic.

Deacon made barfing noises.

"Stop that," their dad said. "No disgusting noises at the dinner table."

"Are you thinking about going?" his mom asked, undeterred by Deacon's little outburst.

"I'm not sure," Henry said, not looking at his mom and stabbing a cherry tomato. He'd show that cherry tomato he was the boss. Even if Henry felt like he wasn't even really the boss of his own life. He could be the boss of the cherry tomato.

"You should ask Jacinta Ramos."

And there it was. His mom and Jacinta's mom were in mom cahoots. The situation was so dire he couldn't even think of a better word than *cahoots*. Thank god no one could read his mind at the moment.

He panicked. He wasn't exactly sure why he panicked. Probably because that was his usual reaction to most suggestions that involved him having to socialize.

He had been pretty cool during the whole conversation with Jacinta the other day, but when he got to homeroom his hands were shaking. Even now, several days and hot showers later, he felt like his mom could smell the flop sweat on him.

"There is no way Jacinta wants to go with me," Henry snapped.

"No one wants to go anywhere with Henry, Mom," Deacon added.

Henry shot him a look.

"Oh, come on, it couldn't hurt to ask. You're friends. You've been friends for a long time."

"No. You're friends with her mom," Henry said, frustration overtaking his worry. "That doesn't make Jacinta my friend.

We get along fine, but I don't think she's even a little bit interested in going with me."

His mom smiled, ignoring his tone for once. Normally there would be a lecture about how it wasn't so much what he said but how he said it. And that he really needed to watch the way he presented himself.

But tonight of all nights, his mom was ignoring his usual coping strategies and staying doggedly on message.

"How could you possibly know that if you don't even bother asking?"

Mom logic. Mom logic could always get the better of him and leave him spluttering for words even when he'd had a perfectly good argument lined up until that moment.

"I talked to her the other day," he said, instantly regretting it. They were never supposed to admit to their moms that they had any contact at school. And it was rare that they did. But Jacinta had sought him out and warned him and now he was stuck at the dinner table trying to dig his way out of a hole of his own making.

"Oh, that's good news! See, she wants to talk to you—you should ask her."

He needed an excuse. "She didn't seem like she was interested in prom." It wasn't a complete lie; they just hadn't discussed her desire to attend.

"But you could try!" his mom said.

He was already exhausted by this topic, and she seemed like she could go another ten rounds at least.

"I'm going to go do my homework," he said, using his only way out.

"Fine, fine, just bring your plate into the kitchen."

He did as he was told and then stomped upstairs as she called after him, "And at least consider it! You never know unless you try."

He closed his bedroom door behind him and threw himself face-first on his bed. All he really wanted in that moment was to go to sleep and maybe not wake up until graduation. Maybe even sleep all the way until he had to leave for college. That wouldn't be so bad. At least he wouldn't have to talk about any of this again.

On the other hand, he would fail his finals and maybe Penn State would rescind his acceptance.

He sat up and rubbed his eyes.

He could do this.

He had to forget everything he had talked about with his mother. He sat down with his homework and tried to concentrate.

Except, three problems into his calc homework and his brain was running in circles.

His mom was right; he wouldn't know if he didn't ask.

But he didn't want to ask Jacinta Ramos to the prom.

He didn't want to go to the prom, period. There was not one little cell in his entire body that had any interest in going to the prom. He would *really* have to want to go to the prom to ever work up the courage to ask someone.

He didn't see that happening anytime in the near future.

Whatever. He had work to do. He moved on to the next problem.

His phone buzzed next to him, and he half expected it to be Jacinta since he had been thinking about her so much. More likely it was Paisley. She'd been texting him before dinner with ridiculous stories from the mall food court.

Instead it was Amelia Vaughn.

Amelia:
Hey, what are you up to?.

Henry:
Calc ☹

They had exchanged phone numbers a while back when they were doing a history project together. But she'd never texted him without a reason before.

He should probably shoot Jacinta a text while he had his phone in his hand, since he had her number and all.

Henry:
Hey, Jacinta. My mom mentioned the prom tonight, so thanks for the heads-up!

He hit send before he could think about it anymore, and then threw his phone under his pillow before getting back to work.

He had calc homework to do and plenty of other things to worry about.

Cameron

It was only 7:45 a.m. Friday morning, and Cameron was having a terrible, horrible, no good, very bad day. It had all started when he'd woken up from a dream where he met Laptop Girl in real life and she laughed in his face when she found out who he was. So that wasn't the best way to start the day.

Then he got in the shower and Landon had used up all the hot water. That was not a rare occurrence. His stepbrother seemed to enjoy his water temperature to be approximately Earth's-core hot.

But on top of that, there was no more orange juice for breakfast, and when he went out to his car it wouldn't start.

It seemed like the battery had died.

Of course, Landon had already left for school and his mom had left for work, which meant there was only one option.

He'd have to ask Richard for a ride.

Cameron went back inside, and Richard was sipping the last of his coffee at the kitchen table while scanning his iPad.

"Hey, um," Cameron said. He never knew what to call him. In his head, he liked to call him Dick, but his mom called him Richard and everyone else in the world seemed to call him Rich. Cameron stuck to "um" most of the time.

"Yes?" Richard asked, straightening his tie.

"My car won't start. Would you mind dropping me off at school?"

Dick looked over at the clock. He didn't have to be at the office until nine, Cameron knew, so this would mean having to leave the house and come back after dropping Cam off, or going into work early.

"Yeah, sure," he said, grabbing his keys.

Cameron followed him out the door and to the car, desperately wanting to sit in the back seat. The thing about Richard was that he probably wasn't a bad guy; he wasn't abusive or mean to Cameron or his mom. Cameron just couldn't stand the way his mom acted around his stepfather. It was like the second she met him she had gotten a personality transplant.

Cameron's dad died when he was seven, so it had just been him and his mom for almost ten years. Until last year when she met Richard on a dating site and the next thing Cameron knew they were getting married. Mere days after announcing their engagement, Cameron's mom was selling the house that Cameron had grown up in and they were moving in with Richard and Landon, in a much, much nicer part of town.

But there weren't much, much nicer people to go along with their nicer part of town. Cameron found them cold and weird.

Richard silently drove him to school. Cameron thanked him as he got out of his car, and Richard merely shrugged before driving away.

Cameron gave the car the middle finger before turning to walk into school.

He passed Henry and Paisley on the way in, and, rather than saying anything to them, he looked away, staring at the lockers next to him like they were the most interesting thing in the world.

Cameron didn't know how to handle anything in his life, but especially not the situation with Henry. It would have been easier to have had a fight with Henry, something that he could have apologized for. But now wasn't exactly the time to stress out about his ex–best friend.

He didn't know how to talk about his family stuff with anyone. Everything seemed to be happening all at once, and more than anything he wanted to focus on leaving Richard's house after graduation and never looking back.

So at the beginning of the school year, he quit the soccer and baseball teams, took two jobs, and totally stopped talking and hanging out with his friends.

Henry Lai was the hardest to stop talking to. Cam hadn't wanted to ghost him. They'd been friends since they were kids, always playing baseball together, but Henry didn't seem to understand that Cameron had other things to worry about now.

Not that Cameron tried very hard to explain it all to Henry. Henry should have just understood. He wasn't much of a talker, either.

More and more it felt like Cameron had made a mistake becoming a hermit his senior year. But it was the only thing he could think to do in the face of all the crap going on at home. He needed something to look forward to, and it was so much easier to cut ties with everyone early before they would all be inevitably cutting ties with one another in June anyway.

Cameron went about his day as he always did, staying quiet in class, eating lunch alone in the library while he scrambled through his homework, and then more classes where he barely spoke.

Except for English.

Except for Laptop Girl.

When he got to class the cart was waiting there. He snagged number 19 as he walked to his seat and couldn't wait to see what Laptop Girl might have left for him.

The very last thing Cameron expected when he opened the document was an invitation to the prom from Laptop Girl. There may have been things he expected less, but he couldn't come up with any, no matter how hard he thought about it.

He had to keep himself busy thinking about other things that would have surprised him, because he was completely unprepared to face the reality of being asked to the prom. Not once during this entire school year had it seemed like the prom would be in the realm of possibility for him, even if he wanted to go.

But now, this girl that he honestly really liked, even though he'd never seen her or met her, wanted to go to the prom with him. And he wasn't sure how to say no to that offer. He wasn't sure how to pass something like that up. It was enough to make him forget the dream he'd had the night before.

Ms. Huang was explaining what they would be working on that day, so rather than spending a lot of time typing up a new message, Cameron just changed the background on the computer to say YES in huge lime green letters.

His terrible, horrible, no good day was actually looking up.

When Ms. Huang set them to work independently, Cameron typed out a quick message to Laptop Girl.

> This is awesome. I never even thought to ask you to prom. We'll have to figure out how to recognize each other. Like both have something lime green on our person, so we can easily tell each other apart from the crowd. I don't have a lot of time right now, but I just wanted to say thanks. And yes. I am into girls.

Cameron hit save and got started on his assignment, unable to wipe the grin off his face for the rest of the period.

Chapter 8

Cora

Cora was desperate for a new coping mechanism.

Over the past week, her feelings about Jamie had shifted. A lot.

For example, his latest text made her cringe.

Jamie:

> Hey, not-babe, are you going to make it to the semifinal game? I know it's almost two weeks away, but I'm only asking because my parents said that you could drive there with them.

She rolled her eyes so hard at the "not-babe" thing. How hard is it to just not mention it? She was allowed to have preferences for what people called her. On top of that, the thought of driving with Mr. and Mrs. Fitzpatrick to the game that was almost an hour away sounded exhausting. Jamie's parents were really very nice, but his dad got a little . . . overheated about baseball and his mom just wanted to feed her hot chocolate the whole time, even if it wasn't cold out.

No one wants to drink hot chocolate when it's above sixty degrees, and it very well might be that warm by then, seeing as how it would be the beginning of May.

Basically, their relationship had gone from steady and non-contentious to Cora pretty much hating everything Jamie did. But how do you break up with a guy after being with him for three years? How do you break up with him when he likes you so much that he decided to go to the same college as you?

After all these years, she finally appreciated her parents making her wait to date Jamie, if only because it was less time they were official. Any way you cut it, three years was a long relationship, but it sounded better than five.

She knew she shouldn't break up with him just because she wanted to all of a sudden. She wanted to at least consider her options a little longer. It could be a passing feeling.

In an attempt to keep her mind busy, Cora had also been trying to keep her body busy. Cold showers and long runs, trying to crochet, listening to audiobooks. Her schedule was overflowing already, thanks to all of her extracurricular activities, but it was like she needed even more hobbies and activities in her life to take up all this brain space.

And now, it all left her even more overwhelmed.

Which was how she ended up alone in her room Saturday night when she normally would have been out with her friends or Jamie. She couldn't deal with even one more minute of socializing.

Her phone buzzed with another text.

Jamie:
You okay? Why aren't you answering?

Cora:
Yeah, I'm fine. I just need to catch up on life.

Jamie:
And you're not mad at me?

Cora:
I'm not mad at you, I swear. I'm not sure about the game. I'll let you know.

Jamie:
That text makes it look like you're mad at me.

He attached a selfie of himself frowning dramatically. She blinked at her phone.

Cora:
What do you want me to say? I told you I'm not mad.

He didn't reply.

Rather than letting this semi-fight eat away at her, she downloaded a meditation app thinking that might be a good thing to try. So, instead of wallowing all night, she got right to it. She read the introduction and directions for the app. She really hoped she'd be able to clear her mind. The whole situation was starting to feel pretty desperate.

As she was about to start the app and the beginner's guided meditation session, there was a knock on her bedroom door.

"Come in?" Cora called, a tone of confusion in her voice. She didn't even know anyone else was home.

Her mom walked in. "Hey, sweetie. I didn't expect you to be home."

"Hey, Mom," Cora said. "What's up?"

"Nothing, just got back from the store. Are you hungry? Are you staying home tonight?"

"Yes and yes," Cora said.

"What are you doing?"

"I might be trying to meditate," Cora said, her cheeks warming at the confession even as she told herself it was nothing to be ashamed of.

Her mom raised her eyebrows and stifled a smile as she leaned on the doorjamb, obviously not wanting to laugh at Cora or make her feel bad for trying. "Are you okay?"

"I'm a little overwhelmed and kind of confused."

"Confused about what?"

"Well, you know. Everything. Nothing. The usual?" Cora offered, hoping that was enough of an excuse.

"Sex. Drugs. Rock and roll?"

Cora laughed then and so did her mom. "Something like that."

"Is it Jamie?'

"Jamie and Teagan and Josie and prom committee and college and yearbook and finals, and, well, everything."

"Now I gotcha," her mom said. "It's a tough time. A lot is going on and a lot is changing."

"Exactly," Cora said. "And sometimes I want to be alone for a little while, you know? To meditate, I guess."

"Well, I'll leave you be," her mom said.

"No!" Cora called after her, leaping off her bed.

Her mom paused.

"I mean, you don't have to go. That's just why I'm home tonight, because I never make time for myself. But, like, being home is part of myself, so you're part of myself?"

"That's actually fairly astute," her mom said. "You know you can talk to me or Dad anytime you feel overwhelmed, right? Like, that's not something you need to feel bad about."

"Yes, Mom," Cora said.

Her mom smiled broadly this time. "Well, I'm going to leave you to this. I know it'll be good for you to concentrate."

"Okay."

"And I'll go downstairs and make us something comforting for dinner. Dad should be home soon."

Cora lit up. "Like mac and cheese with hot dogs?"

"And broccoli, if only to make me feel like I'm not the worst mother in the world."

"Fair enough."

Her mom kissed her on the forehead. "You've got this, Cora, I know you do. You'll figure out what you need to figure out because you're good and smart."

Cora nodded.

"And if you don't figure it out, you're young and I love you anyway."

Cora nodded again, more resolutely this time. Just as she was about to close her door, her mom stepped back toward her.

"And, you know, have you ever considered not doing so much? That wouldn't be a big deal. Pick and choose what's the most important to you. And give yourself a night off sometimes."

"I know. I'm not good at that."

"Well, I'm giving you permission as your mom."

"Thanks, Mom."

"I'll call you when dinner's ready."

With that, Cora shut her bedroom door and turned off all the lights.

She did her best to meditate, but it was almost like she didn't need it now that she'd talked to her mom.

That's how much better she felt already.

And, as it turns out, mac and cheese with hot dogs (and a side of broccoli) is basically a balm for the soul and all that ails you.

Jacinta

Kelsey and Jacinta were ensconced in a pile of blankets on the couch in Kelsey's family room watching *13 Going on 30* on Saturday night.

"I love this movie," Jacinta said, shoving another handful of popcorn into her mouth.

"Seriously," Kelsey agreed. Kelsey's parents were upstairs, and her younger brother and sister had finally gone to bed, so it was definitely time for the sharing part of the evening, Jacinta decided.

"I need to work on operation: PROM," Jacinta said.

Kelsey paused the movie and looked at Jacinta, obviously confused. "Wait, what? You want to go to the prom? Since when?"

"I've sort of always wanted to go to the prom," Jacinta admitted.

"You don't really seem like the prom type," Kelsey said.

"Thanks? I mean, I'm on the prom committee. Obviously I'm interested."

"I didn't mean it in a bad way. But you're not super into dating, or fancy dresses, or dancing."

Jacinta shrugged. "I could be."

Kelsey nodded. "Well, you need a plan."

Jacinta grinned. This was why she always came to Kelsey with stuff like this; she was so good at synthesizing what needed to happen and what the order of operations should be. She started ticking things off on her fingers.

"You need a dress, shoes, all that stuff."

"Yes."

"Did you buy a ticket?"

"Not yet. I don't want to buy a pair and then not find a date and end up with too many tickets. Besides Cora said that due to some mix-up with the venue we have more tickets than we'll ever need anyway and we're going to have to use whatever money we have in our class savings to buy up the rest."

"So what you're telling me is that we're going to have our class reunion at Chuck E. Cheese."

"Maybe if we put it in a high-interest savings account we'll be able to afford Chuck E. Cheese. We might be looking at something more like the school gym."

"That doesn't actually sound all bad to me," Kelsey said, taking a bite out of a Twizzler. "Wouldn't it make sense to go back to school for a reunion?"

Jacinta shrugged; they'd gone way off topic and she was

having trouble honestly caring about their ten-year reunion with the prom looming. "So, most of all I want a date."

"You don't *need* a date."

"Yeah, I know, like I said. I *want* a date, Kelsey. I've never even been on a date. I deserve a date to my prom."

"Hmm," Kelsey said.

"I was thinking about asking Henry Lai?" Jacinta's cheeks warmed at the mention of his name.

"Oh," Kelsey said, her eyebrows knitting together.

"My mom thinks I should ask him," Jacinta jumped in, wanting to preemptively defend herself. "She's way too into the whole idea. But I think he would say yes."

"I wasn't judging you."

"Then, what?" Jacinta asked.

"I don't know, do you think he'd be fun? He's so serious all the time. Maybe you could go with one of Mike's friends. Wouldn't that be more fun for everyone?"

"Maybe for you and your boyfriend, but I think I'd rather go with someone who I actually know."

"Yeah, right. That makes sense," Kelsey said.

"Sorry. I'm sure Mike has great friends. But I don't want to go with someone just for the sake of going with someone. I'd rather go alone if that's the case."

"But you literally just said you want a date so much that it feels like you need a date."

"I know," Jacinta said, frowning. "I know. I'm sort of all over the place. I guess I'm hopeful about finding a date and not having to go with a stranger."

"Well, if you can't find someone, I could set you up. The choice is there."

"Maybe," Jacinta said. "If you think I'll like them and not just because they're convenient for you and Mike."

"Wow, Jacinta," Kelsey said. "I'm really impressed."

"Why?"

"I don't know exactly how to say this, but you don't usually give your opinion. Or it feels like you don't. But lately you're, like, giving your opinion and I think that's cool."

Jacinta smiled and sat up a little taller. "Thanks," she said.

"You are totally welcome."

Chapter 9

Henry

"So, we have a bit of an issue," Paisley said early Monday morning. She'd been waiting for him to come through the back doors of the school, because that was where he always came in.

"I don't like issues this early on a Monday," Henry said as she fell into step with him on his way to his locker.

"Who are you? Garfield?"

"Such timely and humorous jokes," Henry said, yawning.

"It's just that remember when I told you that I sort of mentioned your name for prom king a couple weeks ago?"

"No," Henry said. "You never told me. Was that the thing you had to tell me but never told me?"

"Huh?"

Henry pulled out his phone and scrolled through his screenshots, before turning it to show Paisley the evidence.

"Oh yeah, right. I never told you about it. But thanks for

keeping a screenshot of it." Paisley twirled a piece of her hair around her finger and grinned innocently. "So anyway, no big deal, I mentioned your name for prom king. But! The good news is that we're going to do a king and a queen and a separate prom court! So, like, more people will be up there on stage than ever."

"I'm going to assume that you unmentioned it," Henry said, ignoring her rambling excuse.

"I never had the opportunity to unmention it. It wasn't even an official nomination. But."

"But?"

"Well, it's just that I need you to stay calm and not hate me or kill me. Because I don't think you would fare well in prison."

"Paisley," Henry said.

"So you're nominated for prom king," Paisley said, patting his shoulder. "Okay, I love you, see you around." She started walking off and he grabbed her elbow.

"Wait, what?"

"Cora Wilson read the list of nominees during prom committee, and they're going to be announced during homeroom, and you are definitely on that list."

Henry scrubbed at his face with both hands, trying to reconcile this information.

"Is it really that big of a deal?" Paisley asked. "I mean, maybe you won't win?"

Henry blinked at her. Getting up in front of his whole class to accept an award like this was basically a nightmare for Henry, so of course he would win. He would win and be haunted by it for the rest of his life.

"I just, you know I hate all that attention. Even if I don't win," he said finally.

"Is it really so bad?" Paisley asked. "Like if you have to get up in front of everyone it would be because they all voted for you. And it turned out that after all these years of flying under the radar, you were really making friends. It would only mean good, happy things if you won."

Henry wasn't so sure of that, but he didn't know how to argue this point with Paisley. She would never see it his way.

"I know," he said. "But it's not my thing."

"And I know that. Maybe you could just suck it up and go?"

"Maybe instead you could get me out of it," Henry said with a grin.

"Oh, come on, Henry," she said. "It won't be that bad. It'll be a hot second of torture and then it'll be over. There's also the option of ignoring it completely and just not going."

"I like that," Henry said. "Denial works for me."

"See? You have options!"

"Who are the nominees for prom queen?"

"Pretty much everyone you would expect. Amelia and a couple of her cronies, that chick Josie who's friends with Cora."

"I thought you hate when people use the word *chick*," Henry said, putting air quotes around the word.

"I've decided I want to take chick back," Paisley said.

"What exactly does that entail?"

"Honestly I don't know. I'm just trying to cover the fact that I didn't even notice I was using it."

Henry laughed and turned back to his locker as the first bell rang. "So there's really no way out of this?"

"There really isn't. They're going to announce the nominees during homeroom."

"Who are the nominees for king?"

"Oh right, um." Paisley squinted and looked into the distance for dramatic effect. "Jamie Fitzpatrick, Tag whatever his last name is, and a couple of football dudes."

"Why is dude okay, but chick isn't?"

"Chick is a shortening of chickenhead, and that is a pejorative term used for women who enjoy giving fellatio."

"Fellatio sounds like a type of pasta."

"I believe you are thinking of farfalle, which are the little bow tie ones."

"Maybe. Also isn't dude a word for horse penis?"

Paisley shut her eyes like Henry was being unreasonable and then ignored his question completely. "For the record, Henry, I think you should be king. I think you're the perfect guy for the job this year. If we have to continue this inane tradition, at least let it be someone like you rather than one of the jerk faces and misogynists."

"Jerk faces and misogynists would make a great band name."

Paisley rolled her eyes and shook her head as they took their seats in homeroom. "That's a terrible band name and you know it."

"I don't—" but Henry's words got lodged in his throat when Amelia sat down next to him and leaned over.

Paisley

She could see the exact moment that Henry's eyes glazed over in panic as Amelia Vaughn started talking to him.

Henry was the best friend a girl could ask for, but he was just as susceptible to feminine wiles as any other eighteen-year-old boy.

"I can't remember," Amelia said. "Did I tell you I was going to the prom with Drew? You know Drew? He graduated last year."

"Yes, I know Drew," Henry said abruptly. "But you and I haven't talked about prom, so you didn't tell me."

To Paisley's well-trained ear, she could tell that Henry was doing his robot voice to keep himself calm.

"Well, as it turns out, he can't make it. Something about having to stay on campus for some fraternity thing. I would totally go to that with him, because he totally asked me, but I don't really want to miss my prom for a frat party. I already have a dress and everything."

Henry nodded.

"Shouldn't his semester be over by then?" Paisley asked. Amelia gave her a dirty look.

"Of course, but they still have parties during the summer and they're important." Amelia turned her attention back to Henry.

"I heard that you're nominated for prom king, and I'm nominated for prom queen, and I think it would be a really good idea and like totally fun for us to go together. And campaign together."

Henry stared at Amelia slack jawed.

She smiled. "Right?"

For some reason that word snapped him out of whatever happy place he'd been in.

"Huh?" he said.

"So you will, right?"

"Um, yes?"

"I knew I could count on you," she said, squeezing his shoulder and walking out of the room, since she wasn't actually a member of their homeroom to begin with.

Paisley stared at him.

"Um, I'm sorry," Paisley said. "What did I just witness?"

"Amelia talking to me?" he said, trying and failing to sound casual.

"No, Henry. Not just talking to you. Amelia asking you to the prom and you saying yes." Paisley's eyes went wide. "Were you not there? Were you astral projecting? You can tell me the truth."

"Amelia asked me to the prom?"

"She did and you said yes."

"I did?"

"Yes."

"No."

"Yes. I saw it with my own two eyes. I witnessed it. You looked like you were in some kind of waking coma."

"She's just really intimidating, and her lips are all shimmery, and I couldn't concentrate on what she was saying."

"Boys are gross," Paisley said. "I'm putting that down in the record. But I guess at least you weren't staring at her boobs. You're at least a little more respectful than that."

Henry blinked, obviously still stunned.

"So what are you going to do?" Paisley asked.

"I guess I'm going to the prom with Amelia?" he said as their homeroom teacher strolled in and started taking attendance.

"You really want to do that? I thought you didn't want to go to the prom."

"I don't, but how am I supposed to get out of this? What would I even say? 'Gee, Amelia, I'm sorry I was hypnotized by your lips and didn't realize you were asking me to the prom,'" he said in a goofy voice.

"Yeah, that's not great. She would probably have you killed."

"Her dad's not in the mob or anything, right?"

"I don't know. I don't know much about the mob. I think they prefer it that way."

"I really don't know what to do."

"Well, buckle up, big boy, because you're going to the prom with Amelia Vaughn."

"Don't call me big boy," he said. "Also Vaughn doesn't even sound Italian, so there's probably no mafia relations."

"Well, buckle up, buckaroo, because you're going to the prom with Amelia!" This time she slapped his shoulder for emphasis. "And it probably got bastardized at Ellis Island and her full last name is Vontiglio or something."

"We need to figure out how to get me out of this," he said as he slumped lower in his chair.

"Nope, nope, nope. This is definitely your shit show. It's not my fault that you went into a fugue state because a girl talked to you."

"Come on, Paisley. I need help."

"And I need to not die at the hands of the Northern New Jersey mafia."

"She's not in the mob."

"Of course *she* isn't, but I'm still not sure that her dad isn't."

"This is the opposite of what I wanted to happen," he muttered, his face in his hands.

"I know," Paisley said.

Henry frowned and looked so upset that Paisley had to say something to comfort him.

"Fine, I do blame myself at least a little."

"What? Why?" he asked.

"Well, I mean, I did accidentally nominate you for king, and I might have heard her talking about asking you to the prom the other night at the mall." Paisley cringed away from Henry, as if he was going to hit her, even though Henry would never actually use physical violence on anyone.

"Are you kidding me?" he asked.

Paisley shook her head.

"You could have at least warned me!" Henry said loudly, drawing the attention of everyone in their homeroom. His cheeks reddened.

"I know, I'm sorry," Paisley whispered as the morning announcements started.

"We're going to figure this out," Henry said, his voice tight.

"Yes, we will. I'm sorry I said it was your shit show when I am so obviously implicit in the shit myself."

There was nothing worse than the feeling of guilt that had settled on Paisley's shoulders even though she knew it wasn't entirely her fault.

She'd find a way to help him out.

It was what she did.

Chapter 10

Otis

Otis's leg jiggled nervously under his desk in history class. The girl sitting in front of him turned around to give him a dirty look, and he had to put his hand on his leg to stop it from bouncing.

It had been like this ever since Luke mentioned getting a hotel room after prom. Otis was in a near-constant spiral of panic. He liked Luke, a lot. He wasn't sure he loved Luke.

He also wasn't sure why *hotel room* had to be synonymous with S-E-X. But it totally was. He needed to talk to someone about this and fast before he vibrated out of his skin overthinking it.

He should talk to Luke about it. He knew that. But every time he imagined approaching him about this topic, panic ensued. He chickened out over and over again, all day long, like an ongoing stress dream.

After baseball practice was over, Otis and Tag headed for Tag's car.

Tag's car had a distinct odor. A combination of old gym socks and wet dog or possibly old dog and wet gym socks, it was hard to parse. What was most perplexing was that Tag didn't have a dog.

"What's with the face?" Tag asked as Otis closed the door.

"Have you ever considered cleaning your car and locating the source of that smell? I swear every time I get in here it gets stuck in my nose."

Tag sniffed a few times. "I don't smell anything."

"You've gone nose blind, my friend. I've heard about this ailment. It's a big source of conflict on those Febreze commercials."

Tag rolled his eyes and started the car.

"You're still making that face even though you've lodged your complaint."

Otis rolled down the window. "It still smells like ass in here and Luke got us a hotel room for after the prom."

"Those two subjects are unrelated, right?"

"Yes. But like. A hotel room."

"Make sure you use protection? I'm not sure what you want me to say."

"See, it is totally synonymous with sex, right? Like getting a hotel room means that." Otis paused and dropped his voice low. "Luke wants to have sex with me, right?"

"I guess?" Tag gripped the steering wheel tighter.

"I'm just, like, really nervous," Otis confessed.

"Are you searching for . . . advice?"

"Maybe? I don't even know what I need!"

"I don't know why you would listen to me about anything.

Have you smelled my car? That's pretty damning evidence that I have no idea what's going on with my life."

"So you do smell it!" Otis said, pointing a finger at Tag.

"I do. But I have to pretend I don't."

"There's gotta be a way to figure this out."

"Well, like you said, cleaning up and finding the source. I have a feeling it's a banana peel."

"Well, yeah, that would help, but I was back to the topic of Luke." Otis sighed.

"I'm not really prepared to have the sex talk with you, dude. Maybe Madison would be better for this."

"I listen to you about your 'women problems,'" Otis said, putting air quotes around Tag's favorite phrase.

"You do."

"So it's only fair that you listen to me."

Tag took a deep breath. "You're right, bring it on."

"So Luke—"

"But I don't know how to help you!" Tag said, his voice almost a shriek as he interrupted. "This is too much for a Tuesday."

That made Otis laugh at least. "Ask me something you'd ask a straight guy about sex; it doesn't have to be a big deal."

"I don't think I've had a conversation like this with a straight guy." Now Tag's knuckles were completely white on his steering wheel.

"Why are you panicking?"

"Why are you panicking?" Tag shot back at him.

"Let's try something else."

"Or we could be quiet."

"You're a terrible friend."

"Fine, let's try something else," Tag said.

"Have you ever had sex, Tag?"

"I have indeed. Have you ever had sex, Otis?"

"Like hand stuff or whatever," Otis said, looking out the window.

"And how does that make you feel?" Tag's eyebrows shot up to his hairline in shock at his own question.

"I guess good," Otis said. "You're right. This is too weird."

"Hell no, we're in it now."

"So what do I do?"

Tag chewed his lip for a second. "Maybe you need to mention this to Luke? Like tell him you're nervous? And you guys could still do, um." Tag cleared his throat. "Hand stuff in the hotel room."

Otis mulled that around. "Yeah, like, I know you're right. I don't want to throw a wrench in Luke's big plan."

"God, I hope my mom doesn't have a listening device in my car."

Otis and Tag turned and glared at the bobblehead on Tag's dashboard.

Tag pulled up in front of Otis's house.

"Thanks," Otis said. "For the ride and the talk."

"I honestly can't believe that helped even a little bit."

"You know, I think it did."

"In that case, you can repay me by helping me clean out my car this weekend."

"Not a chance," Otis said as he slid out of the passenger seat.

"Son of a bitch," Tag muttered as Otis slammed the door.

Tag pulled away, taking his stinking, rotting stench with him.

The smell was definitely stuck in Otis's nose. He was definitely going to end up helping his friend try to clean that up someday soon.

Cameron

Cameron had a rare afternoon off from both of his jobs. He really needed the time to study for his upcoming AP biology test. He needed to get maximum points on all his AP exams so he could spend a little less money on college next year. The dream was to get maximum points on bio, history, calculus, and English. If he could place out of those four classes, it was practically like money in the bank and a whole semester that he might be able to skip.

He pulled up in front of Richard's house, which is all he could ever think of it as; it wasn't Cameron's home at all. It was the place he had to live for only a few more months. Maybe weeks if he could find something temporary for the summer. He was eighteen after all. He liked to tell himself that maybe he would make more of an effort if he was going to be here for a while. But the fact that his mom got remarried just before his senior year of high school didn't give him much time to adjust.

Maybe he would make more of an effort if Richard did.

Maybe.

Cameron was even considering taking a few classes at the community college over the summer but needed to find out how he did on his AP exams first. His whole goal in life these days was to get through college without having to take a dime of Richard's money.

As he walked in the house, it was cool and dark, but there was a familiar *clickety-clack* sound coming from the dining room.

He found his mom sitting at the table surrounded by paperwork, gazing glaze-eyed at her laptop as she typed her way through an e-mail. He took the seat closest to her. She looked up a minute later and her eyes went wide.

"How long have you been sitting there?" she asked.

He shrugged. "Like a minute or two."

"You're so quiet sometimes," she said, flipping her hand breezily. "I didn't even know you were home."

Cameron smiled.

"What's up?" she asked, pausing her work and giving him her full attention. It felt like a rarity these days. Like it could be fleeting.

"Um, well, I just wanted to say hi. And to tell you that I'm going to the prom." He said the last part quickly, and all the words ran together.

His mom clapped her hands together. "That's excellent. I'm glad, Cameron. All you do is work and study. It's good for you to have a little fun."

At a different time in Cameron's life, his mom would have taken her time and asked for the details, wanting to know who he was going with or if he needed any money or whatever. But now she shook her head and her smile fell a little.

"I have something that I've been wanting to tell you."

Cameron gripped the straps of his backpack a little tighter.

"I'm pregnant!" she said.

Cameron's mouth dropped open, and he tried to form a couple of words, but it seemed like he was having a delayed reaction to the news. Like it had to course through all the veins in his body before it made its way back up to his brain.

"Aren't you too old?" was the sentence that finally made it from his brain to his mouth.

She rolled her eyes. "Guess not, because I'm three months along. I didn't even realize that I was pregnant. I thought maybe, well. You don't want to hear about this."

Cameron really, really did not want to hear about this. So he didn't protest.

"Well, congratulations," he said. "Do Landon and, um, his dad know?"

"Not yet. I wanted to tell you first. It's just been you and me for so long, I guess it didn't feel right to tell anyone else. I only found out this morning. That's why I'm working from home today."

"Cool," he said.

"You still planning on going to college so far away even now that you're going to be an older brother?" she asked.

"Mom, Ohio isn't even that far away. And it's where I got the best scholarship. I'll see the tiny human sometime."

"Well, I'm due right around Halloween, so hopefully we can work out a way for you to get home around then. I'm sure Richard will be happy to help pay for your travel."

Cameron swallowed back all his feelings. He would not ruin his mom's day with his own negativity.

"Cool," he said again. Even though it wasn't cool at all. "I better go study."

"Cameron. Are you okay with this?" she asked, grabbing his hand as he stood up from the table.

He cleared his throat, willing himself not to sound too emotional.

"Yeah, it's cool. Great even. I hope it's . . ." He paused, searching for the right word or sentiment. "I hope everything is perfect."

She smiled up at him and dropped his hand. "Thank you."

He left the room quickly after that, before his mom could say anything else. He had the distinct feeling that he might cry, but instead he focused on his studying and got down to work.

The next day in English class was at least a laptop day.

Laptop Girl was his only saving grace these days.

I promise to find something lime green to have with me, her message started out.

> I can't promise that I'll buy a lime-green dress. I just don't think I'd look very good in it. But I'll find something. We should try to make sure to both be out on the dance floor for the first slow song, no matter what. I wish I could give you more hints about me, but I worry that it'll ruin the anonymity, and we're so close to meeting each other it'd be silly not to wait until the prom.

He inhaled deeply and finished reading her message.

It was becoming apparent that he really needed someone to talk to about his family stuff. It was getting so bad that he almost walked up to Henry that morning. But what would he have even said? How do you apologize for just not doing anything? Someday he'd figure it out.

For today, he had Laptop Girl.

I haven't decided what my lime green will be, but I know it'll be something cool. Because anything lime green is automatically awesome.

I'm really glad we're going to meet soon. I have all this . . . crap going on in my life, and I can't wait to talk to you about it. You seem like you're such a good listener. Although you'll probably run away crying once I inundate you with my random drama and emotions.

I fear I have said too much.

But I can't wait to meet you.

With nothing more to say, Cameron saved the draft and closed the laptop.

He spent the rest of the period chewing his pen cap and staring out the window.

Chapter 11

Jacinta

When she was invited to join in the shopping trip for her sister's wedding dress, Jacinta was delighted. As the baby of the family, Jacinta was often left out of things that were deemed "grown-up." This outing made her feel like her family was finally taking her seriously now that she was almost eighteen and recognizing her as the adult she was becoming.

It turned out that she was probably only invited because literally every female relative in her family was invited. The trip included: Jacinta, her mom, her sister (obviously), her sister's future mother-in-law, her abuela on her mom's side, two of her tías, her brother's wife, and her brother's wife's sister.

From the very first minute, Jacinta could tell it was going to be the longest Saturday afternoon that she had ever known.

The bridal store associate led the large party up to the second floor, and sometime during her speech about dress fitting

Jacinta checked out of the whole process. There were obviously at least four people too many here and way too much going on. She didn't need to be involved. She'd make sure she put in an appearance when her sister started trying on gowns.

Instead she wandered around looking at bridesmaids' dresses and considering her options. Her "options" meaning how could she trick her sister into choosing the dress that Jacinta liked.

Her mom called her to join them upstairs about fifteen minutes later, and Jacinta stuck around for a bit, honestly enjoying herself. All the abuelas and tías and various family members oohed and aahed at Flora as she came out in dresses that all looked wonderful on her. She was going to be a beautiful bride.

But then she went back to try on dress number thirteen, and if Jacinta knew anything about her sister it was that she wasn't going to buy dress number thirteen. It seemed like a good time to go look at the clearance rack Jacinta had been eyeing across the balcony from where they were.

Jacinta slipped away and started shuffling through dresses.

They weren't arranged by color or size, but that was part of the fun. She didn't necessarily see anything that struck her fancy, and it would probably be tough to convince her sister to select something from last year's line anyway. The Ramoses weren't rich, but they knew what they wanted and they knew how to throw a wedding.

Jacinta got to the end of the rack and stopped in her tracks. There, hanging on a half-broken hanger, was what might have been the most beautiful dress she'd ever seen. Not a bridesmaid's dress; definitely not, it wasn't her sister's style at all.

But it would make the perfect prom dress.

If she hadn't already wanted to go, this dress would have sealed the deal.

She grabbed it off the rack and slipped into the nearest fitting room, hoping that no one from the entourage would notice that she had disappeared.

She slid the curtain closed behind her and started undressing as quickly as she could. The quicker she got this over with the quicker she could be disappointed by how this perfect dress looked terrible on her.

Except. It didn't look terrible.

It was her favorite color, light icy blue, and it looked perfect with her dark brown hair and deep tan complexion, thanks to her Puerto Rican roots. It looked strapless, but it actually had some kind of sheer, gauzy material holding everything in place. She wanted to call it netting, but she was sure that wasn't the proper term. The skirt was short but full and hit right above her knee.

The best and most amazing part was that it fit her like a glove. No dress had ever fit her like a glove before. She had a weird shape. Her mother told her it was lovely any time Jacinta brought it up, but she had broad shoulders and a broad chest, and clothes never looked right on her. She often looked stiff and uncomfortable in dresses, because she *was* stiff and uncomfortable in dresses. If she bought them big enough for her top half, she looked like she was swimming in the rest of it. But this dress was a miracle.

She snapped a picture with her phone and texted it to Kelsey, who immediately texted back a long line of exclamation points, followed by an "OMG, it's perfect!"

Rather than replying right away, Jacinta stuck her head out the side of the curtain and caught her mom's eye. She gestured her over and then yanked her by the arm into the dressing room.

"What do you think of this?" Jacinta whispered.

Her mom gave her a critical once-over.

"Not for Flora's wedding but for the prom," Jacinta added.

Her mom looked at real Jacinta and then Jacinta in the mirror, holding a hand to her chin.

"It's on sale. Final clearance, actually. I need your opinion," Jacinta continued when her mom had been silent for too long.

"Hmm," her mom said. She peeked out the curtain, but Flora had yet to reappear from the back. "Yes. You have to buy it. You look perfectly lovely in it, Jacinta."

"Thanks, Mom."

Her mom slipped Jacinta her credit card and her car keys.

"But do it fast. Go down the back steps over there and buy it in the front. Bring it out to the car and hide it in the trunk and meet me back up here. Best not to tell your sister right now. She probably has some superstition about someone else buying a dress while she's trying on dresses." Her mother rolled her eyes and Jacinta did, too. She couldn't help a little giggle escaping, as her mother was her coconspirator even if it was just about rushing to conceal a dress from Flora.

She did exactly as her mom instructed. The more Jacinta thought about it the more she knew that this was the exact dress for her.

She snuck back upstairs and sat down as Flora emerged in her fourteenth dress.

The group wrapped up their afternoon at the bridal salon

soon after that. Flora decided that she honestly liked the first dress the best and wanted to come back in a week to make sure, after giving herself a little time to think on it.

She had plenty of time, considering the wedding was still over a year away.

On the way home in the car, Jacinta checked her phone. She had a new text from Kelsey.

Kelsey:

I love that dress, but I have terrible news.

Jacinta:

??? Don't leave me hanging!

Kelsey:

Henry is going to the prom with Amelia Vaughn.

Jacinta gasped out loud, but luckily her mom and her sister were so busy talking in the front they didn't even hear her.

Jacinta:

NO EFFING WAY! I should have just asked him when I thought of it. But really, who am I when compared to Amelia Vaughn.

Kelsey:

YOU ARE JACINTA RAMOS!
He would be lucky to go with you!

Jacinta:

I know, it's not even about Henry. I just wanted a date to the prom. ☹ ☹

Kelsey:

And you could still have a date to the prom.
Can I set you up now? Pretty please?

Jacinta:

Seriously? I thought we talked about it, and I only wanted to go with someone you thought I would actually like.

Kelsey:

Of course! And you will like this guy.

Jacinta:

So who is it?

Kelsey:

His name is Brian. He's from youth group at my church. He's cute and kind of shy in a serious way like Henry, since apparently that's your type.

Jacinta:

All right. I'm in.

Henry

Henry had made a terrible mistake. His mom had asked him if he wanted to go to Target with her Sunday evening. He said yes, because he wasn't thinking. When he heard the word *Target* he was really hoping he could find the exact Star Wars T-shirt that he'd been wanting and convince her to buy it for him. Sure he had his own money, but if moms weren't for buying their kids clothes then what was the point.

Unfortunately, it had already been an hour and he was more than ready to leave. It had taken him all of three minutes to find his novelty T-shirt, and now he had looked at everything from sports equipment to books, from kitchenware to office supplies. He was tired of wandering around in his dirty clothes from helping his dad in the yard that afternoon and he really wanted to get home to shower.

He was ready to go. His mom was not.

Apparently she needed to buy towels. Lots and lots of towels. And then the perfect shower curtain to go with those towels. He suggested perhaps that she select the shower curtain first and then the towels to match it, but apparently that was a bad idea. Some sort of interior design faux pas that he didn't understand.

"This is for Flora Ramos's engagement party next month! She wants a particular kind of towel, and I want to make sure it looks just right!" his mother said.

Henry got the heck out of that area, because if he knew his mom at all her next topic of conversation would be Jacinta Ramos and how she still couldn't believe he wasn't going to the prom with her. He didn't have the heart to tell her that he was going with Amelia. He'd let his mom hold on to the Jacinta fantasy a little longer.

He was wandering back toward the electronics thinking maybe he could get his mom to also buy him some new earbuds when he saw a familiar face in front of him.

Oh man, this was going to be awkward.

It was Cameron. Cameron who used to be his friend. And there was no stepping around him.

"Hey," Cam said.

"Hey, you work here?" Henry asked, gesturing toward his name tag and obvious red vest.

"Yup."

"So you quit baseball to start a lucrative career as a Target employee?"

"Basically," Cameron said.

"And how's that going for you?"

"Not bad, not bad. I'm trying to save up some money for college. My stepfather claims he can pay for everything, but I would really rather not get involved with him."

Cameron only ever referred to his mom's husband as "my stepfather," never by his first name and definitely never as "Dad."

"How's everything going with Landon?"

Cam laughed uncomfortably. "It's going. Landon is . . ." He trailed off. "You don't really care about this."

Henry didn't want to agree with him, but he also couldn't disagree. He cared the amount anyone would care that his fellow human had to live with that jackass Landon Rittenbacher. Just thinking the name made Henry's face wince in pain.

"You can admit it," Cam said.

"No, actually I was thinking for the millionth time about how terrible it must be to have to share a house with Landon Rittenbacher."

Cam chuckled and cleared his throat. "How's baseball going?"

"Oh, you know. Not bad, not great."

Cam made a few more feeble attempts to engage Henry, trying to make small talk, but Henry was terrible at small talk and he couldn't understand why Cameron wouldn't put him out of his misery and walk away.

But then Cameron blurted out, "My mom's pregnant!"

"Oh," Henry said, unsure of how to respond.

"I haven't said that out loud to anyone."

"Oh, wow," Henry said. "It's a lot to take in."

Cameron nodded and toyed with the edge of a price sticker that was coming off one of the shelves.

"You know, man," Henry started. He had no idea where that thought was going. He didn't know what Cameron needed or wanted from him.

But then his mom appeared like an angel from the bathroom accessory area.

"Cameron!" Henry's mom said, holding out her arms and pulling him in for a tight hug. Cameron's red hair looked practically radioactive next to her dark black.

"How are you?" she asked as she pulled away. "How is your mom?"

"She's good, thanks." Cameron shot Henry a look that Henry interpreted as "please don't mention the pregnant thing."

Henry kept his mouth shut.

"It's been too long since we've seen you around the house," Henry's mom said, rubbing Cam's arm. "I was saying that to Henry last week."

Cam had the decency to at least look embarrassed. It was his own fault that he and Henry weren't friends anymore, not that Henry was going to say anything like that in front of his mom.

"Yeah, I've been working a lot. I have two jobs actually."

"Two jobs! That's too many jobs! You should be seeing friends and playing baseball. Those should be your jobs!" Henry made a mental note to use these words against his mother the next time she forced him to work at the family store after a long day of school and baseball practice.

"I know," Cam said, frowning dramatically. "But you know how it is. The money is going toward college."

Luckily Henry's mom seemed to take that for what it was worth and let the topic drop.

"Well, we should get going, Henry," she said.

"Yeah, sure," he said at the same moment that Cameron was paged over the loud speaker.

"Good seeing you," Cameron said as he jogged away.

"Such a nice boy," Henry's mom said as they made their way to the front to check out.

She paid for Henry's T-shirt without even noticing since he slipped it in between the full set of towels she'd selected for Flora Ramos.

On the drive home she asked Henry for the millionth time what happened between him and Cameron. And for the millionth time Henry didn't have a good answer for her.

"We stopped liking the same stuff," Henry said. "It happens. Friends grow apart sometimes."

She tsked as she merged onto the highway. "He could probably use a friend."

"I know. I tried a million times last summer. He didn't want to talk. He didn't want to do anything."

"Maybe try some more," his mom said.

Maybe he would. But he would do it on his own terms and not just because his mom thought it was a good idea.

Chapter 12

Cameron

The day after he ran into Henry at Target, Cameron was working the dinner shift at his second job at the pizza parlor. He worked there most days after school until around dinnertime, but they asked him to stay late Monday night since the busboy called in sick. He didn't mind staying. It was better than going home to spend the whole night in his room, bouncing off the walls and wishing he were somewhere else.

He was going pretty quickly through the latest stack of dirty dishes when he heard a commotion out front. He took a quick peek out of the swinging doors, but all he could see was the long hallway that led off to the restrooms and a little sliver of the front door. Not exactly a prime view of the dining room.

A minute later the lone waitress on duty that night came

into the kitchen out of breath. "The high school baseball team is here. Apparently they won some kind of big game tonight," she said dramatically. "And they need like a million pizzas right now."

Cameron chewed his lip. He wasn't one of the chefs, but he would certainly be pulled in if they needed help with the assembly line of toppings.

"Not a great night to be understaffed," the chef said.

The waitress nodded and blew her bangs out of her face. "When are we not understaffed?"

Seeing as how no one had spoken to Cameron yet, he finished the dishes in the sink and then jumped in to help with the pizzas. It really wasn't as bad as the two had made it out. The varsity baseball team only had twenty members. Hopefully Cameron wouldn't be asked to serve them. He hadn't talked to any of the guys on the team since he abruptly quit and wasn't sure what kind of reception he would get.

The chef left to grab something from the walk-in freezer, and in the minutes he was gone someone came through the swinging doors. When he turned it was his boss, Eddie. Everyone called him Eddie, not Ed, not Edward.

"Cameron," he said.

"Hey," Cameron said, keeping his hands busy.

"I know you asked for June first off," he started.

"Yes. It's prom night."

Eddie sighed. "I'm sorry. But I don't have anyone else to work that shift. You know how it is. But I can get someone here around six to relieve you."

"Oh," Cameron said. "That's okay, I guess. The dance starts at seven, and we can't get in after eight. But if someone comes in at six, that gives me plenty of time." Cameron was babbling; he knew it, Eddie knew it, but he had to talk his way through his nerves.

"Good," Eddie said. "You keep working on those pizzas."

Cameron nodded.

He squeezed Cam's shoulder before he left. "Maybe someday you'll have my job if you keep working so hard."

Cameron schooled his face to keep from cringing as the door swung closed behind Eddie. He worked all these jobs to get out of this town, not to take over Eddie's job managing his pizzeria.

Not that there was anything wrong with owning a pizzeria. Cameron just had his sights set to something different. He didn't know what that was, but ever since Laptop Girl had asked him what he wanted to do with his life way back at the beginning of the year, he'd been rolling a bunch of different ideas around, and none of them included owning a pizzeria in the town he grew up in.

Laptop Girl.

What was he going to do about Laptop Girl?

Did he risk losing his anonymity by warning her he might be late for the prom? What if he missed the first slow dance because he couldn't leave work when he needed to?

Maybe he needed to consider a different way of identifying each other.

After work that night, he sat down and typed a message on his phone so that the next time the laptop cart was out in English class, Cameron would be ready with an amendment to how he and Laptop Girl would recognize each other.

I had a new idea, his message began.

> Or not a new idea. But an amendment due to my concern that one of us will get stuck in traffic or something the night of the prom and miss the first slow dance.

The "or something" made it less of a lie, Cameron told himself.

> It's hard since I don't know exactly what this room looks like, but why don't we meet at 8:15 somewhere near the DJ station. And we'll still both have something lime green to recognize the other. And who knows, maybe we'll notice each other long before then. I feel better about having a more concrete meeting time rather than just waiting for the first slow song. What if they don't play any slow songs?! I know, I know. It's the prom, they'll play slow songs.
>
> Anyway, hopefully you're into the idea. I still can't wait to meet you.

Cameron felt better already.

Cora

Cora was in the back seat of Teagan's car after the baseball team's big win at semifinals. It was dark outside and cozy in the car after the long afternoon spent cheering Jamie and the rest of the team on at the game that would help send them to the first round of the state championship.

This was one of those times that Cora had special dispensation to be out on a school night, and she had convinced her friends to go to the game with her so she wouldn't have to drive with Jamie's parents. Teagan and Josie were happy to oblige.

After stopping for dinner on the way home, Teagan was speeding so that she'd be home in time for her favorite Tuesday night show.

"But don't you record it? And can't you just watch on the Internet tomorrow?" Josie asked.

"Obviously, but half the fun is watching it with everyone else on Twitter," Teagan explained. "Like what did people do during commercials before live tweeting?"

"I think I'm going to break up with Jamie," Cora said. As soon as the phrase left her lips she felt a wave of relief fall over her, like all the tension she'd been holding in her shoulders for the past month was gone.

"What?" Teagan and Josie said at the same time.

"But he's perfect," Josie said, shaking her head. "Everyone wants a Jamie."

"Well, maybe it's time for someone else to have a Jamie. Maybe that's my gift to the world."

Teagan looked at Cora in the rearview mirror. "Seriously? You're not joking?"

"I'm not joking. And he's not perfect for me anymore. Something has changed with us lately. I don't even know what it is, but every time I think about spending the next four years with him at school, it's like I feel tied down or something."

"Wow," Josie said. "I feel like my parents are getting divorced."

"Your parents are divorced," Teagan said.

"I feel like my parents are getting divorced all over again," Josie amended. "Happy now?"

"Yes," Teagan said. "But not about Cora and Jamie breaking up. It feels really abrupt from the outside."

Cora shrugged. "Not to me it doesn't. I've been thinking about it for a while. It's like, I love him but I'm not in love with him. And because he's great doesn't mean we're great together or that we have to stay together forever."

"That's pretty brave," Josie said.

Cora tipped her head to the side. "Is it, though? Like, we've been together a long time, probably too long by high school standards. And we made all these plans to stay together in college. Is that even healthy? There's like a huge buffet of people out there. I might not even really like boys?"

"So you're breaking up with him because you're a lesbian?" Teagan asked.

"No, that's not what I mean. I mean, I might be like bi or something, I haven't even really considered other people because I've always been with Jamie. You guys have had a million crushes each."

"You've had crushes," Josie pointed out.

"On celebrities. But in real life it's almost like I've been blind to everyone who isn't Jamie. I don't know. I guess my point is, it's time to try something new. We're not married. Why do I always act like we are?"

"Because you're a good and loyal person," Teagan said.

Cora had to smile at that. "Thanks."

"It's true, you really are," Josie agreed.

"Do you really think you're bi?" Teagan asked. Cora couldn't see her face, but her voice was normal and not strained as if she was worrying Cora was about to try to make out with her.

"I don't know," Cora said. Her thoughts drifted for a moment to the way her lab partner Madison's hair fell in front of her face when she was using the microscope. Cora had always admired the way Madison's hair fell, but maybe she was really admiring Madison.

"Well, if you are, that's cool," Josie said. "I don't mean, like, I just mean, I'm cool with that."

"Yeah, me too," Teagan said.

"Thanks," Cora said, grinning at her friends' slightly awkward declaration. And she knew it was true when the subject changed.

"What are you going to do about next year?" Teagan asked.

"That is a good question," Cora said. "It's too late to switch schools. My parents already put down a deposit. I might just have to suck it up and go to BU. And it was my idea to go there in the first place!"

"It's a big school, so maybe you won't have to see him that much," Teagan offered.

"When are you going to tell him?" Josie asked.

"I don't know. I want to do it like right away. I feel like I'm lying to him at this point, but I don't really want to break up with him before prom. That feels sort of mean, you know?"

"I guess. I don't know what's meaner," Teagan said. "Isn't it a little bit like stringing him along at this point?"

Teagan pulled up in front of Cora's house, and Cora leaned against the front seat to look at them. "Thanks, you guys, for listening and for saying nice things to me."

Teagan put the car in park. "Of course and always."

"Now go home and watch your show."

"Yes, ma'am," Teagan said, saluting Cora.

"Text me if you need me," Josie said.

"Yeah, me too," Teagan said.

Cora didn't want to leave her friends and go out into the cool night air, but it was time. Teagan honked as she pulled away from the curb, and Cora felt like maybe she'd be able to accomplish this. Like maybe she'd be able to break up with Jamie. She definitely felt better suited for the task now that she knew she had her two best friends by her side.

Chapter 13

Lizzie

The laptop cart was ready and waiting at the front of the classroom when Lizzie walked into English class Friday afternoon. The cart had been absent for nearly a week.

About time, Lizzie thought. She had missed their conversations.

She opened up their shared document to see what else he had to say. After Lizzie read the brief message a couple of times, she worked on writing back for most of the rest of the period. She couldn't stop smiling, just thinking about the reality of meeting him. Though Mystery Boy was right, it was better to have a concrete time to meet up.

After telling him she agreed with the new plan, she added some more thoughts.

Is it weird that even though we still don't know exactly who the other person is I suddenly feel a lot more vulnerable? (Don't worry; I'll answer that for myself. Yes. It's weird.) I guess the idea of meeting you and you meeting me and therefore meeting each other. Yeah, so that's super redundant.

But anyway. I'm really glad you want to go with me. Or meet me there. Are we going together if we're meeting there? I don't know how that works.

Lizzie wrapped up the message soon after that, feeling like she was babbling an awful lot. The rest of the period dragged on, but as soon as the bell rang Lizzie sprinted off to her locker.

Two seconds after she got there, Madison came up next to her.

"So," Madison said, her eyes wide with an unspoken question. "How was English class?"

Lizzie leaned against her locker and sighed dreamily. It was proof of Madison's loyalty that she didn't make fun of Lizzie's heart eyes.

"He wanted to talk more about logistics and meeting up and everything. He keeps saying how happy he is that we're going to meet."

Madison let out a loud whoop and leaned on the locker next to Lizzie's, getting comfortable. "And you're obviously pleased with these developments."

"I do feel happy. I feel like I'm going to the prom with a boy and I never expected this to happen to me."

Madison tsked. "As your best friend, I can totally tell you this was going to happen for you."

"You couldn't know that," Lizzie said, slamming her locker shut.

"Are you working tonight? Let's hang out and celebrate

your happiness. I have plans with Otis, but you should come along. Maybe he could offer a male perspective on Mystery Boy."

"I am not working, and I would love to hang out with you and Otis, but why do I need a male perspective on Mystery Boy?"

"Well, you know, why is he still being so secretive? Who is he? That kind of stuff."

"Sure." Lizzie didn't think she wanted to know who he was yet. She still kind of liked the anonymity, but that seemed like something Madison didn't understand.

"Cool, I'll pick you up at seven."

As promised, Madison was outside Lizzie's house at seven o'clock. Lizzie jogged to the back door of the car and got in.

Madison pulled away from the curb. "Do you guys want to go to the diner? I want home fries with cheese on them."

"Um, why have I never gotten home fries with cheese on them? That sounds magical," Lizzie said.

"It's definitely magical."

As they slid into the booth at the diner, Madison said, "I filled Otis in on the gist of what's going down with you and Mystery Boy."

"And what do you think?" Lizzie asked.

Otis put his menu down. "You really have no idea who this guy is?"

"None whatsoever."

"What if he's grotesque?" Otis asked.

"Do we even go to school with anyone who's truly grotesque? Are we not all God's creatures?" Madison asked.

"I'm serious. There's that dude. You know that guy," Otis said, snapping his fingers, trying to remember.

"I have no idea who you're talking about," Lizzie said.

"Well, okay. But what if you see Mystery Boy and you're just not attracted to him?"

"I mean, I've still had a lot of fun talking to him all year. I still want to meet him; he doesn't have to be the Hottest Hottie from Hotville."

"I like that. Hottest Hottie from Hotville. I'm going to use that," Otis said.

"I suppose I'll allow it," Lizzie said as the waitress came for their order.

After she walked away, Otis looked at Lizzie appraisingly.

"So, let's take it back to basics. You have a secret admirer."

"I wouldn't call him a secret admirer; it's more like a double-blind friendship."

"Hmm, yes, so scientific, so specific," Otis said, opening a packet of sugar and dumping it into his coffee. "And you really, really have no clue who it could be? Like you've gone through all the possibilities?"

"I haven't gone through any of the possibilities," Lizzie said. It was time to put her foot down. "I honestly like the romantic comedy aspect of it. I've gotten used to not knowing. And now I want to wait. It's only a couple more weeks."

"He's never dropped any useful hints? Nothing?"

"I used to try to figure it out at the beginning. I even e-mailed the document to myself so I could take my time reading it. But I don't want to do that anymore. I really, really don't want to know."

"OMG, let me read the document," Otis exclaimed, stirring his coffee. "I'm sure I could figure it out."

"You just said OMG," Madison pointed out to Otis. "You're practically turning into Luke these days."

"He has a lot of influence on me," Otis said.

Madison rolled her eyes and turned to Lizzie. "If he reads the document, then I definitely get to read the document."

"Hell no. That's my private business. And his private business. No one is reading the document," Lizzie said, pointing at Otis.

Otis pouted.

Their food arrived, and everyone dug into their order.

After a few more minutes, it was obvious that Otis wasn't going to let go of this topic anytime soon.

"Have you ever considered that it's not double blind?" Otis asked.

"What do you mean?" Madison asked.

"Have you ever considered that he knows who you are, but you don't know who he is?" he asked with an eyebrow raise.

Lizzie had definitely never considered that possibility.

"Oh my god," she said. "What if he knows who I am but I don't know who he is?"

"That's what I'm saying," Otis said.

"How have we never considered that possibility?" Madison asked.

"It never even struck me. Not once." Lizzie shrugged and looked around the diner. "It's like everyone is a suspect now. He could be following me."

"He probably doesn't know," Madison said.

"But he might," Otis said.

"He might," Lizzie agreed.

Henry

In his head, Henry listed the things he should be doing. Writing his final paper for English, studying for the AP calc test, taking a jog, or texting Paisley. Instead he was lying facedown on his bed and pretending it wasn't Sunday night, pretending that he didn't have school in the morning.

He sort of wished he could text Cameron, but he'd actually deleted his number back in November at Paisley's urging. Henry hadn't thought much about how Cameron was feeling back then with his mom's remarriage and all. He didn't think about what Cameron was going through. It wasn't because Henry was a bad friend; at least he didn't think so. It was more that he didn't know how to navigate the murky waters of whatever was going on with Cameron. And now his mom was pregnant?

Henry had no idea how to "be there" for Cameron. But he had a distinct urge to try, just like his mom had advised.

It required an emotional quotient that Henry didn't possess. He got good grades, and he was going to a good college in the fall, but he lacked something in the area of empathy. He could have tried harder to be there for his friend. But how do you put all of that in a text? It had started feeling like they'd never really been that close in the first place, even though they'd pretty much been best friends up until junior year. Cameron

117

was second to Paisley, and that was only because Henry had known Paisley since nursery school and had met Cameron in kindergarten.

Back when Cameron had started pulling away, not returning texts, saying no to hanging out, and quitting the baseball team, it had felt like it wasn't Henry's job to worry about him.

But maybe it was his job. Maybe that's what he got wrong.

He flipped over onto his back, and his phone beeped next to him. For a second he believed it was Cameron, as if just thinking about him was enough to start a conversation.

But it wasn't Cameron. It was Amelia, sending him a picture of her dress so he knew what color corsage to buy her. Henry covered his face with his hand. He didn't want to deal with this.

His phone beeped again. This time it was Paisley with one of her wild stories from the mall food court. A woman had gone off on her about putting an extra pump of liquid cheese on her potato.

Paisley:

Anyway, I long for the day that I'm not in the customer service industry. What's up with you this fine Sunday evening?

Henry:

Are you busy?

Paisley:

If I was busy I wouldn't be texting you.

Henry:

But is the boss man coming soon to stop you from texting?

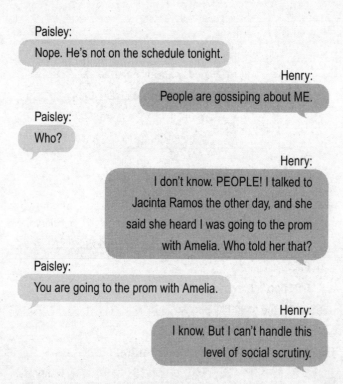

Paisley:

Nope. He's not on the schedule tonight.

Henry:

People are gossiping about ME.

Paisley:

Who?

Henry:

I don't know. PEOPLE! I talked to Jacinta Ramos the other day, and she said she heard I was going to the prom with Amelia. Who told her that?

Paisley:

You are going to the prom with Amelia.

Henry:

I know. But I can't handle this level of social scrutiny.

Paisley texted back a series of emojis that equated to "What do you want to do about it?"

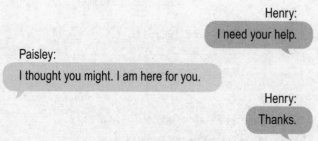

Henry:

I need your help.

Paisley:

I thought you might. I am here for you.

Henry:

Thanks.

And then he remembered something that happened the other day while the baseball team was riding home on the bus.

Henry:

So, you should probably know that the other day I might have mentioned to the guys on the baseball team that you don't have a date for the prom. And some of them might try to ask you this week.

Paisley:

WHAT? Is this your revenge for me nominating you for prom king?

Henry:

No. Yes. Maybe. Fifty/fifty.

Paisley:

Fifty percent revenge, but what's the other fifty percent?

He could almost hear her incredulous tone.

Henry:

Mostly I want you to go to the prom so we can be miserable together.

Paisley:

Sigh. You are the worst, Henry Lai.

Henry:

There might be a pool involved.

Paisley:

They made a BET about who could get a date with me? Who on the baseball team even cares that much! And you let them? I thought you were a feminist, Henry.

Henry:

I didn't "let them" do this, as much as I watched in horror as it all went down.

Paisley:

I repeat: You are the worst.

What do you even get out of this?

Henry:

It benefits me since I want my friend to go to the prom!

She stopped responding after that, but Henry imagined he was going to get his ass handed to him sometime soon.

Chapter 14

Paisley

When Henry told her that the guys on the baseball team were going to ask Paisley to the prom, she only halfway believed him. It seemed like the kind of thing Henry would say in jest and the guys would have a good chuckle over, but that no one would actually see through, even if there was hypothetical money on the line.

So, when she arrived at school Monday morning, it wasn't even on her mind. Which was why when she got to her locker she was so surprised to see a single balloon tied to her lock, with the word *PROM?* emblazoned on it in thick black marker.

She sighed and shook her head, looking around to find the culprit of this silly, harmless little prank. But no one was in the vicinity, definitely not anyone on the baseball team. By lunch, her secret prom suitor had still not revealed himself.

It was only when she popped the balloon and a small piece

of paper the size of a fortune from a cookie floated out that she learned it was Stewart Smith asking her. But if he wanted to go to the prom with her, he was going to have to actually speak with her face-to-face.

Even knowing that meant she'd have to reject him face-to-face, it didn't worry her. It shouldn't be her problem to track him down when she didn't even want to go.

Garrett Yi was standing by her locker after lunch.

"Hey," he said.

"Hey," she said.

"I hear you don't have a date for the prom and was kind of wondering if . . ." He trailed off and held his hands up.

He was sort of cute, and he got points in style for not having any style.

"I'm sorry to say I'm just not interested in going to the prom," she said, wrinkling her nose. "It's not you, it's the prom."

"Oh well," he said, walking away. "Thanks anyway."

She tried to ignore the way his neck glowed bright pink even from so many feet away. Paisley was not one to wallow in guilt. It wasn't worth it. She knew she'd have a terrible time at the prom. She didn't want to go and she didn't have to go.

When she found Henry during lunch, she backed him into a corner. "How many more, Henry?"

"How many more what?"

"How many more guys are going to ask me to the prom?" she said, poking him in the chest between each word to emphasize that she was in a take-no-shit kind of mood.

"Um, well, I know at least four of them put money in the pot, but there might have been more that I didn't see."

123

"Who gets the money if I don't say yes to anyone?"

Henry shrugged. "I don't know the rules of this particular gentlemen's agreement."

Paisley scoffed and went about her day. But she had a great idea during gym class. When she got home that night, she used some random leftover T-shirt-making stuff from her days as an Internet fangirl. She had bought a bunch of printable iron-on T-shirt transfer sheets and was going to start an Etsy shop for fans of a certain boy band she had been pretty passionate about in middle school.

And the beginning of high school.

And part of the middle of high school.

Fine, she had been obsessed with One Direction right up until Zayn left the group.

And it was right around when Zayn left the group that she lost all interest in starting an Etsy shop, but she'd already lost the receipt for the iron-on T-shirt transfer sheets.

All this to say, she was going to make a T-shirt printed with the phrase *It's not you, it's prom.*

The next day when Tyler Lewis approached her in the hallway, all she had to do was unzip her sweatshirt and point to the phrase. He turned on his heel and booked it in the other direction.

Paisley was smug with joy over her idea.

But this meant she was either going to have to make another T-shirt tomorrow or wash this one tonight. It honestly seemed easier to make another T-shirt. Especially when Madison came up to her after school.

"Um, that T-shirt is awesome and where did you get it?"

"I made it," Paisley said.

"Any chance you'd be willing to make me one?"

"Get me a plain T-shirt and I definitely will."

"I'll bring it by later; we could have a T-shirt-making party."

Paisley grinned. Maybe she should start an anti-prom T-shirt Etsy store.

The next day was sort of a letdown. Not one guy from the baseball team approached her. It was kind of annoying, seeing as how she spent all that time last night making T-shirts with Madison.

At least she had a few new shirts and some fun ideas for making money off other people who didn't care about the prom.

When she went outside after school, Derek Rodriguez was standing there with a single yellow rose, like his whole life was an episode of *The Bachelor*.

"Hey, there," he said.

"Hey," she said.

"How about we go to the prom together?" he asked. There was something unsettlingly smooth about Derek.

Paisley lifted the sweater she'd put on over her T-shirt.

"*It's not you, it's prom,*" Derek read. He looked her in the eye. "So that's a no, then?"

Paisley nodded.

"Dammit," he said, and walked away, still holding the yellow rose.

She pulled out her phone and texted Henry.

Paisley:

HOW MANY MORE?
HOW MANY HENRY?

Henry:

I DO NOT KNOW.

125

You're annoying when you're sassy.

She slid her phone in her back pocket and threaded her way to Madison's car, finding solace in the back seat while Madison drove her and Lizzie to their respective homes.

Thursday and Friday were quiet. It seemed that the message was out there.

Paisley Turner was not going to the prom with anyone.

Jacinta

Kelsey and Mike picked up Jacinta at 6:30 p.m. on the nose. They drove over to the Olive Garden, where Brian met them out front. For some reason Kelsey loved the Olive Garden no matter how much other people made fun of it. She was not one to be swayed by the opinion of others.

Brian was definitely cuter than Jacinta had expected, even cuter than Kelsey had described. And much cuter than any of the pictures that Jacinta had found of him on social media. Apparently the camera was not his friend.

He had the kind of smile where you could tell he still wore his retainer every night. Which reminded Jacinta, she needed to start wearing her retainer every night. It'd be worth it if her teeth looked as good as Brian's.

Another plus for Brian was that he held the door open for her. Jacinta was easily impressed by even the most basic manners. She really did believe it was the little things in life that sometimes meant the most.

The four of them got seated pretty quickly in a booth, and their waitress brought over bread sticks that Kelsey immediately attacked as if they were her last meal.

Brian smiled and offered the bread stick bowl to Jacinta before taking one for himself. Another point for him.

Sadly, things plateaued after that and Jacinta couldn't find anything else to give him points for.

He was okay. He didn't have much to say, which wasn't really a bad thing, but Jacinta was having a hard time imagining spending a lot of time with him. He wasn't exactly making an impression with his quiet politeness.

She sighed inwardly and hoped no one noticed her eye roll. Why couldn't she be the kind of person who was lucky enough to have a date from their class? Why did everyone else get to go to their prom with someone from school, while Jacinta had to scramble to find someone, anyone, willing to spend an evening with her?

It wasn't doing great things for her confidence.

Focus on Brian, she told herself.

The food arrived and truth be told, Jacinta's meal was better than she expected, so at least the night had something going for it.

Kelsey dragged her to the bathroom before they ordered dessert.

"So, what do you think?" she asked.

"He's not really doing much?"

"What do you mean?"

"I mean, he's barely said a word."

"He's shy!" Kelsey insisted. "You need to get to know him. You're shy, too."

"Okay. Yes. But like he needs to do something to make me

want to get to know him. Like leave some kind of impression. Right now I'm imagining being at the prom with him and neither of us saying a word for four hours."

"Well, I'll be at the prom, too, and Mike, of course, and we can help keep the conversation going."

"I appreciate your optimism, but I'm honestly not sure this is going to work out," Jacinta said, placing a hand on Kelsey's arm.

Kelsey frowned dramatically. "Come on. Give him one more chance. Ask him a question."

"I can't ask him a question when you're sitting there staring at us like we're about to do a song-and-dance number. That's probably not helping his shyness, either."

"Okay, fine, I'll have a conversation with Mike, and you have one with Brian."

"Fine. Let's go."

They settled back into the booth, and Brian and Mike both smiled at them.

Kelsey started a quiet conversation with Mike, and Jacinta took her moment.

"So what are your postgraduation plans?" Jacinta asked.

"Um, you know," Brian said, nodding.

"No," she said with what she hoped was a carefree laugh. "I don't actually know. That's kind of why I asked."

"Oh right," he said, and laughed at himself. She liked his laugh at least. "I'm going to Rutgers."

"Cool, cool."

"What about you?"

"I'm going to Penn State actually."

"Nice. They're rivals."

This was the worst conversation known to man, and Jacinta had no idea how to keep up her end of the bargain when this kid couldn't offer anything interesting. She decided to try something random.

"What was your favorite TV show when you were a kid?"

Brian smiled and seemed to think long and hard about this question. Jacinta really appreciated the time he put into it. A solid minute passed before he answered.

"Is it weak if I said *SpongeBob*?"

Jacinta laughed with surprise. "Why would that be considered weak? Doesn't everyone love *SpongeBob*?"

"It's kind of obvious, you know? Like of course everyone loves *SpongeBob*. I feel like I should have a more highbrow answer." His cheeks reddened when Jacinta giggled.

"I don't think there are a lot of highbrow shows for little kids. And really it's a better answer than, say . . . *Caillou*."

"Oh hell, yeah. If I said *Caillou*, then you could be sure I was a psychopath."

The conversation only got better from there, and when the check came they all walked out of the restaurant together.

Brian grabbed Jacinta's hand to stop her in the middle of the parking lot. Kelsey and Mike walked ahead of them.

"Thanks for, you know, going out with me," he said.

He was maybe kind of adorable. "You're welcome. Thanks for paying. You really didn't have to do that."

"That's what the guy is supposed to do, right?"

"Sure, if you want to be old-fashioned about it." Jacinta smiled to show him she was teasing.

"So, Kelsey mentioned that you needed a date to the prom."

"She did, huh?"

"Yeah, I'd be happy to go with you."

"I'd be pretty happy to go with you, too," Jacinta said. And she meant it.

"As long as it's not June first."

Jacinta's jaw dropped. "It's totally June first."

"Oh, that's the night of my graduation. It's private school. We finish earlier than public. I didn't even think of it."

Jacinta patted Brian's arm, comforting him, even though now she was down another possible date for the prom. "It's okay. I really did have fun tonight. Maybe we could see each other again sometime."

"Totally," Brian said with a grin. They exchanged numbers, and Jacinta tried not to feel like the whole night was for nothing.

She slid into the back seat, and Kelsey turned around expectantly. "So?"

"He can't go to the prom. It's the same night as his graduation."

"Oh," Mike said.

"Oops?" Kelsey said.

Chapter 15

Otis

When Madison texted to see if Otis wanted to go to a late movie Saturday night, he knew he should have said no. His curfew was eleven; he definitely wasn't going to be allowed to see a movie at ten.

But it was getting late in his senior year, and it was a movie he really wanted to see that probably wouldn't be in the theater much longer, so he said yes.

And the little voice inside his head cheered, because just maybe he'd get in trouble and maybe then he wouldn't even get to go to the prom or deal with any of this hotel room stuff. Considering how strict his parents were, it didn't seem all that far-fetched.

For example, one time his older sister told them she was going to a daylong volleyball camp and went to the beach instead. She was grounded for the rest of the summer. Like seriously grounded. On-lockdown grounded for over a month. She practically wept with joy and kissed the floor on the first day of school.

Otis had never really gotten into big trouble with them, so maybe it was time to see exactly how strict they were.

He slipped past his mom in the living room just after nine and said he'd be right back, making sure to close the door quick before she could ask any questions. His dad was out of town on business, and his mom always went to bed early. She'd never even notice what time he got back as long as he didn't wake her up.

Madison and Otis bought their tickets and went into the theater. Otis put his cell phone on silent as soon as he got into Madison's car and decided not to look at it out of fear his mom might be asking too many questions.

The movie took his mind off the situation completely and eased his worry, especially when he saw that he didn't have any texts from his mom after the movie was over. There was no way she'd still be awake when he got home.

When Madison invited him back to her house after the movie, he didn't even think twice about saying yes. Madison's mom was loose about Madison's curfew and she wasn't even home when they got there. In fact, what eventually woke Otis up after he and Madison fell asleep watching Netflix was Madison's mom setting off the burglar alarm coming into the house.

When he got back to his house, he tiptoed through the front door. The TV was off and there was a pile of pillows and blankets on the couch. He was sure his mom was under it, which meant he was definitely, 100 percent going to win this round.

He was patting himself on the back, literally, as he stepped into his room and slipped off his shoes.

But when he turned on his bedside lamp, there was a mound under the blankets on his bed, in the shape of his mother. The shape was unmistakable.

He panicked. There was no way around this. Unless he pretended he'd been in the basement all night or something. But they didn't have a finished basement, so unless he had been down there using the treadmill or doing laundry for the past—he glanced at his alarm clock—six and a half hours, neither of which his mother would buy, he was screwed. Completely screwed.

(So screwed he might not be allowed to go to prom and could avoid having to talk to Luke about the hotel room. That was the silver lining.)

His mom was still definitely asleep. Maybe he could curl up next to her and convince her she had sleepwalked into his room.

As he was going through a variety of other scenarios, she woke up and stared right at him.

"Well, hello, Otis."

"Hi, Mom."

She sat up, throwing off the quilt his oma had made him when he was five.

"Fancy seeing you here, in your room, at four in the morning."

"I was in the basement," he said, his voice high pitched and squeaky like he's twelve.

She tsked. "Keep your voice down and don't wake up your sisters."

133

"Okay," he said. And then he decided to try a different tactic. He yawned and stretched. "Well, I'm exhausted. Guess I should get back to sleep."

"Where were you?"

"The basement?"

She stood up and shook her head, walking slowly to the door.

"You're grounded," she said over her shoulder.

"Wait, for how long?" Otis asked.

"Let's say forever."

"Can't we negotiate this?" he asked, his hands going clammy at the thought of having to tell Luke he couldn't go to the prom with him. He'd made a huge mistake.

"It's four o'clock in the morning. I'm not negotiating anything. You snuck out of the house, didn't tell me where you were going, then lied when you got home and ruined my sleep. You wouldn't have pulled this if your father was home."

He couldn't deny that.

"I'm sorry," he said.

"I'm sure you are, but we're done discussing this."

As she pulled the door closed behind her she said, "Good night."

Otis threw himself down on his bed.

He knew enough to let it go for now. There was no reason to try to discuss it with his mother. But he would bring it up in the morning, and if that didn't work he would wait until his dad got back and figure out a way to make them listen about the prom.

He flipped over onto his side and squeezed his eyes shut.

Except maybe it was fate getting him out of the whole hotel

room mess and whatever embarrassing situation was sure to happen there.

If he couldn't go to the prom, he wouldn't have to talk to Luke about how nervous he was at the prospect of what the hotel room entailed.

He'd put in an effort, because that's what Otis did. He was stubborn and he loved a good debate. But if didn't work, it didn't work.

He'd have to accept it and so would Luke.

Lizzie

When Lizzie arrived at Madison's house Sunday afternoon, Luke's car was sitting out front. If she had known Luke was going to be there, she would have asked him for a ride instead of waiting for her dad to get up after working the night shift.

Madison's mom let her in, and Lizzie ran up the stairs to Madison's room where she could hear an argument in progress.

"All I'm saying," Luke said through the crack in the door, "is that he wouldn't have gone out last night if you hadn't invited him."

"Well, all I'm saying is that if he knew he'd get in trouble he shouldn't have said yes!" Madison retorted.

Lizzie knocked loudly on the door. "I'm coming in!" she yelled through it.

Madison was standing on one side of her unmade bed, and Luke was standing on the other. If Lizzie hadn't known better she would have thought they were having a very heated argument about the best way to make a bed.

"So," Lizzie said in a sugary-sweet voice, dragging out the *o*. "I take it everyone is having a lovely Sunday afternoon?"

Luke crossed his arms and huffed out a breath. Madison slumped into her desk chair and stared out the window.

"I feel like I'm about to play referee here."

Madison turned to look at Lizzie. "Otis and I went out to a late movie last night, and he got caught sneaking back in. Luke thinks this is somehow my fault."

"It's totally her fault that Otis got into trouble! He might be grounded from the prom," Luke said.

"I'm confused. How is this Madison's fault?"

"Thank you!" Madison said. "That's what I want to know, but he doesn't have a good answer for that question. His logic is baseless."

"Madison lured Otis out of his house."

"Why would she lure him out of his house?"

Luke scoffed but didn't answer.

"No, I'm serious. This is a serious question. I don't understand your use of the word *lured* here."

"Neither do I," Madison said.

"Well, I guess," Luke said, "she lured him out by offering to go see some dumb movie that I didn't want to see, so of course he went with her."

Lizzie looked at Madison. "I didn't want him to get in trouble. You can even read the texts. I specifically asked if he would get in trouble for going out late."

Lizzie read the texts. "This is pretty damning evidence that she was not trying to get him in trouble," she said to Luke.

Luke sat down on the end of Madison's bed. "I know."

Lizzie turned to Madison. "And since when are you allowed out so late?"

"My mom was on a date, and I knew she wouldn't be home until really late."

"Oh," Lizzie said. "She did look a little tired when she let me in."

Madison nodded.

"Anyway," Lizzie said. "You both realize you're being ridiculous, right?"

"Yes," Luke said.

"Yeah," Madison said.

They both seemed so resigned.

"Hug," Lizzie demanded.

Madison got up and sat next to Luke, giving him an awkward side hug that lasted all of three seconds.

"Hug like you mean it," Lizzie said.

This time they hugged full on and Luke rubbed Madison's back. "I'm sorry," he said. "Otis has just been really weird lately. Like he doesn't want to go to the prom with me."

Madison pulled away from him. "Don't be silly. Of course he wants to go to the prom with you."

Luke shrugged.

Lizzie sat down and leaned her head on his shoulder. Madison did the same on his other side.

"Otis likes you a lot, and he wants to go to prom with you," Lizzie said.

"Thanks, guys," Luke said. "Now let's talk about something better. Like how is Mystery Boy, Lizzie?"

"He's fine," Lizzie said, sliding to the floor. "But prom is so expensive!"

"Oh," Madison said. "Otis and I were talking about

everyone chipping in and getting a limo." She turned to Luke. "See! There's proof he wants to go to the prom with you."

Luke rolled his eyes. "That's just proof that he wants a limo."

"So you're telling me that I just used the majority of my most recent Hot Potato paycheck to buy a ticket to the prom and now you want me to chip in for a limo?"

"Well, maybe we could just go in Luke's car," Madison said.

"I didn't even know you decided you were going to prom," Lizzie said.

Madison shrugged. "I need to see what happens with Mystery Boy. Obviously."

Lizzie smiled and shook her head. "But seriously all this money for one night! Such a waste."

Luke looked her earnestly. "You're going to be one of those people who get married at city hall, aren't you?"

"Yes. It's financially reasonable. I'll use the money I would have otherwise spent on a wedding to go to grad school or something."

"So wise," Madison said.

Lizzie wasn't feeling very wise. She felt like she was hemorrhaging money. Hopefully Mystery Boy would be worth it in the end.

"Hey, not to totally change the subject," Madison said. "But do you guys ever think that Cora Wilson might be into girls?"

"I have never once thought that about Cora Wilson, because she's been in a relationship with Jamie Fitzpatrick since birth," Luke said. "But I realize how closed minded that sounds and am therefore open to the discussion."

"I agree with Luke," Lizzie said. "On both counts."

"Well, I would like to discuss this with the group." Madison grabbed a notebook from her bag. "I have a list I've been keeping in biology since we're lab partners. I think my gaydar is finally starting to work."

Chapter 16

Cameron

"Do you have the book we need for English?" Landon asked from the door of Cameron's room.

Cameron turned in his chair to look at his stepbrother. The two boys weren't friends at school, and when their parents got married last year it didn't exactly make them friends at home, either. Suffice it to say, this was not a usual occurrence.

Cameron went through his backpack while Landon lingered by the bulletin board on the far side of Cameron's room, acting very interested in Cameron's work schedule that was tacked there.

"Here," Cameron said. Landon walked over and grabbed the novel, practically skipping out of the room without so much as a thank-you.

"Hey, wait," Cameron said.

Landon turned around.

"Do you think everyone at school hates me?" Cameron asked. It wasn't exactly what he wanted to say, but the opportunity to talk to Landon about this had never really presented itself before. Landon might actually be able to give him the best, most unbiased answer to this question.

Landon had approximately the reaction that Cam would have expected, had he planned to ask the question in the first place. He glanced longingly at the door and the hallway to freedom, but then turned around.

"Hate is a really strong word," Landon said.

"Then what word would be better?" Cameron couldn't shake the feeling that Laptop Girl would take one look at him on prom night and run screaming in the other direction when she realized that she'd been communicating anonymously with the school pariah all year long. When he'd chosen the full-on hermit life, he obviously hadn't factored Laptop Girl into the equation.

"I think you act weird, so everyone acts weird."

"Have you ever heard anyone talking about me?"

"Well, yeah. They're not exactly delicate around me. I honestly don't think most people even know our parents are married."

"So what do they say?"

Landon shrugged. "I heard someone say you were dealing drugs and that's why you stopped talking to people and aren't around anymore."

"What? Who?"

"I don't know. I didn't see them. I just heard them. I wasn't exactly running to find out who it was and defend your honor."

Cameron rolled his eyes. "Thanks for that."

"Honestly, Cam. I haven't put that much thought into this."

"You thought about it enough that when I asked if people hated me you had a pretty good answer."

Landon sighed and took a seat on Cameron's bed. "When someone changes like you did, and totally falls off the grid, people are going to talk."

"But why would they assume I was doing drugs?"

Landon shrugged. "Why not? People love to gossip. I mean, I don't love to gossip. But it's part of human nature."

"Okay."

"Like the other day I heard that Amelia Vaughn asked Henry Lai to the prom. And apparently that's true."

"That doesn't sound true."

"I know! That's why it was so crazy. So I ended up asking Amelia about it. And it's a real thing."

"Are they, like, dating?" Cameron could not imagine Henry even talking to Amelia without having a mild panic attack, forget actually going to the prom with her, or dating her.

"I don't think so," Landon said. "I didn't get that impression at least."

"People really do love to gossip."

"And sometimes the rumors are true."

"Well, except for the people who have been saying that I'm dealing drugs. They're lying."

"Well, yeah, but they're obviously an asshat who's looking for attention."

"I messed up," was all Cameron said in response. He had a lot of thoughts happening all at once. But he had obviously messed up if he somehow ended being a rumored drug dealer.

"I guess. I don't really understand why you decided to

become a hermit senior year. But you probably aren't totally messed up."

"You really think so?"

"Believe me, I'm a certified peer counselor."

"Oh my god. You're not going to try to score some kind of volunteer hours on this, are you? Are you using me as a charity case? I knew you were being too nice."

Landon held up his hands defensively. "I swear I'm not. You asked and I answered. Teen angst happens to be something that I was trained to discuss, but that's not why I'm discussing it with you."

Cameron narrowed his eyes at his stepbrother. "Why do you always talk like a middle-aged man?"

"I don't know. I didn't know I did that," Landon said with a shrug.

"Well, whatever. High school's almost over anyway," Cameron said, speaking his most recent motto out loud.

"Exactly." Landon was about to leave, but then he stopped. "Are you really going to the prom?"

"Um, yeah, seems like it."

"Wow."

Cameron nodded.

"I'm not even sure I'm going to the prom, and I'm on the actual prom committee."

"You're not going?"

"Emma can't come up for it. It sucks having a long-distance girlfriend."

"I wouldn't know about that," Cameron said.

"I'll get this back to you later," Landon said, gesturing with the novel for English class.

Cameron waved and continued working on his final paper for English.

Cora

It was Jamie's eighteenth birthday, and all he really wanted was to go to the new Japanese fusion restaurant that had just opened in town. His parents had gotten him a gift certificate and everything.

All Cora wanted to do was break up with him. But what kind of heartless bitch breaks up with a guy on his birthday?

At least they were doing something different this year. For Jamie's past three birthdays they'd gone to Ruby Tuesday at the mall and then to the movies.

"Do you ever feel like we're in a rut?" Cora asked after the waitress took their order.

"Us?" Jamie asked. "Aren't we too young for that?"

"Jamie, anyone can get stuck in a rut. They're not just for super old, bored, or married people. And we've been a couple longer than some super old, boring married people. It's totally possible that we're in a rut."

"What kind of rut?"

A text alert pealed off from her phone.

"Just one sec," she said, grabbing her phone from her bag. It was a text from Madison about their final bio lab of the year. She suddenly felt far more alert and she really wanted to write back. After a moment of thought she decided to save it for later. Cora could have a fun text chat with Madison when this dinner was all over as a reward. She slid her phone back in her bag after putting it on silent.

Jamie was staring at the flickering candle in the middle of the table when she looked back at him.

"Anyway," she said to catch his attention. "My point is we've done the exact same thing for the past three years for your birthday."

"But we're doing something different this year. So it's not a rut!" he said, sitting up straight and pounding his hand on the table to punctuate his point.

Cora shook her head. He was too cute for his own good sometimes.

"Or maybe it's a rut," he amended a moment later. "But even if it is, next year we'll be in a new city with new people. That'll force us out of our rut."

"I worry sometimes about that."

"About the new people? Don't worry, Cora, I'll be there, we can still hang out."

"That's what I worry about," she muttered.

Her phone went off in her bag, even louder this time. Instead of silencing it, she must have put it on full volume.

"Sorry," she said, not even looking at the screen, just feeling around for the silent button.

"So what do you worry about?" Jamie asked. "'Cause I worry about stuff, too."

"I worry that we're going to use each other as a crutch and not meet anyone. That we're going to get stuck in a rut in Boston. Not the exact same one as here, but a different one. And we'll never meet new people because we spend all our time together."

Jamie thought about that for a full minute. "Well, we

probably won't be in the same dorm. There's a whole bunch of different ones. We could even make sure we're not in the same dorm. That would help probably. Then we can introduce each other to a lot of different people." He wrapped up his monologue with a big smile like he had solved world peace. "I'm gonna run to the bathroom. Be right back."

Cora swirled the straw in her glass of soda and pulled her phone out, opening up the group text she had with Josie and Teagan.

Cora:

He's testing my patience tonight.

Josie:

You can't break up with him on his birthday!

Teagan:

You could. It'd be a little mean. But it's starting to feel like you're only staying with him not to be mean. And either way, he'll be sad.

Josie:

That's true. Maybe it would be nicer to break up with him. But I still say that's too mean for his birthday.

Teagan:

All right. Yeah, maybe. You probably shouldn't ruin his birthday.

Cora:

Do you two even need me for this conversation about my life? ;)

Teagan:

Maybe not.

Cora:

Good, 'cause Jamie's coming back to the table.

He was walking toward her and grinning from ear to ear. Cora sucked in a deep breath. Would it be horribly selfish to rip the Band-Aid off and break up with him on his birthday?

Josie:

Keep us posted!

Cora responded with a string of heart emojis, but before she could slide her phone away, a call popped up from the prom venue. She stood.

"I'm sorry," she said to Jamie. "I have to take this. I have no idea why they would be calling me."

It turned out that the call was actually a wrong number and from a different Sheraton entirely.

Jamie had his arms crossed when she returned to the table. He handed her a Snickers bar.

"Where did this come from?" she asked. "Also it's your birthday and I'm supposed to get *you* gifts."

"It's my birthday and you can't even give me your full attention."

"I said I was sorry."

"Did you?"

"Um, yes," Cora said. "I said it every time we were interrupted. I don't know what to tell you. I don't have control over who contacts me."

"You could turn your phone off completely or put it on airplane mode or something."

"Yes. You're right. That's what I'll do right now." She exaggeratedly put her phone in airplane mode and stuck it in her purse.

She leaned toward Jamie and smiled. "Now, please, tell me where the candy bar came from."

He rolled his eyes but then grinned again. "Well, there was a kid out in the foyer by the host stand who wanted to sell candy in the restaurant and the manager told him they don't allow solicitors in here. But I felt so bad for the kid that I decided to buy a candy bar for each of us. I'm pretty sure I made his whole night. He was such a scrappy kid I wanted to buy every single piece of candy he had, but I definitely didn't have enough money for that."

"Thank you," Cora said, mustering up all her sincerity. "And I really am sorry."

"You're welcome," Jamie said. "And I accept your apology."

That was Jamie in a nutshell. How could Cora break up with a guy like this on his birthday? It would probably leave her with bad karma for the rest of her life.

There was no way to break up with him.

She could suck it up and stay with Jamie a little longer.

There was no reason to ruin the end of senior year.

At least not yet.

Chapter 17

Jacinta

"I have a brilliant idea!" Kelsey said as she ran up to Jacinta in the hall Thursday after school.

"I am terrified."

"Don't worry. I'm not setting you up again. At least not really. I suppose it could kind of be called a setup, but it would maybe depend on who you asked."

"This is not helping my fear," Jacinta said.

"You should ask Landon!"

"Landon has a girlfriend in Canada." *Also*, Jacinta added silently, *it would feel like taking your castoffs, Kelsey*, not to mention that she didn't particularly like him.

"She's in Texas actually."

"Same difference. Texas, Canada, they're far, but not that far."

Kelsey paused. "I think Texas is actually farther than

Canada. Like it definitely is. We could drive to Canada in like six or seven hours."

"Yes, thank you for this geography lesson. But you know what I mean. Also there's no way Landon would want to go with me anyway. And this situation doesn't exactly scream 'dream date.' If anything, it screams 'Jacinta Ramos: Girlfriend Placeholder.'"

"Oh, come on. I think he would be cool with it. He wants to go, but Emma can't come from Texas to go to the prom. He doesn't want to go alone. It would just be about having someone to hang out with, you know?"

"You didn't already talk to him about this, did you?"

"Of course not. I had the idea and came right to you."

Jacinta rolled the idea around in her head for a minute. Maybe it wouldn't be so bad, going with Landon. It would solve a lot of Jacinta's issues. And it wasn't so much that she didn't like Landon, she just had a lot of opinions about him. But he and Kelsey had broken up amicably, and he wasn't a complete douchebag.

"You know what? I think I will ask him."

"Yay!" Kelsey cried, hugging Jacinta tight.

"But I think I should run it past Emma."

"I think that's totally respectful of you."

Henry was walking down the hall ahead of them. Jacinta grabbed Kelsey's arm and pulled her to a stop. "I'm still having trouble believing he's really going to the prom with Amelia. I heard they might be dating."

"Maybe it's a rumor," Kelsey said. "I swear the gossip mill has gone into overdrive lately. I've heard some of the weirdest things."

"Like what?"

"Something about Ms. Huang dating one of the other teachers."

"I hadn't heard," Jacinta said with a shrug.

On her way to the final class cabinet meeting of the year, Jacinta sent Emma a Facebook message basically requesting her permission to ask Landon to the prom, even though Jacinta had never met Emma in real life. Landon and Emma had met last year at Harvard Model United Nations, and almost immediately thereafter, Emma had followed all of Landon's friends on social media.

When the meeting was over, Jacinta checked her phone and Emma had said yes. She said she was happy that Jacinta checked with her first, though, and really appreciated her thoughtfulness and would she mind exchanging numbers in case they needed to be in contact in the future.

Jacinta rolled her eyes a bit at that. She would never understand why people took high school relationships so seriously. It was high school. There was nothing serious about it.

Since she was on her way home and would pass Landon's house anyway, Jacinta decided to pop in and ask him face-to-face.

As soon as she rang the doorbell she knew it was a bad idea.

Not just going to his house to ask him, but asking him at all. It was a really bad, really weird idea and she hated how she felt. She was about to turn and leave since no one had answered the door, much to her relief, when a vaguely familiar figure walked out from the side of the house.

It was Landon's stepbrother, Cameron.

"Oh, hey," Jacinta said.

"Hey, hi, sorry, I was looking for the cat. I don't think anyone else is home."

He was empty handed. "Did you find the cat?"

"Yeah, but she didn't want to go inside anyway."

"Okay," Jacinta said. "I forgot that you lived with Landon."

"Or does Landon live with me?" he asked seriously.

It was like a logic puzzle that Jacinta had no idea how to answer.

"Ha," was all she said.

Cameron seemed okay with her weak laugh and smiled at her. He moved to open the front door.

"Do you want to come in? Why are you here?" He shook his head. "Sorry, that's kind of rude. I just meant, like, are you here to see Landon or are you selling magazine subscriptions or something?"

Jacinta couldn't quite keep up with this kid. He was all over the map.

"Um, yes, I'm here to see Landon."

"Like I said, he's not here right now, but he should be home soon, if you want to wait."

"Okay, I think I'll wait."

Cameron plopped down on the top step. "I'm locked out anyway. Damn cat."

Jacinta sat down next to him. "I'll keep you company."

For as weird as Cameron was, there was something sort of interesting about him. She'd heard a lot of rumors about him at school, but she had no idea if any of them were true or who to believe.

"So," Cameron said, nodding his head.

"So."

"What do you need Landon for?"

"Well, I was thinking I might ask him to the prom? I know he has a girlfriend, but I actually already talked to Emma and she said since she couldn't make it that it would be okay to ask him."

"Interesting. Like some kind of reverse medieval dowry."

"I mean, not really. I don't think Emma is getting anything out of this . . ." Jacinta trailed off, trying to make sense of her life at the moment. "Are you going to the prom?"

"Oh, um, it's weird and sort of complicated," he said.

That sentence seemed familiar to Jacinta, but before she could figure it out, a car pulled into the driveway.

Cameron's mom and Landon got out. Jacinta wouldn't have recognized this woman as Cameron's mom out on the street, but in this context she was immediately recognizable.

"Oh, hello," she said.

Landon waved but his face held a question.

"Hi, I had a question for Landon," Jacinta said. It felt like the trees, the lamppost, and the porch overhang were all dripping with awkward.

"Cameron, help me with the groceries and leave Landon to speak with . . . Jacinta, right?"

Jacinta smiled. "Yup, that's me!"

Cameron and his mom went inside.

"So, what's up, Jacinta?" Landon asked.

"Well, I was sort of wondering if you wanted to go to the prom. With me?"

"I'd have to check with Emma . . . ," Landon said, with a tone that made it pretty obvious that he wasn't interested in going with Jacinta.

"I hope you don't mind, but I actually already messaged her. I kind of wanted to get her okay before I even talked to you about it."

"Oh, that was cool of you," he said, his body language changing in an instant when he realized that Jacinta might not be an evil boyfriend stealer.

"Yeah, so, I was hoping that maybe we could go together, with Kelsey and Mike, of course, as friends. It might be fun, and I already found a dress."

"That does sound fun. Thanks." Landon smiled. He seemed actually pretty surprised and happy about Jacinta asking him. "I'll see about getting a ticket tomorrow. I wasn't sure I really wanted to go alone."

"I understand."

"Well, I have to study," Landon said.

"Sure, I should get going. I haven't even been home yet after school, but once I got this idea in my head I wanted to see what you thought first, you know?"

"Totally."

There was a weird moment between them when Jacinta felt like maybe they were supposed to hug, but that seemed wrong.

"Well, thanks," she said.

"Bye," he said.

As Jacinta drove home she couldn't stop thinking about the weird encounter she'd just experienced, with Landon's stepbrother definitely being the weirdest of them all. She'd have to figure out what his deal was, because he was definitely a character.

But at least she had a date to prom. Even if the whole

situation was a pale comparison to what she had wanted prom to be like.

She sighed at her own patheticness. Would it never end?

Henry

Henry was exhausted.

Baseball was exhausting.

Being gossiped about was exhausting.

Amelia was so exhausting.

She wasn't even his girlfriend and her mere existence in his life was taking its toll.

But the worst part, the most terrifying part, was the gnawing guilt in his stomach every time he thought about telling her he didn't want to go to the prom with her. That's what was really keeping him up at night.

He knew he should be happy she wanted to go with him. That he should be grateful even. Wasn't it every guy's fantasy to go to the prom with the most popular girl in school?

But that didn't stop him from not wanting to go with her.

He honestly still wasn't sure if he wanted to go at all. He didn't have much time to decide, though, and he'd already bought a ticket. But he could just stay home at the last minute.

On top of everything else, being the hot topic of gossip was new for Henry. He didn't like it. He preferred living his life under the radar. That was way more his speed.

It was way more Paisley's speed, too. He knew he was

starting to get on Paisley's nerves, which was why he made plans with her for Thursday night. Not to mention the whole issue with the baseball team. She was totally not thrilled about that. He would need to make it up to her someday.

Paisley's mom had her book club that night, so they could spend the evening on Paisley's couch eating whatever they wanted without parental supervision. Or parental eaves-dropping, which is what would have happened at Henry's house.

When they sat down with a meat supreme pizza and a large bottle of generic birch beer to split between them, Henry jumped into complaining again.

"I'm pretty sure I'm giving myself an ulcer," he said.

"I'm pretty sure you're giving me an ulcer," Paisley said as she handed him a slice of pizza with so much meat on it you could barely see the cheese. "I also think you really, really need to let Amelia off the hook while she still has time to find another date. What you're doing isn't fair to either of you."

"But I don't want to hurt her feelings."

"Maybe you should have thought of that before you said yes."

"I didn't even know I said yes! Remember? I was in a fugue state brought on by her lips and her natural scent. She was intoxicating."

Paisley rolled her eyes. "I don't know that her perfume is natural. I'm pretty sure you can buy it by the bottle at any Macy's store."

"You know what I mean."

"I don't really know what you mean, but I'll take your word for it."

"So what should I do?"

"You need to tell her you don't want to go with her. Plain and simple."

"She's going to hate me. I don't like the idea of people hating me."

"You could blame it on me if you want."

"Why? So she can hate both of us?" he asked.

"The good news is that I don't care whether Amelia Vaughn likes me or not."

"How would I blame it on you?"

"Just tell her that"—Paisley paused to finish chewing a big bite of pizza—"you feel bad because you forgot that you told me you'd go with me a million years ago. Like sophomore year or some crap like that. And I only recently reminded you about it, and now I'm being a complete bitch."

"You're not a bitch." Henry dropped his voice low on the last word.

"Tell her it was a bet! That we made a bet and I won and you totally forgot. This would be mutually beneficial because then I would feel even less guilt about saying no to the entire baseball team."

"You really wouldn't care if I threw you under the bus like that?"

"I really would not care. Especially if it meant that I didn't have to listen to you whine and bitch anymore."

"Have I really been that bad?"

Paisley nodded. "You need to call her."

"No way! Can't I mail her a kindly worded letter?"

"I don't trust the postal service to get her that in time."

"A postcard with some kind of beautiful vista on the front.

Possibly a beach landscape, something soothing so she doesn't kill me."

At that moment, Henry's phone chimed.

He looked at it like it was a bomb about to go off. "Oh god, oh god. It's definitely going to be her. I don't think I can handle it."

He unlocked his phone and handed it to Paisley, covering his face with his hands.

"She's asking about a boutonniere. And what color your tie is."

"I need to wear a specifically colored tie?" Henry asked from behind his hands.

"I mean, you don't have to. But some guys do I guess."

Henry lowered his hands and let out a long sigh. "Give me the phone. I need to put both of us out of our misery."

"By both, do you mean you and her, or you and me? Because I should be included in this no matter what. I have been miserable."

He took his phone from Paisley and started crafting a text message.

"What do you think?" he asked Paisley after he finished.

She read it out loud. "Amelia, I'm so sorry to do this to you, but I have to go to the prom with my friend Paisley. It turned out I had already said yes to her a while ago and I totally forgot. I'm sure you understand. Sorry."

Paisley shrugged. "I would feel rejected but would walk away quietly. I'm not Amelia, though. I'm sure she'll find something to argue, some loophole, but it works in my personal opinion."

Henry hit send. He sat back and tried to relax.

"Can I do something for you? A massage or something?"

He looked over at Paisley. "You would give me a massage?"

"Not really. But you seem so stressed out."

"I am stressed out! I've been telling you I'm stressed out!"

"Okay, okay," Paisley said, raising her hands defensively.

"You realize what you've done to yourself, right?" Henry asked with a wicked grin spreading across his face.

"What do you mean?"

"You have to go to the prom with me now."

"What? No. I got you out of the prom."

"Um, no. You got me out of the prom with Amelia."

"Oh shit. I am the worst. I hate me. Everyone should hate me."

Henry's phone pinged. He took a deep breath and looked at the screen.

Amelia:

Fine. Turns out Drew can go anyway, so I was going to have to ditch you.

Henry showed it to Paisley. "Oh yeah, she hates you."

"You know, I think I'm actually okay with that. I'm just so relieved. I can feel my ulcer going away already."

"It doesn't work like that, but whatever you need to tell yourself to get through the day," Paisley said, patting him on the head.

"Thanks, Paisley. This was really excellent."

She burped. "That meant you're welcome. In case you couldn't tell."

Chapter 18

Paisley

Paisley wandered around the prom dress section of Macy's searching not for the perfect dress but for any old dress that she didn't absolutely hate. She hated a lot of dresses, so this was a challenge.

Most of them were too short or too long, too puffy or too flat. She wasn't supermodel tall, and she did not have the boobs for a lot of the styles. And why was it too much to hope to find a dress with pockets? She'd be so much more comfortable through the whole evening if she had somewhere to stick her hands when she didn't know what to do with them.

"How do I let him talk me into these things?" she muttered as she circled another rack. The only good news was that most of the dresses weren't too expensive, even though she hated the idea of spending any of her hard-earned Hot Potato money on a dress she'd only wear once.

Her mom had offered to give her money for it, but it felt wrong. Paisley had gotten herself into this mess; she didn't need a bailout from her mom.

She was well aware that if she hadn't accidentally nominated Henry for prom king neither of them would have to go to the prom.

This dress was her penance.

She grabbed a black spaghetti strap number in a heavy satin with a peacock feather print across the front in whites and blues. She didn't love it, but it had pockets, which after more thought had started to feel essential. Far more important than liking anything else about the dress.

In the fitting room, she stared at herself in the mirror, sticking her hands in the pockets and posing casually in one direction and then turning to pose casually in the other direction.

It honestly wasn't so bad. She looked pale but not sickly in the dark, rich fabric, and it came in at the waist, making her feel feminine and a little bit flirty, even if she wasn't a flirt.

She couldn't resist giving a spin in the mirror, ignoring the goldfish-printed socks on her feet that totally ruined the look.

At sixty-eight dollars it was too good to pass up. Especially since she'd been willing to spend a hundred if she had to. She might even be able to wear this to her cousin's wedding next fall.

There was a knock on her dressing room door just as she started another round of twirling.

"Do you need anything? Anything I could help with?" the saleswoman asked.

"No, I'm fine, thank you," Paisley called back, feeling exposed. She quickly slid off the dress and put her Hot Potato uniform back on. Her shift started in fifteen minutes, so twirl-ing time was definitely over.

Paisley purchased the dress and even had enough time left to run it out to her car. She didn't want to get cheese sauce on the satin.

When she got to the potato stand a few minutes later, Lizzie was there and Madison was seated in her usual hiding spot.

"You should really get a job here; I'm sure we're hiring," Paisley said.

"It's way more fun coming in to bother you guys. Besides, babysitting has been far more lucrative for me."

"The potato business is nothing to frown upon," Lizzie said in a fake haughty voice. "Potato futures are looking up."

"What does that even mean?" Paisley asked.

"I have no idea, but sounded funny in my head," Lizzie said.

The girls laughed.

"So here's another funny thing, at least to me," Paisley said. "I'm going to the prom."

"Ugh. So am I," Madison said.

"Me three," Lizzie said.

"Yes, Lizzie, we know all about you," Madison said. "So why are you going, Paisley?"

"Henry needed a favor."

"Henry is no longer going with Miss Amelia Vaughn?" Lizzie asked, placing a scandalized hand on her chest.

"He is not," Paisley said with grin.

"She must be on the warpath."

"I don't know," Paisley said. "She was out sick today. Why are you going, Madison?"

"Well, I want to see what happens with Mystery Boy, obviously," Madison said. "But also. It's the prom. I might as well go."

"Well, at least we can all have fun together," Paisley offered.

"Ugh, fun," Madison said.

But Paisley did feel a little better knowing her other friends would be there.

"Come on, maybe it won't be so bad," Lizzie said.

"Ever the optimist," Paisley said.

"I'm definitely sneaking booze in," Madison said.

That worked for Paisley.

Otis

Otis's dad returned from his business trip Friday night, but Otis knew enough to wait until Saturday to talk to him. The prom was less than two weeks away, and he'd already blown his opportunity with his mom. She was a firm no on the whole situation.

After mowing the lawn on Saturday afternoon, Otis found his dad out in the garage looking through a box of pool supplies for a pool they didn't even have.

"How was your trip?" Otis asked.

His dad held up a length of tube. "Do you think your sister could use this for a robot she needs to make for the science fair?"

"Jillian's participating in the middle school science fair?"

His dad rolled his eyes. "Your younger sister," he clarified.

"A working robot or a model robot?"

His dad paused. "I don't know." He threw the tube in the laundry basket where he was apparently gathering things for Lindsey's project.

"And my trip was okay." His dad eyed Otis thoughtfully. "I hear you had a little adventure."

"Funny you should bring that up."

"Oh, very funny I'm sure."

"Listen, I understand that I deserve to be punished. I shouldn't have gone out, but I would really like to explain why I should be allowed to go to the prom." Otis had decided to make a good show of arguing about his punishment with his dad even if he was feeling more and more relieved about this turn of events.

But his parents would be suspicious if he didn't say anything at all, hence how he ended up in the garage with his dad on a Saturday afternoon.

His dad sucked in a breath and rubbed the stubble on his chin.

"I understand that, but I don't need to hear your case, Otis. If you were so worried about the prom, you should have thought about that before you snuck out in the middle of the night."

"I wasn't thinking about the consequences." *Lies!* the little angel voice in Otis's head said.

"I know. I'm quite sure you weren't, and that's why we need to make sure that you really feel the consequences."

"But what am I going to learn if you take this away? That keeping a promise to Luke isn't important? Are you really setting the right example?" This argument was so weak, and yet his dad seemed to be buying it.

His dad rolled his eyes and chuckled. "I do feel bad for Luke. I'm not going to lie."

"So don't punish Luke for something dumb that I did!" Otis threw his arms up in the air to punctuate this sentiment. He might as well give the performance of a lifetime.

"Otis, it isn't just that you went out past your curfew; it's that you made your mother worry."

"She was so worried she fell asleep."

His dad gave him a warning look. "She's always exhausted, especially in the wee hours of the morning. Her sleeping is not what's on trial here."

"I didn't think she would even notice," he said. His excuses were sounding worse and worse. His dad was going to realize this was a farce soon enough. Better to start wrapping things up.

"She always notices. She called me in the middle of the night, frantic that you weren't home. She checked where your phone was and realized you were at the movies and that you were probably safe. But you gave her a good scare, not being where you were supposed to be."

"But she saw me leave! How scared could she be?"

"This is also not a debate or discussion about what emotions your mother did or did not experience."

"I know." Otis crossed his arms and leaned against the garage wall. This was actually going better than he had hoped.

"You're almost an adult, Otis," he said. "This close." He held his fingers a half an inch apart. "But you need to remember your actions have consequences, and from now on when you're off on your own, you'll keep this experience in mind and think twice."

"But—"

"No buts."

Otis frowned, but there was a little bubble of hope rising in his chest. He had put up a decent fight, and he was still not allowed to go. So this really was fate keeping him away from the prom and whatever was going to happen in Luke's hotel room.

For a split second he thought about talking to his dad about that, about what to do about *that*. His parents had been remarkably cool when he came out to them, and they both were pretty fond of Luke, but did any parent really want to talk about sex with their kid? Any kind of sex?

Otis had to assume the answer was no.

He walked back into the house, relieved that at least if nothing else, there'd been no discussion of confiscating his cell phone.

He shot off a text to Madison.

Otis:

> Don't tell Luke, but I probably won't be allowed to go to prom.

Madison:

> OMG. You are going to be in so much trouble with him!

Otis:

> I'm already in so much trouble with my parents. But I'm hoping for a last-second parole.

He was really hoping that if he mentioned this to Madison it would eventually get back to Luke and solidify his case.

Madison:

There's no way. Your parents are really good at sticking their ground. You can't out-logic them.

Otis sighed. No matter how relieved he felt, he was going to carry this guilt around with him for a long time. He'd give it one more try next week. Maybe there would be a change of heart in the Sorenson house.

Maybe Otis would have a change of heart himself. Anything was possible.

Chapter 19

Lizzie

How Lizzie had made it to the week before prom without realizing that she needed a prom dress was beyond her comprehension.

Subconsciously, she'd hoped something would have miraculously appeared in her closet just in the nick of time. But that wasn't going to happen. And every possible dress she tried on from her closet and her mom's closet definitely didn't fit and definitely didn't give her the confidence to meet Mystery Boy.

She even gave in and called her cousin. She was a few years older than Lizzie, but maybe she'd have something Lizzie could borrow. Unfortunately, none of her clothes fit Lizzie right, either. Some of it was too big, but none of it was going to work.

What was worse was Lizzie had no idea how she was going to get money for a dress. She'd used up whatever money she had from her most recent paycheck on her prom ticket, and she wanted to make sure she had enough for whatever they might do after prom. She was definitely cash flow poor. She had a savings account, but there wasn't even that much in it, and she was going to need it next year to buy books for college way more than she needed a prom dress.

She finally had to give in and talk to her mom about it. She got up early before school Tuesday morning, much earlier than she had to, so she could see her mom before she left for work.

"Good morning, honey," her mom said, punctuating the greeting with a big yawn while she poured coffee into a thermos.

"Hey, Mom."

"What's up? This is pretty early for you to be awake."

"I kind of decided to go to the prom."

"Well, that's nice."

"And I paid for my ticket, and everything is taken care of, but I don't have a dress. I thought for sure I'd be able to find one by now. I went through every dress in this house, and I even called Aggie to see if she had anything."

Lizzie slumped down in a kitchen chair.

Her mom went through the cabinets. "I have just the thing," she mumbled as she moved around canned goods.

"I can't even begin to fathom what you're looking for in the kitchen cabinets."

Her mom stood on her tiptoes and rooted around in the back of the cabinet before pulling out an envelope.

"Here you go," she said with a grin.

"What?" Lizzie asked, taking the envelope. There was a small stack of singles and a couple of fives stashed away in it.

"It's not much, but I'm sure it's enough to get something on clearance or maybe from the thrift store."

"Oh my god, Mom," Lizzie said, jumping up to hug her. "What was this for? I don't want to take money for the electric bill or something."

"Nah, this is fun money that I've been squirreling away all year, knowing that you might need something for graduation. I was going to give it to you anyway. But now you can use it for your dress."

Lizzie squeezed her mom even harder, and her mom squeezed back. "Thank you so much."

"I'm just glad you came to me," her mom said.

"You have no idea. I was close to selling off my hair or something."

"I don't know if that actually works outside of old movies," her mom said.

Lizzie bounced into school that morning. All in all, there was forty-three dollars in the envelope, and she was sure she could find something for that much. When she saw Madison she ran up to her.

"Do you have plans later?"

"Aside from softball practice? No."

"I need to go prom dress shopping."

"Oh, me too. I was going to wear something from my closet, but I don't know. None of it felt right. Do you think we go to one of those schools where they won't let girls wear tuxedos to prom?"

"I honestly don't know," Lizzie said.

The rest of the day dragged on, and then waiting for Madison to finish with softball practice dragged on, and then it was finally time to go dress shopping. Lizzie had honestly never been this excited about shopping before. It was definitely the joy of having money coupled with the relief of having money.

They walked into the mall just after six.

"Can we shop first and then eat?" Lizzie asked. She wasn't sure she'd even have money for food, but this way she'd have a better chance at being able to eat.

"Yeah, sure. I think it'll help us choose quicker."

Madison walked them toward Lord & Taylor.

"Any chance we could try Macy's first? Or even JCPenney?" Lizzie asked. She struggled to find an excuse for this request, then shrugged. "They tend to have a better selection of plus-size dresses and are more in my price range."

"Sure, but since when do you need plus-size dresses?" Madison asked, turning on her heel and walking in the other direction.

"Since I'm plus size."

"But you're, like, not fat," Madison said. No one had ever quite been so blunt about this before with Lizzie. "Not that there's anything wrong with being fat. It's just not a word I would use to describe you."

"I'm fat enough."

"What size do you wear?" Madison asked.

Lizzie hesitated. She hated talking about stuff like this. It was why she avoided shopping with friends, even people she trusted like Madison.

"I swear I'm not going to put it on blast to the whole school or something. But it'll help when we're trying to find dresses together."

Lizzie felt a little wave of relief. "Right. Um, a 16 or an 18, depending on the cut. And I can't really wear junior's sizes. They don't exactly fit my stomach. Or my arms." She blushed but Madison was still all business.

"All right, we've got this under control," Madison said. "For the record, I'm an 8 or a 10 if you see anything good for me."

Instead of veering toward the junior's section in Macy's, they took the elevator upstairs. But Madison didn't go to the back of the store to the plus sizes, and instead went toward the formal dresses.

"Do you really think they'll have my size over here?" Lizzie asked.

"It's worth trying, right?"

They split up and started searching. Every dress that Lizzie looked at was way too expensive, and every dress that Madison held up for her had the same exact problem.

And that's when she saw it. The promised land.

Also known as the clearance rack.

She walked over and found a section of size 16 dresses; most of them were still too expensive, but one of them was thirty-five dollars. It wasn't exactly what she wanted. It was red and short and might not look great on her. But the price was right so she might as well try it on.

She showed it to Madison.

"That's not exactly what I would have picked out for you, but I like it."

Lizzie was shocked by how much she liked it. It gave her a waist and a little bit of cleavage and actually made her feel slim and feminine.

When it was time to check out, Madison had picked up a white sparkly jumpsuit and she offered to put Lizzie's dress on her card.

"I get points and you get an extra fifteen percent off."

It was hard to say no to.

And it left her with more than enough money for dinner at the food court.

They just avoided the Hot Potato stand. Both of them were sick of potatoes.

Paisley

Paisley had been tiptoeing around the school for a few days after Henry had rejected Amelia, not because she was afraid of Amelia, but because she had zero interest in confrontation.

Amelia seemed like she'd be a hair puller if a fight ever got physical and Paisley wanted to avoid that at all costs.

But all that came to an end when Amelia stormed into the second-floor bathroom while Paisley was washing her hands. She barely even had time to react, or dry her hands, when Amelia was standing next to her, staring her down in the mirror.

"Hi," Paisley said brightly, spending much too long drying her hands in an attempt to mask the fact that they were shaking.

Confrontation was seriously the worst.

Amelia put her hands on her hips.

"Please don't beat me up," Paisley said. Turned out that in

the face of going one-on-one with Amelia Vaughn, Paisley became a whimpering mess.

Amelia rolled her eyes. "I'm not going to beat you up."

"Oh good, that's a relief." Paisley skirted around Amelia in the direction of the door. "I'm just gonna head out in that case. You know, things to do, people to see."

"No, I want to talk to you."

"My mother is dating a cop!" Paisley yelled. That was a lie.

"I'm seriously not going to do anything to you."

"Fine. So, what's up?" Paisley asked, remaining close to the door for a quick getaway if necessary. "I'm not going to apologize for going to the prom with Henry. He's my best friend. It's how things go sometimes."

Now Amelia actually looked kind of sad. Maybe Paisley had been reading her all wrong.

Amelia's shoulders dropped and she crossed her arms. "I don't understand why he doesn't want to go to the prom with me." She held up her hand. "And before you go defending him, you can't tell me that this wasn't what the whole thing was about."

"I thought you were going with your boyfriend anyway?" Paisley asked.

"Yeah, I talked him into it. But it would have been more fun to go with someone still in high school. Drew is just going to complain the whole time. I don't know. It's not as much fun with him as it used to be. Also we broke up."

"Oh. Well, Drew must still be pretty into you if he agreed to go to the prom with you even though you broke up."

Amelia shrugged half-heartedly.

"Listen, Henry is kind of a weird dude," Paisley said,

choosing her words carefully. "He's awesome. And I love him. But I think he feels like he got pushed into the spotlight this year and keeps getting more attention than he really wants or likes to have."

"He's a really good pitcher," Amelia said. "Of course people took notice."

Paisley smiled and nodded, because it was nice that Henry was getting acknowledged for his talents.

"I was so focused on wanting to be prom queen and on finding a king, you know, to be queen with, I kind of didn't realize he wasn't into me?"

"I think there are plenty of guys who are very into you, and Henry doesn't hate you or anything like that."

"Then why won't he go to the prom with me?"

This conversation was hitting rough terrain, and Paisley was not sure she'd be able to handle it if Amelia started to cry. "Henry likes to live under the radar, and you live over the radar."

"But why did he say yes in the first place?"

"I feel kind of bad and weird talking to you about him like this," Paisley said, scrunching up her nose.

"I know. I get it. I'm kind of embarrassed. It sucks, getting rejected."

"Yeah, totally," Paisley agreed, even though she had done more than her fair share of rejecting recently. "And I guess Henry said yes because he's not very good at saying no."

"I guess I don't want to go with someone who doesn't want to go with me anyway."

Paisley nodded. "I'm not gonna lie, Amelia. This conversation went in a completely different direction than I ever would have expected."

Amelia's expression changed quickly from sad to her usual resting bitch face. It was like the bathroom had turned into a freezer. She stuck her finger in Paisley's face.

"Don't you dare ever tell anyone about this conversation. I will deny the whole thing, and I will make your life miserable."

Paisley backed up a step. She was going to say something snarky about how unless Amelia planned to stalk her post-graduation, she wasn't going to have a lot of luck ruining Paisley's life. But she held her tongue. Mostly because she was a little scared again.

"Okay," Paisley squeaked out.

"And never, ever mention this to Henry. I have a reputation to uphold, and he doesn't need to know about any of this. For once in your life follow the girl code."

With that, Amelia tossed her hair over her shoulder and stalked out of the bathroom.

Paisley looked at her refection in the mirror quizzically. "Did she just come in here to talk to me?"

She shrugged at herself.

"At least the conversation ended in a more expected way than it began," she said.

Paisley decided to stop talking to herself and go back to physics.

She had never been so surprised and then disappointed over the span of a single conversation.

Chapter 20

Jacinta

Jacinta wondered about the futility of doing homework at this point in her senior year. Would it really make a difference, in the scheme of things, if she just skipped this reader reaction paper for the short story they read in English class? Would Ms. Huang actually fail her?

Unlikely.

On the other hand, it could affect her overall grade and might lower it enough that she wouldn't be exempt from the final. And she really wanted to be exempt from that final. She didn't need to waste multiple hours taking an essay exam about all the books they'd read throughout the year. That sounded painful, especially when the alternative was to write the reaction paper that was sitting in front of her.

As she jotted down notes and tried to get her thoughts in order, her phone rang.

Jacinta was confused.

She hadn't heard her phone ring in a long time, not since she had finally convinced her mom to start texting her last year.

She looked at the phone, and the screen told her that Emma Lim was calling.

Why on earth would Emma be calling on a Thursday night? Jacinta answered. "Hello?" She sounded like a cartoon bear.

Did her voice always sound so weird when she answered the phone, or had she legitimately forgotten how to do this?

"Hey!" Emma said.

"Hi," Jacinta said.

"I know we talked the other day, and I hope I'm not interrupting anything, but I wanted to talk to you about something."

"Ooooo-kay," Jacinta said.

"So, as it turns out, my parents were planning to surprise me with a plane ticket to New Jersey next weekend. When I told them about how Landon's friend was going to the prom with him they finally told me that they had this plane ticket. And I'm going to be staying with my cousins or whatever. And it's like all worked out."

"So, you're coming next weekend?"

"Yeah, it's so weird how late your prom is. I'll already be done with school by then. But I didn't think I'd really have the money for this trip. Then like I said, my parents wanted to surprise me. Surprise!"

"So, I'm not going to the prom with Landon?" Jacinta asked, trying her best to keep up, but there was a lot of information coming from Emma.

"I mean, of course you should still go. But I'm going to be surprising him. So I was hoping you could help me with that.

And we can all go as a big group. Won't that be so much fun? Landon, me, Kelsey, Kelsey's boyfriend whose name I can't remember, and you!"

That honestly sounded like torture to Jacinta. Hooray for being the fifth wheel. This was the opposite of what she wanted.

"I need you to make sure that there's a ticket for me."

Jacinta blinked slowly and shook her head.

"What were you going to do about a ticket if your parents had gone through with the surprise?"

"Oh, um, I don't know," Emma said offhandedly. "Are they a lot of money or something? I don't really understand these northern proms."

"Can you hang on a second?" Jacinta asked.

She didn't wait for Emma to answer. Instead she grabbed a pillow and screamed into it for ten seconds. She was pretty sure she knew exactly what was going on. Emma had decided that she didn't want Landon to go to the prom with another girl, so she begged and pleaded with her parents to let her come for the weekend.

That was seriously the only explanation.

Jacinta picked her phone back up. "Sorry about that. So, here's the thing. This northern prom is at a hotel and it costs a hundred dollars a ticket." Before Emma could complain about the price, she chattered on. "And it would have been even more since we're having it at a fancy hotel, but our class is really good at fund-raising."

"Oh, ours was in our school gym, so it wasn't—"

Jacinta cut her off. "So I'm going to have to go talk to the head of the prom committee and find out if there are any tickets left. Okay?"

"Sure, that's so nice of you. I'll PayPal you the money."

Jacinta had kind of been hoping that part would deter Emma a little bit, but apparently not.

Jacinta was filled with the kind of rage that was usually reserved for slow walkers and people who texted during movies.

And Jacinta knew that it was actually really sweet of Emma to want to do this, but Jacinta wasn't sure why she needed to be involved. It all felt kind of passive aggressive.

"Do you want my e-mail address so you can PayPal me?" Jacinta asked after realizing that Emma had been quiet for an awfully long time.

"Yeah, that'd be so great. Thank you so much. I know you can figure this all out for me. I really appreciate it."

"Yeah, cool, you're welcome," Jacinta said. Then she spelled out her e-mail address.

"I really can't wait to see Landon's face when I show up on prom night. I'm going to need all the information, like where you all are taking pictures and things like that. What kind of dress do you have? I guess I'll wear the dress I wore to my prom."

Jacinta was 99.9 percent sure that she was supposed to ask about Emma's dress and offer details about her own, but she couldn't handle this conversation even one more second.

"Well, that's good," Jacinta said. "I really should go, though. I still have homework to do for tomorrow."

"That's so weird! Graduation is on Tuesday for me."

"That's great," Jacinta said. "Bye."

She hung up without waiting for Emma's goodbye.

She lay back down on her bed and decided to scream a little more. It felt so good the first time around. Might as well keep it up.

She wasn't sure how she got involved in stuff like this, but it solidified the fact that she would never be anything but a background character in her own life. She needed to learn to take a stand. And she thought she had. She thought she was getting better.

But how do you tell someone else's girlfriend not to go to the prom with them? Jacinta didn't have that kind of moxie, and it really was not her place to say things like that.

At least now she wouldn't have to deal with the awkwardness of whether or not to slow dance with Landon. And if she was being absolutely honest with herself, she hadn't been really that excited about going with him anyway.

She sucked in a deep breath and went back to her desk.

Might as well keep working on her reaction paper. Though being exempt from the English exam didn't even feel like a big deal anymore.

Cora

Cora was just closing up shop in the student government office on Friday during lunch. She didn't want to have to stop back here after school, considering it was a long weekend and all. But she needed to make sure all the prom money was safe and sound. She gave a quick count and locked the safe.

When she turned around, Jacinta was standing at the door.

"Hey, what's up?" Cora asked.

"Well, I was wondering if we could still buy prom tickets."

Cora's eyes narrowed. "I mean, I guess. I think today is the last day to make changes. It's going to take some rearranging of tables, I think. And don't you already have a ticket?"

Jacinta nodded and then dove into the story of how Landon's long-distance girlfriend conveniently decided that she wanted to go to the prom with Landon after Jacinta had already made all the plans to go with him as friends.

No matter how stressed out Cora was, and at this point in the school year she was pretty stressed out, she couldn't make Jacinta feel worse, no matter how much she wanted to guilt her.

Between wanting to break up with Jamie, the prom coming up, and finals looming, Cora had had it with high school. But Jacinta was obviously really sad about this turn of events, so Cora put on her cheerful-acquaintance hat and did her best to deflect.

"Well, that bites. Are you sure you want me to get her a ticket?" she asked, hoping maybe Jacinta would say no.

Jacinta rolled her eyes. "It does bite, right? I'm not making this up or being sensitive? Like this is all so sudden. She seemed totally normal about the idea. She lives out of state. I live here. Landon and I are friends. Why would she change her mind at the last second? It's just so convenient that her parents bought her a surprise ticket."

"It does seem really convenient," Cora agreed.

Jacinta nodded sadly.

"Are you okay?" Cora asked.

And that was it, that was all it took for Jacinta to start crying. Not big, dramatic sobs, but her eyes filled with tears and then spilled over. Cora understood.

"I feel like I hold everything back, like all my opinions, so that I never hurt anyone's feelings and yet I still get shit on?"

Cora nodded. That wasn't exactly what her life was like, but it felt like a shade of her own issues if not her exact issues.

"I'm so sorry, I shouldn't have laid this all on you. I'm so sad and everything feels so weird lately? For months now." Jacinta sniffled.

Cora nodded again. "I think a lot of us have been feeling that. It must be a senior year thing."

"And I didn't even want to go with Landon, but I can't exactly explain that to anyone, you know? Like I don't want to hurt his feelings, and I don't even feel like I can say it to Kelsey because she dated him, and I'm sure she thinks he would make a great prom date. So I'm left with all these thoughts and nowhere to put them. And now I'm here, telling you. I am so sorry." Jacinta wiped her eyes and sniffled a few more times before Cora could locate the box of tissues and hand them to her.

Cora made comforting noises, unsure about what to say.

"Is there anything you want to talk about?" Jacinta asked. "Misery loves company."

"Honestly?"

"Of course, you just listened to me."

For some reason, Jacinta's earnest inquiry felt like a dam breaking somewhere inside Cora, like she couldn't hold back for even one more minute.

She shook her head, because if she spoke, she would definitely start to cry.

"Well, just know that the offer stands."

"I don't even know where to start," Cora said, tears welling up in her eyes. "And once I start I'm not sure I'll be able to stop."

"I've got time. Ms. Huang has a substitute today, so I'm sure we won't miss much if we're late."

"I want to break up with Jamie," Cora blurted out, and then the floodgates really opened. She was crying so hard she couldn't even make any sound.

Jacinta came over to her and wrapped her in a warm hug. Cora melted into her, and for a second they both just sniffled.

Cora pulled away and took a breath, grabbing for the tissues herself.

"Sorry," she said. "I don't mean to be so dramatic."

"Um, did I or did I not just get super dramatic with you?" Jacinta asked.

"I wouldn't say super dramatic."

"Do you feel any better?"

"I do."

"Do you want to talk more?"

"I do," Cora said, but then she glanced at the clock. "But we should really get to English, even if Ms. Huang has a substitute."

Jacinta nodded. "But just know the offer stands. If you need a friendly ear."

"Thanks," Cora said. "I'll keep it in mind."

The two girls walked in the direction of their English class, making a quick stop to wash their faces in the girls' room along the way.

Chapter 21

Henry

It was Memorial Day weekend, and Henry needed to pick up his tuxedo from the mall, because he definitely would not have time to before the prom on Friday. Of course the whole place was packed and forcing Henry to play his usual school hallway game of trying not to touch anyone in the long corridors. There were children and strollers and people crawling up the walls, or so it seemed.

If he hadn't promised to give Paisley a ride home after her shift at work, he would have turned and walked out, abandoning the tuxedo and just wearing his baseball uniform to the prom. Paisley wouldn't have minded.

When he turned into the storefront of the tuxedo rental shop, it was immediately quieter, cooler, and a more relaxed atmosphere than the mall proper. He took a deep breath. This was far more his speed.

And there at the counter was Cameron Wyatt, obviously waiting for his own tuxedo rental.

Henry scratched at his forehead and cleared his throat.

"Hey," Cam said.

"Hi," Henry said, squinting toward the curtain separating the counter from the back of the store.

Cameron drummed his fingers on the counter.

"Have you been waiting long?" Henry asked.

"Um, you know, a little while."

More awkward silence.

Cameron blew out a long breath.

Henry had the distinct urge to turn around and flee. "I feel like there's something we need to talk about," he said instead. This was not the place that Henry had ever envisioned a conversation with Cameron happening, but maybe that was for the better. Less pressure to live up to in his own head.

It was just that more and more lately, Henry couldn't stop thinking about his former friend, and he didn't want to have regrets in life.

"All right." Cameron was obviously taken aback, but Henry needed to get his thoughts out before he lost his nerve.

"I hate talking about this crap, but it sucked that you stopped talking to me, all right? I didn't know how to talk to you because you know me. That's not, like, my strongest quality. So I kept waiting for you to come to me."

Cameron nodded but didn't interrupt, so Henry continued.

"But I guess I wanted you to know that I don't hate you or anything. That's not what the problem is or was. I didn't know how to deal with you not talking to me all of a sudden, but I definitely didn't hate you. I just didn't know how to deal with being ignored."

"I didn't know how to deal with everything going on with my mom and her getting remarried. I didn't like how she was acting, and I didn't know how to talk about it without sounding like a jealous kid." Cameron's cheeks flared with red, as if guys aren't supposed to talk about their feelings this way. "Anyway, I didn't know how to deal. It was just a thing that happened. We don't have to talk about this at all."

"I'm the one who brought it up," Henry reminded Cameron.

"Right, yeah," Cameron said, letting out a long, slow breath.

"I'm sorry I didn't . . . I don't know, try to be friends again, or something. I don't know exactly what I'm sorry for, and I'm also sorry that I can't be more specific than that."

"I'm sorry," Cam said. "For everything. And that I can't be more specific than *that*."

"In that case, I totally forgive you."

"I totally forgive you," Cam said with a shrug. It was like neither boy could stop himself from shrugging after nearly every uncomfortable thing they'd said.

"So, does anyone actually work here? Have you like talked to anyone?" Henry asked, changing the subject.

Cameron nodded. "I gave them my ticket like eight years before you even walked in."

"Does this mean you're going to the prom?"

"Um, yes," Cameron said.

"Do you need a place to sit? Because Paisley and I are going, and we had to do some table rearranging and ended up with mostly empty seats."

"You wouldn't mind?"

"We definitely have room for you." Henry grimaced. "Do you have a date? This feels like a really nosy question, seeing as how we've barely talked in the past year."

"I have a date, but it's a long story," Cameron said.

"We might have time," Henry said, trying to peek into the back of the store to see if there were any workers around.

Of course, at that moment, a guy came from the back room.

"Here you go!" he said cheerfully, handing a garment bag to Cam.

Cameron looked at it. "I didn't order a red tuxedo."

"No?"

"I would remember that," Cam said. "I did order a lime-green shirt, though."

"Ah yes, the chartreuse."

"Is that another word for lime green?"

"Yes." The guy disappeared behind the curtain.

Henry leaned on the counter, about to ask more about Cameron's complicated prom story, but Cameron spoke up first.

"I thought you were going to the prom with Amelia Vaughn."

"Uh, yeah," Henry said. "That was a thing that was happening for like five minutes. Turns out my prom story is kind of complicated, too."

"I think we have time," Cameron said.

Paisley

It was so busy in the mall, Paisley hadn't checked the clock in hours. Time had no meaning when the only reason you were put on this earth was to serve baked potatoes to the masses.

"Why are people even at the mall?" she muttered as she

pulled another vat of sour cream from the refrigerator in the back. "Don't people go to barbecues anymore? Or the beach? Isn't this the unofficial beginning of summer?"

Her boss John poked his head into the back. "You ever coming out?" he asked.

"Yeah, I'm coming, I'm coming."

It wasn't until nearly three, long after traditional lunchtime had ended, that there was a lull in the lunch rush. John was leaving for the day, and Paisley was going to be alone at the counter until the dinner people came in to relieve her.

"You sure you're gonna be okay?" John asked for the millionth time.

"Of course. Just get out of here before I change my mind."

With that, he fled through the back door and Paisley was alone. There were still plenty of people in the food court and the mall in general, but no one else was looking for a baked potato. Thank god. She wasn't sure if she could pour even one more ladle of melted cheese.

After organizing and wiping up behind the counter, she made herself a lovely cocktail of Hawaiian Punch and Coke. Paisley settled in to wait for her coworkers to come in and relieve her. Only an hour left, she noted, looking at the clock.

When she turned back around, there, standing in front of her, was Stewart Smith.

"Hi," he said.

"Hi," she said.

"So, when should I pick you up on Friday? Also where should I pick you up? I don't know where you live," he said with an uncomfortable chuckle.

"What are you picking me up for?" she asked, trying to

remember if Henry had mentioned they were going with other guys from the baseball team.

"The prom."

"Um. I never said I'd go to the prom with you."

"You never said no," he said, waggling his eyebrows.

"I never said anything," Paisley replied, slurping the last of her drink through her straw.

"Come on, go to the prom with me, please?" he said. And then he leaned in, conspiratorially. "We could split the money from the bet."

She angled toward him. "How much are we talking about?"

"Forty bucks," he said.

She snorted as she stepped back. "Hell no."

"Oh, come on, please? I assumed all this time we were going together. Now I won't have a date."

"What about Margie Showalter? She asked you and you said no."

His jaw dropped.

"Oh yeah, I know about that. You can't make me feel guilty for rejecting you. If you can reject people, then so can I."

"I just assumed we'd go together. I thought . . ." He trailed off and shrugged.

"You never even talked to me! This is literally the first conversation we've ever had."

"But you could totally go with me."

She threw up her hands in frustration. "I'm going with Henry."

"Wait a second, why would Henry act like you didn't have a date when you were going with him all along?"

"Well, back then he was going with Amelia, but that, um,

fell through," she said, not wanting to air Henry's dirty laundry. "And it all kind of started because he was getting back at me for something. It's a very long story. But I promise you, I'm happy to be going with him now. Or at least not super crabby about going with him."

"You could have told me no," Stewart said.

"Are you kidding me?" Paisley asked, her eyes wide. She picked up a plastic knife and broke it.

Stewart flinched. "Okay. Fine."

He turned on his heel and walked away into the crowd. Paisley shook her head and watched him go.

Henry appeared next to her with a too-big grin on his face. "So what was that about?"

Paisley picked up another plastic knife. This one was harder to snap, but she managed to get through it.

"Yikes," Henry said.

"Stewart Smith," Paisley said through clenched teeth, "still thought I was going to the prom with him."

"Aw, poor guy."

Paisley shook her head again. "I hate boys. They are all the worst. Prom is the worst. And I also hate potatoes."

"So, you wanna leave?" Henry asked.

"I would love to, but I'm still waiting for people to relieve me."

"So you wanna make me a chili and cheese potato in the meantime?"

"Listen, Henry. I'm not going to waste another knife, but please imagine that I broke another one."

"So that's a no on the potato?"

"I will make you a potato, but only because I have to be

here for another fifteen minutes anyway. And also because I recognize this Stewart Smith stuff isn't really completely your fault."

Henry grinned.

"But it's not free."

Henry frowned and Paisley made him a potato.

"I'm watching you, buckaroo," she said, handing him his potato. "Your good mood is suspicious."

"I'll tell you all about it in the car," he promised.

Chapter 22

Lizzie

Luke pulled up in front of Lizzie's house, and she shaded her eyes from the late afternoon sun. It was hot for the end of May, but in a good way, like she could feel her bones thawing out from winter finally.

"Hey," he said as she slid into the front seat.

"Hi." He leaned over the center console to give her a hug. Even at this awkward angle, Luke was a very good hugger. He hugged with his whole body.

"A million thank-yous for agreeing to entertain me this afternoon," Luke said as he pulled away from the curb. "Otis remains on lockdown, so I feel like I'm grounded, too. And it's just too nice to stay home."

"Totally," Lizzie said, buckling herself in.

"Do you mind going to the mall?"

"I suppose, if we must," Lizzie said dramatically.

"I know it's your day off and all. We'll avoid the food court. I'm craving one of those sour cream and onion pretzels from that kiosk by the fountain."

"Works for me," Lizzie said. They drove most of the way in silence, and Lizzie enjoyed the warm air coming through the open windows. She imagined that she had been a dog in a previous life because it took all her control not to stick her head out and really feel the breeze.

After a quick stop at the pretzel kiosk, Lizzie sipped the biggest lemonade money could buy and Luke ate his pretzel while they wandered around, mostly window shopping. He stopped a few times to check out shoes.

"I'm always in the market for brightly colored sneakers."

Which reminded Lizzie. "I still need to find something lime green to wear to the prom so Mystery Boy recognizes me."

Luke gasped. "You haven't found anything?"

"That's a little dramatic," Lizzie said. "I have almost a week."

"But lime green is so specific. And you have a red dress, so it has to be something just right."

"You're right. It does need to be just right."

After that, their shopping excursion became much more focused. Store after store, Lizzie couldn't find anything that would look good with her dress.

"Let's check one more place," Luke said, pulling Lizzie toward a small boutique-type store with a font so fancy on the sign that Lizzie had trouble reading the name.

Lizzie stopped. "There's no way. Everything in there is so expensive."

"Oh, come on," Luke said. "We have to at least try."

The answer to Lizzie's problem was right at the front of the store. A short necklace made of several strands of lime-green ribbon with a fake red rose attached to it. And it was only $9.99.

Luke saw it the same second she did.

"Unbelievable," he said. "And look at how cute it looks on you."

Lizzie turned to look in the full-length mirror in the middle of the store. It did look cute on her. It was a much bigger statement piece than she would have normally picked, but at least Mystery Boy wouldn't be able to miss it.

As they waited in line to pay, Luke got a text message.

"What?" he said to his phone as he read the message.

"What?" Lizzie asked. The clerk rang her up, and when she was done paying she had to lead Luke out of the store because he was still staring slack jawed at his phone.

"What is it?" Lizzie asked again when they'd sat down on a bench in the center court of the mall. "What's wrong?"

Luke shook his head and handed his phone to Lizzie. "I can't even read it out loud. I might cry."

Lizzie took his phone. A line of long texts from Otis filled the screen.

> Otis:
>
> It's official. I can't go to the prom. I thought for sure my parents would let up on this, but I know there's no use in continuing to argue with them.

Lizzie's jaw dropped.

Otis:

I'm so sorry to disappoint you like this. And I know I should have probably waited to tell you in person, but I just feel so guilty. I hope you can forgive me.

Lizzie looked at Luke. "This is terrible!" she exclaimed. "Of course he feels guilty." She rubbed Luke's arm while he sat on the bench staring sadly at the ground.

"I don't even want to go to the prom without him," Luke said in a quiet voice.

"That's okay," Lizzie said. "I don't think anyone would be shocked if you didn't go. But you know, Madison and I will still be there. And a bunch of people from the GSA. We can still have a lot of fun together. Otis is important, obviously, but he's not the only friend you have."

"I just, I had this whole thing planned," Luke said, his shoulders deflating even farther. "I got us a hotel room for afterward."

Lizzie smacked his arm. "What? You never told me that!"

"I know, I didn't want to jinx it or act like I was bragging about getting a room with my boyfriend. But Otis never even seemed all that interested in it."

"I'm so sorry, Luke," Lizzie said. She wasn't sure how many other ways she could say it. She was biting her tongue to keep from dragging Otis through the mud, even if he deserved it. But he and Luke were actually still dating, even if this news made it feel like a breakup.

"But I think you should go to the prom," Lizzie said. "And

I think you should use the room. Madison, you, and I can have an awesome hotel sleepover party."

"Seriously?"

"Sure! Does it have a pool?"

"Yeah," Luke said.

"Come on. That would be totally fun. We'll even split the room with you," Lizzie said, calculating how much money that would cost. She didn't want to dip into her savings, but at this point she would do anything to cheer Luke up.

"You'd really do that for me?" Luke asked.

"Of course."

"You're the best Lizzie to ever Lizzie," he said.

"You're the best Luke to ever Luke," she said.

"God, we're adorable."

He gave her a quick hug, and they headed back out to his car, both of them chattering away about the epic hotel slumber party they would have on prom night.

Cora

Cora was filled with regret.

An hour ago, Teagan and Josie had texted her to see if she wanted to go to the movies with them. She had said no. Of course now as the movie was starting, nothing sounded better than sitting in a dark, cool room and getting lost in someone else's world.

Cora was antsy and anxious and not having the best long weekend. She wished that she could go back to school. And even though she'd regret having those thoughts in the morning, right now she had too much energy and nowhere to put it.

Her parents were at a barbecue at one of her dad's coworkers' houses. Cora had begged off, but now even that sounded better than being home.

She could call Jamie, and he would find something fun for them to do. But it would also likely involve his family, seeing as how it was a holiday. And Cora wanted to become less entwined with Jamie's family. Calling him and going over to his house wasn't the best way to do that.

After pacing her room for another ten minutes, she decided to lace up her sneakers and go for a run.

Cora wasn't exactly what you'd call a runner.

She liked the idea in theory so much more than in practice, but even if she jogged for a minute or two here and there, and walked the rest of it, she'd at least feel more productive than she did at home.

On her way down the street, she spotted someone walking a dog and almost diverted to the other side, since the dog seemed to be a little out of control.

Cora wasn't afraid of dogs, but that didn't mean she wanted it to jump on her, and she definitely didn't want to get muddy dog prints on her brand-new running sneakers that she'd just pulled out of the box.

As she was jogging across the street, she realized the person walking the dog was actually Jacinta Ramos. She stopped and waved.

Jacinta waved back and was promptly tugged off balance by the dog as he lunged in the direction of a squirrel, and landed in a heap on the nearest lawn.

Cora went off course again, in the middle of the street, and ran over to Jacinta.

"Are you okay?" she asked, putting her hand out to help Jacinta up.

"I'm fine," Jacinta said, dusting off her butt. "This dog, though, is not going to be fine."

Cora was pleased to note that it didn't jump up on her; seeming content with causing Jacinta to have fallen down, the dog was now sitting on the sidewalk panting.

"Do you need me to get anyone or call for help?" Cora asked.

"Really, I'm fine. I'll have a bruise on my ass, but whatever. I don't know how I get talked into these things. I'm dog sitting for a neighbor, and taking Rocky here for a walk seemed like a good idea."

Rocky panted and smiled his doggy smile.

"What's up with you?" Jacinta asked.

Cora shrugged. "Want me to walk with you? In case he decides to declare mutiny again?"

"That'd be awesome, but I don't want to interrupt your run."

Cora scoffed. "It was a fake run. I don't really run. I'd rather walk with you any day."

Jacinta grinned and they set off in the opposite direction.

"Hey, so remember that time that we had synchronized emotional breakdowns?" Cora asked.

"Hmm, yeah, that sounds familiar," Jacinta said.

"Does the offer still stand to talk more?"

"Yes. That was a forever offer," Jacinta answered, even as Rocky nearly ripped her arm out of the socket while he ran to sniff at a telephone pole. "So what's up?"

"So on top of wanting to break up with Jamie, I feel like college has been sort of ruined and I'm not sure I even want to go to Boston anymore," Cora announced.

"Wow, that's big. That's a big deal."

"I know. And I haven't said it yet, and I didn't have anyone to talk to today, and holy crap it feels so good to say it out loud!"

"What about—"

Cora held up her hand. "But I don't want to talk about it in terms of other people yet, just in terms of what the reality would look like if I didn't go."

"All right. I think I get it," Jacinta said, nodding. "So what are you going to do?"

"Well, that's the thing, isn't it? My parents already put money down. I took placement tests; I filled out the roommate survey. What can I do?"

"You can go for the first semester or year and then transfer. That's always an option."

Cora nodded. "Yeah. I keep reminding myself that, but it's like my brain is being super dramatic about all of this."

"Well, let's think about this logically. You could find out if any of the other schools you applied to have later deadlines for accepting admittance. You'd still lose your deposit, but maybe that would work?"

"Maybe," Cora said. "I hadn't really considered that."

"Is there somewhere you have in mind instead?"

Cora shrugged. "No. And it sucks because Boston was my idea. I shouldn't have to give it up for Jamie. See, my cousin went to Harvard and we went to visit her there once when I was ten. And I knew that was where I wanted to go to college. But it became pretty apparent that I wasn't going to get in, you know, when I realized that I was just a normal overachieving student and not a supernova overachieving student."

Jacinta nodded. "Ah yes. That realization."

Cora smiled. "So somewhere along the line, Boston became the new dream."

"Have you considered talking to him about this?" Jacinta asked. "I know you said before you didn't want to talk about this in terms of anyone else, but you brought him up and really he's pretty entwined in all of this."

"No, I know. But I'm not going to talk to him until after prom. It feels really terrible to break up with him beforehand. Just way too mean, no matter how much I'm sort of over him."

"I can see why you needed to get this off your chest."

"Right? It's been eating away at me all day. I swear I was about to get an ulcer."

Jacinta smiled. "And who knows, maybe you'll like it and won't want to transfer. Maybe it'll suit you. Or maybe Jamie will transfer."

"I appreciate your optimism."

"And really, it's so silly to change your plans for just one boy."

"I know. Thanks for listening."

"You're welcome," Jacinta said as they turned a corner. "Well, this is Rocky's stop. But seriously, if you need someone else to talk about this, text me anytime."

"I might take you up on that," Cora said. She gave Rocky one little pet, and then Jacinta walked up the long driveway to the back door of her neighbor's house.

Cora turned on her heel and started to run. She felt freer than she had in years.

Then she got totally out of breath and decided to walk.

But she still felt pretty free.

Now she had to make it through prom.

Chapter 23

Cameron

Things were seriously looking up for Cameron during the week leading up to the prom.

For starters, on Tuesday before school he'd had an actual conversation with his stepdad over breakfast. It wasn't anything earth shattering or life changing. As usual they were the last two to leave the house before work and school, but rather than sit in silence they talked about baby names.

Richard had been in an increasingly good mood since Cameron's mom had announced her pregnancy, so it wasn't even really that shocking when he struck up a conversation with Cameron. And yet, Cameron was mildly shocked.

"Your mother thinks we should name the baby Richard Jr. and call him RJ."

Cameron wrinkled his nose but didn't say anything, not wanting to offend his stepfather.

"I feel the same way," Richard said. "If I'd wanted an RJ that's what I would have named Landon."

"And we don't even know if it's a boy yet."

"We don't. She just seems to think it's a boy."

"I don't know," Cameron said, finishing off his last spoonful of Frosted Flakes. "Might be nice to have a girl."

"I said the same thing!" Richard exclaimed. "And your mother seemed surprised that I had this opinion."

Cameron smiled. "And what would she want to name it if it was a girl? Richardette? Richardina? Is there a female version of Richard?"

"I honestly have no idea, but hopefully with both of us working together we can talk her out of this one," Richard said.

Cameron put his bowl in the dishwasher and was halfway out the door before turning around. "Have a good day at work, um, Richard," Cameron said.

"You, too, Cam," Richard said.

Between the good interaction with Richard and his conversation with Henry over the weekend, Cameron decided to take a chance sitting with the baseball guys at lunch that day.

After some gentle ribbing along the lines of, "Cam? What the hell? I thought you moved or something," the guys all settled in and acted like it wasn't even a little weird that Cameron was there.

Henry smiled as he took the seat next to Cameron.

"Are you lost?" he asked Cameron.

"Maybe. I feel like I time traveled back to last year," Cameron said honestly.

And that's really how he felt. Like he had gone back in time. Or maybe like he was finally stepping out of a fog; all those terrible, sad feelings that he didn't know what to do with were starting to fade away.

In English class, he was relieved to see the laptop cart. There was a time when not having a new message waiting from Laptop Girl would have made him worry she didn't like him anymore. But not today, not for new and improved Cameron. New and improved Cameron was logical and figured they probably just hadn't used the laptops in her class.

And he was grateful to get one more shot with laptop 19 this year. Ms. Huang hadn't been bringing the cart in much, and Cameron really wanted a copy of the document preserved for him. He put it on a flash drive and shoved it deep in his backpack.

He didn't want to sit around reading the document every day for the rest of his life or anything, but he thought maybe if he found it in five or ten years, it might be something fun to read.

Or he might want to delete his awkwardness.

He'd let future Cameron work that out.

After that, the week kept getting better.

He didn't have to work Thursday after school because Eddie felt so bad about making him come in on Friday. The good news was that Eddie didn't know all the seniors got out of school at twelve thirty the day of the prom or Cameron was pretty sure his boss would have asked him to come in for the lunch shift, too.

But not having to work on Thursday meant he had time to go to his mom's first ultrasound with her and Richard.

The whole experience was weird, but he was glad not to miss it.

And he might even take Richard up on his offer to pay to fly Cameron home from college for the baby's birth.

Maybe.

The last thing he did Thursday afternoon before heading home after his mom's doctor's appointment was stop at the florist to pick up a matching boutonniere and corsage for him and Laptop Girl. They were both lime green.

He thought for sure he'd get a weird look when he ordered them, but apparently lime was a very popular color this year.

Cameron stood in his bedroom making a list of everything he needed to take with him to school the next morning to go from school to work to prom. It was going to be a crazy day, but twenty-four hours from that moment, he could be with Laptop Girl.

He couldn't wait.

Otis

Otis sucked in a deep breath as he walked into school the morning of the prom. It was time to confront reality and actually talk to Luke face-to-face. He'd been dodging him for the majority of the week, even faked sick on Wednesday just to avoid the awkwardness between them.

He had halfheartedly tried to talk to his parents one last time that morning, but Otis knew when to quit. The irony was not lost on him that after not wanting to go, now that he wasn't allowed to go, he sort of wanted to go. Especially now that he'd heard their private hotel room had turned into a slumber party with Lizzie and Madison. Why couldn't that have always been the plan?

"Oh, hey there," Luke said, grimacing when he saw Otis. "I was starting to wonder if your parents had locked you in the basement and I was never going to see you again."

"I'm so sorry about the prom!" Otis blurted out before he could lose the nerve. "I thought I could talk my parents into commuting my sentence or something, but I couldn't. It's over."

Luke blinked at him and then frowned. "I guess I was hoping for a last-minute reprieve, too. Because it was literally one time. One mistake. You have a clean record otherwise! You're a first-time offender!"

"I know that, and you know that, but apparently it's about learning that actions have consequences."

"But don't you already know that?"

Otis shrugged. "I thought I did." The guilt was likely to eat Otis alive. No wonder he'd been avoiding Luke.

"Well, this sucks so hard. I don't want to go to the prom without you," Luke said, taking Otis's hand.

Somehow all of this was worse because Luke was so sad instead of angry. Otis was prepared to take on the wrath of Luke; he wasn't prepared to take on sad, disappointed Luke.

"You'll still have fun with Lizzie and Madison and them," Otis said. "At least you get to go."

Luke's chin wobbled, making Otis feel a million times worse. "I know, but I'm going to be thinking about you all night long. Maybe I shouldn't go, either. Would your parents let me come over and hang out with you?"

"I don't think that's part of my grounding," Otis said. "I

don't know how long I'm grounded for, mostly because I'm afraid to ask, but I promise I'll make this up to you."

Luke sighed. "The prom is a one-time thing. There's no way to make it up to me, not really. We either go to the prom or we don't. And we're not. So there's sort of no way to make it up to me."

"Yeah, I know, I'm sorry," Otis said, fiddling with the dial of the lock on the locker next to Luke's. "I owe you a grand romantic gesture when I'm finally not grounded."

"You know, I just . . . I wish you hadn't gone to the movies with Madison. Was it really that important to sneak out and ruin this?" Luke asked.

"It wasn't. There's no way it was. But I wasn't really thinking like that. Who could have guessed that the punishment for sneaking out would be no prom? This isn't the way my parents usually handle these things."

LIES! the angel voice in Otis's head screamed. It seemed to be the only word it knew.

"You know. This is like the one time in high school I thought I was going to have this, like, perfect high school moment that I'd actually want to remember. Us in our tuxes, taking a limo, slow dancing, getting a hotel room. I know some of that stuff didn't work out, because limos are ridiculously expensive, but it was still mostly going to go as planned. It was still going to be this whole memorable event."

Otis frowned; he really didn't know what to say. Although he was kind of relieved that Luke seemed to be getting angrier the longer this monologue went on. Angry Luke made sense in this situation.

"I thought after like a couple years of homophobic garbage

my boyfriend and I were going to have this awesome prom experience. But no. And like, you kept telling me everything would be fine, so I kept my hopes up. But you must have known you were in such bad trouble, and it took you a week to finally admit it to me."

"I don't know what else to say besides I'm sorry."

Luke's nostrils flared. "Yeah, whatever." And with that he stormed off.

Luke didn't look back.

Which made Otis feel even worse. The pit in his stomach grew larger. He couldn't believe how terrible he felt about disappointing Luke. It was beyond anything he could have imagined.

Everything would be fine. Otis didn't have to go to prom and he would totally make this up to Luke someday.

Someday he'd come up with the perfect grand romantic gesture.

He promised himself he would find a way.

There had to be a way.

Chapter 24

Paisley

Paisley heard the buzzer for her condo go off several hours earlier than Henry had said he'd be there. She figured it was the mail carrier getting confused about unit numbers again. Luckily, Paisley's mom was home to get the door and she didn't have to pause what she could only describe as "Hair Jenga."

Paisley was using bobby pins to create what she hoped was a stunning updo, but it might actually have been the world's tiniest bun. It was impossible to create an updo from a growing-out pixie cut. On the other hand, it'd be great if the prom got attacked and she could just yank out a couple of bobby pins to use as weapons. That seemed like something that could feasibly happen at prom.

Paisley could hear Henry and her mom exchange pleasantries in the living room, followed by Henry's plodding steps down the hall before he stopped and knocked on her bedroom door.

"Come in," she said, realizing in that moment that she didn't have anything like an appropriate bag or purse for a formal event.

When Henry walked in, her head was stuck in her closet, where she was looking for a small canvas bag that she bought on the Internet a while ago. It had a rainbow unicorn on it and would have to do for a clutch.

After thinking about it for a minute, she decided it was kind of the perfect clutch.

She leaned out of the closet.

"Hey!" she said. "You're like three hours early and you're not even dressed."

He threw himself down on her bed. "Maybe we don't have to go?"

"Henry, come on, we've been over this."

She stood up and dusted herself off, holding the canvas bag.

"You look nice," he said. "Especially your hair."

She narrowed her eyes at him. "Don't lie to me, Henry Lai."

"I'm not lying!" he said, holding up his hands defensively.

"Well, fine. Your hair looks nice, too. More formal or something."

He touched it, as if he forgot he'd gelled it back. "Yeah, I thought it would look fancier this way. I don't know if I really like it, though."

"So why so early?"

"I'm nervous."

"Aw, poor buckaroo," Paisley said. "Where's your tux?"

"Hanging in the living room," he said.

"So you're gonna watch me get ready? 'Cause that's not creepy."

"I didn't think I'd watch you get dressed," Henry said. "But I couldn't stay in my house for another thirty seconds. I kept pacing around. My mom was way too enthusiastic, and my brother kept asking stupid questions. I had to get out of there."

"I have to figure out my hair mess," she said, handing him her laptop. "As usual, you are not permitted to check my browsing history."

Henry lounged on Paisley's bed while she got ready, in and out of the bathroom, around in circles in her room, digging deep into her closet in search of the shoes she had only bought the other day but that had become buried in the interim.

"Henry, it's time to get dressed," Paisley said a half hour before they were supposed to leave. Henry sighed and went to gather his tux. When Paisley heard the bathroom door click shut, she threw off the pajama shorts and T-shirt she'd been wearing and slid her formal wear on.

If the dress looked half as good as it felt, maybe this night wouldn't be so terrible.

She examined herself in the mirror for a minute before Henry knocked at her door. When she opened it, he stood sheepishly in the doorway, looking quite dapper in his tuxedo.

Paisley led the way back into the living room, even though Henry obviously knew how to get there. Her mom made them go outside to take pictures next to some bush with a lot of flowers on it.

"I'll be sure to send these to your mom, Henry," Paisley's mom said.

"Thanks, that'd be great," he said, trying to hold his fake smile. At least Paisley's mom knew enough not to force them into awkward prom poses. She was satisfied with Henry throwing an arm around Paisley's shoulders.

"You smell nice," Paisley said as they broke apart. He smiled.

"Thanks."

After that it was time to actually suck it up and go to the prom.

"You're a really good friend, Paisley," he said as they got into the car.

"Thanks, you're a good friend, too."

"I can't even begin to tell you how much I appreciate you going to the prom with me. Like you have no idea how much this means, that you would do this. Even though you really don't want to go."

Paisley moved far away from Henry, as far as she could get in the confined space. "This isn't where you confess your love for me, right?"

"Paisley," Henry said seriously, looking her in the eye.

"Oh god, oh no, I thought you promised it would never come to this!"

"Paisley, I don't love you like that."

"Oh thank god."

They pulled out of the parking lot of Paisley's condo community.

"But that means you do love me, right?" she said.

"Yeah," Henry said with a grin. "But only as a friend."

"And you better keep it that way, buckaroo." Paisley pointed a threatening finger at him.

"Well, I know you're serious since you're giving me the pointer finger."

She wagged it at him a few times, to show how serious she was.

"Let's go to the freaking prom now."

"Yes, let's," Henry agreed.

Cora

Teagan and Josie came over after school so that the three friends could all get ready for prom together. Cora figured it was probably because she was the only one of the three of them that had her own bathroom.

Also Teagan was so much better at makeup than the other two, they would have begged her to help them no matter what. This way, it was more convenient for everyone involved having them all together in the same place.

Teagan did her own makeup first, because it only seemed fair, while Cora and Josie worked on their hair and went through a variety of jewelry options, each vetoing the other's ideas one after another, until finally Teagan said, "OMG. Both of you just wear whatever damn earrings you want to wear."

While Teagan did Josie's makeup, Cora painted her toenails to match the awesome peep-toe heels she had bought special for prom night.

"I'm going to be really relieved when this night is over," she said. The thought had been following her around all afternoon, and it felt good to get it out in the open.

"Are you going to break up with him tonight?" Josie asked, turning to look at Cora and in the process making Teagan draw a line of eyeliner across Josie's cheek.

"Dammit, Josie, you gotta hold still," Teagan said, grabbing for a tissue to clean up the mess. "And of course Cora isn't breaking up with him tonight. Right, Cora?"

Cora chewed her lip and dabbed polish on her pinkie toe. "As relieving and wonderful as it sounds to just rip the Band-Aid off this relationship, no. I'm not going to break up with him tonight. Could you even imagine?"

Cora let herself daydream about a dramatic breakup on the dance floor for a hot second before getting back to work on her nails.

"It would be next-level evil to do it tonight," she said firmly.

"Agreed," Josie said.

"And thirded," Teagan said.

It was Cora's turn to have her makeup done, and Teagan took her time putting everything in place to make Cora glow.

"But what if, hypothetically, I broke up with him tonight," Cora said.

Teagan paused, mascara brush hovering in front of Cora's face. Josie's jaw hung open from across the room. Neither of them answered.

"I'll take that stunned silence as a no," Cora said after a minute.

"Even just waiting until tomorrow would be nicer," Teagan said.

"You've made it this long," Josie added.

By the time their dates arrived for pictures, Cora felt a little less resolute about breaking up with Jamie. She'd never done anything so dramatic before. And there was a pressure building up behind her eyes, like this was the moment to do it, no matter how ill timed it was. She couldn't get the thought out of her head.

The boys waited downstairs for their dates: Jamie; Tag, who was going with Josie; and Dave, Teagan's date.

Jamie smiled at her so wide as he slid her corsage on her wrist. Cora felt like her smile was a lie, like he'd be able to tell she wasn't happy. But he didn't say a word while Cora's parents lined them up to take pictures next to the fireplace, and then instructed the group to go out on the lawn for a few outdoor shots.

While they were outside, Cora's heel got stuck in the grass. Not only did Jamie make sure she didn't fall, he even leaned down to pull her heel out and still maintained his grip around her waist. He was damn near Superman, and Cora had to make it through the night, no matter how painful it sounded.

"No worries, babe," he said after she thanked him.

Jamie made everything harder by being a good person. He was cheerful, he was kind, and he was helpful. The very least she could do for him was at least not ruin his night. But she was really sick and tired of being called babe.

I will not break up with him tonight, I will not break up with him tonight, Cora thought as they finished pictures.

She glanced at the other two couples as the pictures were taken, observing their body language. Dave and Teagan had been involved in an on-again, off-again thing for the past two years, and they seemed pretty on tonight. As for Tag and Josie, he was the kind of guy that could make anyone laugh, and Josie was laughing a lot.

Cora looked up into Jamie's face. He grinned his megawatt grin.

Before she got in the limo, Cora's dad proudly showed her one of the pictures he'd taken with his new camera. "Not just a cell phone picture for my little girl," he said.

Again, Cora was struck by the body language of the three couples. Josie and Tag were laughing uproariously. Dave and Teagan were leaning into each other like they were the only two people there.

Jamie, for his part, looked casual and calm, while Cora looked uncomfortable in his arms. Why couldn't she have realized all of this sooner? Why did it have to happen now?

I will not break up with him tonight, I will not break up with him tonight. She continued rolling the phrase around in her head as they got into the limo and drove away.

I will not break up with him tonight.

Maybe if she thought it hard enough, she'd start to believe it.

Chapter 25

Lizzie

The day had finally arrived after what seemed like months and years of waiting.

The last week leading up to the prom had totally flown by, and Lizzie was more than ready to get this night started.

Her nerves were so on edge she was having trouble putting on her mascara. She had to keep stopping to take deep cleansing breaths and remind herself that tonight was going to be fun and only full of good things.

Like Mystery Boy.

She grinned so big at the thought of meeting him that she had to pause again in her makeup application.

When she finally finished with her makeup, she put her finishing touch on, the lime-green necklace. Then she stood back in front of her full-length mirror and looked herself up and down. She was really happy with what she saw. Everything from her hair that she'd worked really hard to curl, to the earrings she borrowed from her mom, to the dress she'd gotten on mega sale, and the black-heeled sandals she'd bought at a thrift store that she'd never gotten to wear before, all made her feel completely prepared for the night.

Lizzie's phone vibrated in the little clutch bag that her mom was letting her borrow.

Luke:

I'm on my way!

Lizzie:

You're pretty early.

Luke:

I know, but I have a quick stop I need to make before we head to the prom.

Lizzie tried not to wonder too much about what the quick stop was. If Luke made them run late and risk the possibility of not being allowed in, she would literally hitchhike to the prom if she had to. She was not going to miss her moment with Mystery Boy for whatever detour Luke wanted to take. Lizzie decided to see if Madison had any insight.

Lizzie:

What's up with Luke?

Madison:

I don't know, but he's giddy for someone whose boyfriend isn't going to make it to prom.

Lizzie slid her phone back in the clutch and walked out into the living room, feeling a little silly in her heels, especially when one got caught on a loose carpet thread.

Both of her parents were in the living room, grinning. Her mom was holding the old camera, like, a real camera that required film and everything.

They took her picture standing next to the front door and each gave her a hug.

"Have fun tonight!" her dad said. "And be careful."

It all felt like something out of someone else's life. She couldn't believe this was really happening to her.

When she slid into Luke's car, Madison was in the front seat, putting the finishing touches on her makeup. "He picked me up so damn early I didn't have time to finish my lips," she complained.

"Yeah, why are we leaving so early?" Lizzie asked.

"I just. I need to see Otis. I yelled at him this morning, and we haven't talked since. I tried to call him but he didn't answer. And no matter how mad I am about what he did, I don't want him to think I hate him."

He drove to Otis's house and parked out front. Luke picked up a few small stones from the road and pelted one of the upstairs windows. A minute later, Otis opened it and leaned out.

"Well, this is surprising," Otis said.

"Romeo, Romeo? I hope you don't think I hate you, Romeo," Luke said.

"Wow, you went old school with this latest movie reference." Otis laughed. "I don't think you hate me. What are you doing here?"

"I wanted to see you on prom night and tell you that I promise to take a million pictures."

"Thanks," Otis said, looking sad.

"I wish you were coming!" Luke yelled.

"I wish I was coming, too." And then a light went on behind Otis's eyes. "Wait right there."

Lizzie felt like she was watching a great love story unfold, even if she was slightly annoyed that time was ticking by. She kept reminding herself they still had almost an hour before the dance even started.

Otis

Otis leaned on the windowsill and looked down at his friends, Luke in his white dinner jacket, Lizzie in her red dress, and Madison in her sparkly jumpsuit. He wanted to be with them more than anything he'd wanted in his life.

"I wish I was coming too," Otis said. And he meant it. But then he had an idea. "Wait right there."

He threw on his navy-blue suit. He'd had every intention of renting a tux, but once he realized his parents weren't budging, that had fallen apart. He looked in the mirror above his dresser and ran a hand through his hair, hoping the messy look would work for Luke. He stopped in the bathroom and swallowed some Listerine because there was no time to swish and spit. He'd grown out of his own dress shoes, so he stopped by his dad's closet and borrowed a pair of his.

There was no way Otis wanted to live the rest of his life with this level of guilt about missing the prom. It was time to be brave.

He'd promised Luke a grand romantic gesture to make things up to him. It might as well be now.

Otis was prepared to go out in a blaze of glory.

His parents were in the living room, watching the evening news.

Otis grabbed the remote and muted it, then stood in front of them and made sure he had his parents' full attention. He folded his hands in front of him as if preparing for a presidential address.

"Hello and good evening," he said formally. "I know I'm grounded. But I have to go to the prom. My boyfriend is outside, and I know I'll regret it forever if I don't go."

His dad opened his mouth to speak, but Otis held up his finger. "For the record, I didn't plan this rebellion and neither did Luke. He loves grand romantic gestures, so he stopped on his way to prom to throw pebbles at my window and tell me that he wasn't mad. This mutiny is my idea."

He tried to gauge his parents' response to his monologue, but they were both sitting on the couch with their jaws dropped.

"You can ground me for the rest of the school year, for the entire summer, I don't really care. You can even ground me while I'm away at college, though I'm not sure how you would accomplish that. But suffice it to say, I need to go to the prom with my boyfriend. I said yes to him when he asked. And it is a responsibility I'm going to uphold."

His dad stood up with a grimace, but his mom tugged on his hand.

Otis began inching toward the front door. He cleared his throat, preparing for further declarations, but then he caught his mom's eye and she mouthed, "Just go."

So, he went.

Otis opened the front door and called over his shoulder, "See you tomorrow!"

He jogged down his front walk, yelling at Madison, Lizzie, and Luke to get in the car. The girls slid into the back seat, and Otis made a dramatic leap through the already-open passenger door. It was like something out of an action movie even though no one was chasing him.

"Go, go, go!" Otis said, drumming on the dashboard, full of too much energy.

Luke drove off, and it wasn't until they were stopped at a light on Main Street that what happened finally got through Otis's brain and he started to laugh.

Lizzie and Madison started to laugh in the back seat.

Luke started to laugh so hard he had to actually pull over out of fear of crashing because he couldn't see through his tears of laughter.

Luke took Otis's hand and threaded their fingers together over the center console.

"And you say you never do anything grand or romantic," Luke said, kissing him square on the mouth. "That was by far the most romantic thing I could have imagined."

"Thanks," Otis said.

Madison leaned up from the back seat. "So like how much trouble do you think you're going to be in, when this all shakes out?"

"So much trouble," Otis said, leaning against the headrest and laughing again.

"Do you think it'll be worth it?" Lizzie asked.

Otis squeezed Luke's hand. "I know for a fact that it will be."

"Aw, that's so cute. I love it when you're so cute," Luke said.

An *I love you* was on the tip of Otis's tongue. But he'd save it for a better time, when Madison and Lizzie weren't staring at them from the back seat of the car.

"Well, that's the cutest thing I've ever seen," Madison said to Lizzie in the back seat.

"So darn cute," Lizzie agreed.

"We should probably get the hell out of Dodge before your dad comes after us," Luke said, pulling out of the spot where he'd stopped.

"Oh god, seriously. You should have seen his face as I fled the house. I'm shocked there's not a SWAT team coming after us."

That set everyone off laughing again.

It was going to be a great night.

Chapter 26

Jacinta

Jacinta took her own car over to Kelsey's house for pictures before the prom, mostly because she wanted to be able to drive herself home afterward. Especially now that she was going to the prom alone. She didn't need to drag the night out any longer than necessary.

As Jacinta drove down Kelsey's street, she realized that her mom hadn't even given her a curfew for the night. Jacinta's usual curfew was eleven, but that was when the limo was picking them up from the venue after the prom, so her mom knew that Jacinta wouldn't be home by then.

Jacinta laughed giddily at the thought of the freedom this night had given her. She was wearing a pretty dress and she had no curfew. She could go anywhere.

That thought took her by surprise. Because she'd been looking forward to the prom, even with all her date issues. But now, the idea of not going suddenly felt like the best idea she'd ever had.

When she got to Kelsey's house, there were no available parking spots close by. The limo had arrived and was taking up most of the driveway.

Jacinta drove around the block, and when Kelsey's house came back into view she got to observe the moment Landon saw Emma.

Jacinta was happy that Landon was happy, but suddenly she was even happier at the prospect of just not going. She pulled to the end of the street and looked back, making sure that no one had noticed her car passing. When she felt it was pretty clear, she turned left, away from Kelsey's house, away from the hotel, away from the whole evening.

Toward freedom.

Her phone beeped and booped in the passenger's seat. She knew she couldn't leave them hanging, so she pulled over and sent a few texts without really reading the ones she already had.

One text went to Kelsey, saying they could leave without her and that she wasn't going to make it to the prom. She offered no further explanation, and another little thrill went through her.

The next text she sent was to Landon, saying she hoped he had a great time with Emma.

The third and final text went to her mom, promising she wouldn't get home too late.

Jacinta chewed her lip.

Then she decided to turn off her phone.

The world was her oyster; she could go anywhere as long as she didn't get home too, too late. She could even drive around and then meet up with everyone after the prom. Or she could keep driving. Forever.

The prom had been her dream, but around the time Emma got involved it had started to feel like a commitment that Jacinta wasn't interested in. Jacinta had kept going along with everything because her friends wanted her to. But she didn't have to do things just because she was supposed to. Life didn't have to work like that. She could do something else.

But she really wasn't sure where she should go. She sat at a red light, thinking about her options.

The mall, the diner, and the movies were out. None of them sounded like fun at the moment; she wanted to be outside. She wanted the breeze to ripple through the skirt of her dress.

She drove around for twenty minutes blasting her "get psyched" playlist. What did she want?

The answer was ice cream. Jacinta really, really wanted ice cream.

She decided she'd go to the ice cream place on Main Street and get "dinner." Followed by "dessert" at the pizzeria next door. Eating dessert first was a minor rebellion, but she liked the decadence of it.

Jacinta parked about a block away and walked to the ice cream shop. The breeze blew through the trees and rustled her hair. She had put it up in a ponytail, and her sister had helped her make ringlets with the curling iron, but now she'd let it down and it tickled her shoulders as she walked down Main Street.

She ordered the most elaborate thing on the menu, a banana split, and ate sitting at the café table outside. She watched the cars drive past and thought about where her friends were at that moment. They had probably just arrived at the venue.

As she stood to throw away her empty ice cream bowl and turned to go into the pizzeria, Cameron Wyatt came stumbling out, barefoot.

"Hey," Jacinta said.

"Oh, hey," he said, obviously flustered. "You look nice."

"Thanks," she said. "You look . . . nervous."

He pulled on a pair of socks. "Aren't you supposed to be at the prom with my stepbrother?"

"Well, it's kind of a long story, but I promise I didn't stand him up."

"What happened?" Cam asked, leaning down to tie his shoes.

He seemed like he was in a big rush, but he was asking, so Jacinta decided to give him the abridged version of the story while he continued getting dressed in the middle of the sidewalk.

It turned out he was a pretty good listener.

Cameron

Cameron had watched the clock from behind the counter at the pizza place. It was suspiciously empty for a Friday night, as if everyone in town was going to the senior prom and not just the seniors. There had been a rush of orders between five and six, but now it had completely slowed down.

The clock ticked past seven. The dance had begun and Cameron wasn't there.

He could still make it there without a problem. He'd have to be fast, because if he got there after eight, he wouldn't be allowed in and the venue was a solid half hour away. But he could do it.

The door jangled open at the moment that Cameron considered slipping into the restroom to put on his tuxedo. He couldn't leave the register unmanned, and the only other people working were the chef in the back and a waitress, Heather. Unfortunately, Heather had been on a fifteen-minute break for at least thirty-five minutes.

He really didn't want to stand Laptop Girl up. The anxiety of that thought was enough to make him want to leave the pizza place immediately. But he knew if he ran off like that, the reality was that he'd be fired. He needed the money.

When his replacement finally showed up, Cameron knew he was going to be cutting it awfully close. He ran into the employee bathroom and set the timer on his phone for three minutes. He opened up the garment bag that held his rented tuxedo, but first he closed the lid on the toilet. Tonight was not the night to drop something in it.

Unfortunately, the tuxedo was far more complicated than he could have possibly imagined. The fly on the pants wouldn't work, and the cuffs on the sleeves of the shirt wouldn't button properly.

The timer on his phone went off long before he was anywhere near finished getting dressed. He decided to just keep moving.

He ran out of the pizzeria and right into Jacinta Ramos. He had already come to terms with the fact that he probably wasn't going to make it to prom, so he might as well chat with Jacinta for a minute.

Cameron listened intently as Jacinta told a brief story about Landon's girlfriend, Emma, and her surprise for Landon.

"Emma annoys the crap out of me," Cameron said. He looked at his phone and sighed.

"Seriously, are you okay?" Jacinta asked. "You look a little . . . nauseous."

"Um, well, I'm kind of supposed to be at the prom."

"I kind of gathered that, but you won't be allowed in after eight. And the venue is at least twenty-five minutes away."

"Yes. I'm aware of all of this. But the person who was supposed to relieve me at work ran late. So it looks like I'm not going."

Jacinta nodded sympathetically.

"I was really hoping to make it," Cam said. Although another glance at the clock told him he was shit out of luck. It was already 7:45. His shoulders deflated.

"I'll never get in now."

"It doesn't seem like it," she said. "So did you have a date? Are they going to be super pissed? Can you text them?"

"It's a weird story. I technically don't know who my date is. I kind of thought you might be her for a second. But you're not wearing any lime green."

"Wait, what? Who?"

"It's kind of an embarrassing story. You probably don't want to hear about it."

"Try me," Jacinta said.

"There's a girl, and, um, we've been exchanging messages on one of the laptops in Ms. Huang's class, and I was supposed to meet her tonight at the prom."

Jacinta's jaw dropped.

"I thought maybe you were her, just for a second, but I don't know how you would have known that I was working late at the pizza parlor and wouldn't be at the prom to meet you."

"Why aren't you at the prom?" Jacinta asked, and he could see the moment her mouth caught up with her brain. "Why are you wasting time with me? Why would you stand her up?"

"So you know who it is?" he asked.

"I one hundred percent know who it is."

"Who is it? Can you text her? Do you have her number?"

"No, you dumbass, you have to go to the prom!"

"I can't. Ms. Huang said that they weren't letting people in after eight. There's no way we'll make it there in time. We're both too late to get in."

"But why aren't you there?" she asked again.

"I told you! I had to work late. Somebody called out, and the waitress was late getting back from break, and my boss is a real pain in the ass."

"You could have just left when you were supposed to leave."

"I mean, that's nice in theory, but I need the job. I need the money for college next year. I can't wander off because I have a girl to meet at the prom."

"You're not much of a romantic."

"Says the girl who minutes ago was going to get a slice of pizza instead of going to the biggest dance of her high school career."

Jacinta stood up. "It doesn't matter! We need to come up with a plan! You have to meet . . . Maybe I shouldn't tell you who it is yet. Maybe we still have another option."

"Oh yeah?"

"Yeah," Jacinta said resolutely. "You finish getting dressed and I'll drive."

He shrugged and followed her. He didn't have anything to lose.

Chapter 27

Lizzie

On a scale of one to ten, Lizzie's excitement level was somewhere in the thousands. To quote *Mean Girls*, the limit did not exist.

Madison, Otis, Luke, and Lizzie had arrived at the prom right at seven o'clock. After they found their table, Lizzie took the seat with the best view of the main entrance.

Luke and Otis headed toward the dance floor, but Madison hung back.

"Don't you want to mingle or something?" Madison asked. "The DJ is starting up; why don't we dance?"

"I am going to sit here and wait for Mystery Boy to come in."

"Suit yourself," Madison said. "I think it would be more fun to occupy your mind until eight fifteen, but good luck."

Lizzie was practically bouncing out of her skin with excitement, but she knew that if she went to dance, she'd miss the moment he arrived. And she wanted to see him, whoever he was. Even if they'd promised to meet at eight fifteen, she had a feeling she would know who he was right away. She watched couple after couple come through the balloon arch at the door. To her relief, she did see several groups of singles that had all come in together, so she didn't feel like she stuck out too much.

But there were two things working against Lizzie.

1. Lime green was very popular. Boys were coming in with ties, boutonnieres, even sneakers that were lime green.
2. All those lime green–wearing boys had a date.

She believed in Mystery Boy, but she had some nagging worries.

Why wasn't he early? She was early because she was excited to meet him. What if he wasn't as excited? She stared at the banner above the balloon arch.

A PROM TO REMEMBER! it declared in glittery letters. She hoped it would be a prom to remember for good reasons and not bad reasons.

Her friends came and checked on her a few times, trying to coax her onto the dance floor. She would join them for a song or two, but then always went back to her post, her eyes glued to the door.

As it edged toward eight, Lizzie swallowed down her anxiety. She wasn't usually the type of person to get her hopes up like this.

She spent a lot of time feeling proud, almost smug, about her ability to remain realistic in the face of even the best news, or the biggest hopes and dreams. It all started when Lizzie was eight and her mom told her that she was going to win a family trip to Disney World.

Lizzie dreamed about that vacation every night for a week. She started cutting out everything Disney related she found in old magazines and made a collage. She told her friends about it.

It never happened. Lizzie's mom didn't win. And Lizzie learned from that moment on not to get her hopes up.

But this time, this dance, this boy, had gotten into her head. She had started to allow herself to believe that this might happen. That her big night might be a reality.

To be fair, she did have a little bit of fun even while she waited. Her group of Madison, Luke, and Otis were fun people in general. It wasn't like she was alone, sulking in a corner. They made sure to keep her mind off Mystery Boy.

And she told herself that even if Mystery Boy didn't show up, she might not have the best night of her life, but dammit, she was going to stay and make the most of it. She was too practical to not stay and have dinner and dessert. To not dance in the dress that her mom bought for her by saving a dollar here and a dollar there.

So she danced with Otis. And then she danced with Madison. Then she danced with Luke. And they all danced in a group.

Around eight, Madison snuck her away from the ballroom and gave her the last swig of coconut rum that she had somehow smuggled in.

"A little liquid courage," Madison said as Lizzie downed the last bit and coughed. "Just be cool."

"I'm cool, I'm cool," Lizzie promised. "But how did you get this in here?"

Madison took the empty bottle and shoved it in a faraway trash can.

"I might have stuck it in my underwear."

"Lovely. No wonder it was so warm. And"—Lizzie paused, searching for another word to describe the rum but failing—"and warm."

Madison giggled. They turned and went back into the ballroom, and Lizzie felt a little better. And a lot less bitter.

Along with wondering about Mystery Boy, she was also starting to really wonder where Jacinta was. She marched across the dance floor to Kelsey to ask her, still counting down the minutes and seconds to eight fifteen. It was getting close.

"Is Jacinta okay?" she asked.

"Well, hello there," Kelsey said. "Jacinta is fine."

"Where is she? Wasn't she supposed to be here?"

"What are you, her mom?" Landon asked.

Lizzie rolled her eyes. "No, I was just wondering where she was."

"Ignore him," Kelsey said. "He got stoned on the way here. He can't help being an asshole." Landon's girlfriend giggled next to him.

"Is she stoned, too?"

"No, she's honestly just annoying," Kelsey said, whispering in Lizzie's ear.

"Makes sense."

"Anyway, Jacinta sent me a text, letting me know that she wasn't going to make it to the dance or something, but she never really gave me a reason. She just didn't show up. At least we know she's not dead somewhere."

Lizzie must have looked as horrified as she felt.

"I'm sorry. I shouldn't joke like that," Kelsey said.

Lizzie nodded. "But you're right, I'm relieved to know she chose not to come and that she's not stuck somewhere."

At eight fifteen on the dot, she went to their agreed-upon meeting spot. Maybe she'd missed him coming in, maybe she hadn't noticed some subtle lime green on one of the guys that came in alone. Maybe he was there and she just didn't know it. She stood by the dance floor for five minutes, even timing it on her phone so she would know when to give up.

If he didn't come, all she had to show for this night was a dress she might never wear again, a ticket she wasted money on, and a sinking sensation in her stomach that she had done something wrong, that somehow this was her fault.

When the timer on her phone went off, she had to face the reality of the situation. It was 8:20 and she had been stood up.

Lizzie had let her hope get the better of her.

Cameron

Of course there had been traffic on the way to the prom.

Jacinta was driving as fast as she could now that the lanes had cleared up, but it still felt too slow to Cameron.

"We're so late," he said as he fiddled with his tie in the vanity mirror and tried to watch a YouTube video about tying bow ties at the same time. He honestly didn't understand why they were still trying. They needed a miracle.

Jacinta glanced over at him. "You know there's no shame in a clip-on bow tie."

"Yeah, but the tux rental place just gave me this one. I didn't ask for it or anything."

"I don't think your mystery date would mind if you didn't have a bow tie. She'd definitely understand."

"I want things to be perfect," Cameron said. But that was good news about the bow tie, because he was honestly getting a little carsick trying to look in the mirror while trying to tie it.

"So late," he muttered again, looking at the clock.

"We know we're late. Repeating it won't make us less late. And it's not the point anyway. We're going because you need to get you-know-who's attention."

"She's not Voldemort. You could just tell me who she is."

"And take all the fun out of this?" Jacinta asked. She peeked at her phone while they were stopped at a red light. "I am a little worried that when she realized you weren't gonna show up she left and maybe joined a religion that doesn't allow phones, because it's been twenty minutes and she hasn't responded to my good-news text."

"Can I see what you wrote?"

"Hell, no," Jacinta said, shoving her phone out of his reach. "Then you would see the contact information."

Cameron was nearly bouncing in his seat at the thought that the identity of Laptop Girl was that close at hand.

"What are we gonna do if she left? Do you know where she lives?" he asked.

"I do know where she lives. But we're not going to stalk her. We'll figure it out. She's bound to check her phone at least one more time tonight."

"Before the full indoctrination takes hold," Cameron said.

It took a second, but then Jacinta burst out laughing.

"This isn't worth it," Cameron said, heaving out a frustrated sigh. "She's not going to be that into me anyway. She's probably heard that I sell drugs behind the pizzeria. And Ms. Huang is going to think I'm totally irresponsible."

"Hey, whoa. What's with all this pity party stuff? Ms. Huang is going to understand that you have other responsibilities and you were at work. Voldemort is just going to be psyched you showed up. She'll understand about work, too."

"The Voldemort thing isn't exactly relaxing me."

"You started it," Jacinta said simply.

Cameron had to smile. He almost had no choice. It felt better to smile than to keep worrying in the same thought circles. He couldn't seem to relax his shoulders, like they were creeping up to his ears with each passing minute.

"And for the record, since I didn't address it earlier, no one thinks you sell drugs from behind the pizza parlor. I've never heard anything like that. From anyone."

"That's good news at least." Cameron patted the arms of his button-down shirt, feeling wrinkly and disheveled.

As they pulled into the hotel parking lot, Jacinta looked over at him. "You know, maybe instead of trying to look perfect you should leave the top couple of buttons open and roll your sleeves."

He shrugged and did as he was told as they got out of the car.

"Just calm down," Jacinta said.

"Easy for you to say." He leaned against the hood of her car. "Do you have any other pearls of wisdom?"

She walked up to him and messed up his hair. He'd wet it down in the bathroom, trying to make it look more presentable.

"There," she said. "Now it matches your look."

"What's our next step?" he asked.

"Now we wait," she said, looking at her phone.

Cameron shook his head. "I can't wait. I'm going to try to get in. Maybe no one is watching the door."

Cameron jogged across the parking lot with Jacinta trailing behind him.

When they got to the front door, Mr. Muehler, the shop teacher, was standing there.

"You kids are late," he said.

"But we got held up," Cameron said.

"Unless you were literally held up, at gunpoint or something, and have a police report, I can't let you in. Ms. Huang's orders."

Cameron shook his head, wishing he could somehow persuade this man to let him in. Maybe if he explained it was for true love.

Not that he was in love with Laptop Girl.

And not that Mr. Muehler seemed like the kind of guy that would get all gooey about teenagers in love.

"But he has to get in there to meet someone. Maybe you could go get her for us at least?" Jacinta asked, making her voice as sweet as possible.

"I can't leave my post. You two will sneak in then for sure."

"Please?"

"Doesn't matter because if she leaves the prom she won't be able to get back in and neither will you."

Jacinta looked at Cameron.

"I don't want to ruin her night," he said.

"You two need to move along. No loitering out here."

Before Cameron could argue that Mr. Muehler was technically loitering, Jacinta grabbed him by the arm and pulled him away.

"Come on," Jacinta said. "We have other options."

Cameron huffed out a breath and followed her back to the car.

Chapter 28

Henry

"Why are we still here?" Henry asked Paisley as they swayed on the floor to the slow song currently blasting from the speakers.

"Because we have to stay until the coronation."

"I think we could dance this one dance and leave."

"That doesn't sound like a fun prom."

"I would say all my goals would have been met. One dance. Avoiding Amelia. No public humiliation."

Paisley rolled her eyes. "We're staying."

As far as terrible things go, prom night was not quite as terrible as Henry had assumed it would be.

But in his mind, they had done what they'd set out to do. Upon arriving at the prom, they got their picture taken, and they danced to a slow song. It felt like the night could only go downhill from here.

It wasn't his idea of a great time, but the food was okay and Paisley seemed happy. They danced to every slow song, but Henry drew the line at dancing to fast songs. He didn't know what to do with his hands when he was sitting, and he certainly didn't know what to do with his hands when he was dancing.

There were just some things he wasn't prepared to do.

"Is it time to go yet?" Henry asked.

"I repeat, we have to stay until the coronation," Paisley said, pulling back and twirling under Henry's arm and then forcing him to do the same.

"I'm not much of a twirler," he muttered, glancing around the floor.

"Who are you looking for?" Paisley asked.

"Uh, no one," Henry said.

Paisley stared at him until he felt like she could read his mind.

"Fine, I was looking for Cameron. He said he was coming."

"It's so weird that you guys are talking again."

"I guess."

Paisley let the subject drop as the music changed.

"You're going to have to learn to dance someday," she said as she took his arms and tried to move him to the upbeat music.

"I don't think I do."

"What are you going to do in college?"

"Is there a lot of dancing in college? Here I thought I was supposed to be getting an education and preparing for my career."

"There's a lot of partying in college."

"So?"

242

"You're never gonna go to a party? You're never going to want to dance with someone at a party?"

"I mean, I'm pretty sure I'm an eighty-year-old man in an eighteen-year-old's body, so it seems unlikely to me that I'm going to suddenly catch the dancing bug because I'm at a frat party."

Paisley shook her head and let him go back to the table to sit out the fast song while she danced with Lizzie and Madison. He sat at the table and watched her shake and shimmy on the dance floor. And then he watched other people.

No one seemed concerned with how they looked, but they all seemed to be having a lot more fun than he was.

He would never be cool. He needed to stop trying to be cool.

And with that thought, he joined Paisley on the dance floor. He still didn't know what to do with his hands, so he shoved them in his pockets and tried to swing his hips to the beat.

Paisley helped a little, getting him moving, and the next thing he knew his hands were out of his pockets and he was just dancing. It was probably not the greatest thing to watch, and he would never want to see it on video, and he would definitely never be a contestant on *Dancing with the Stars*.

But he was dancing, at least until Ms. Huang stood up to make an announcement.

The announcement.

"It's that time that everyone has been waiting for. The announcement of the class court and our prom king and queen. I have just a few words to say first."

Henry had a terrible feeling in his stomach. He started to

back away from the dance floor, from the lights, from Paisley. If he moved slowly enough maybe no one would even notice he was leaving.

"I am so proud of this class for taking it upon themselves to shake the usual tradition and add a court to this year's festivities," Ms. Huang was saying.

There were mild cheers and applause from around the dance floor.

Henry inched closer to the door.

"Ladies first!" Ms. Huang said into the microphone. She looked at her card. "This year's prom queen is Amelia Vaughn!"

The cheers and applause were loud as Amelia made her way up to the DJ booth. There wasn't a proper stage, but there was a small rise in that part of the room.

Ms. Huang placed a tiara on Amelia's head and gave her a red rose.

"And your prom king is . . ." Ms. Huang searched the room with a grin. "Henry Lai!" The room erupted into much louder cheers this time. He was apparently the king of the people.

Bile rose in Henry's throat, and he slipped out the back door.

"Where is Henry?" Ms. Huang asked, her voice muffled in the hallway but still clear enough to motivate Henry to move faster.

He headed for a nice, private bathroom stall, figuring that was the one place that Paisley wouldn't be able to follow him.

He just needed a few minutes to himself.

And maybe to throw up a little bit.

Paisley

Paisley walked into the men's bathroom like she owned the place, prepared to tell all the guys who were in there to get the hell out.

As it turned out, perhaps men didn't linger in the bathroom the way women lingered in bathrooms, because it was deserted. Maybe because this bathroom was totally bare bones compared to the ladies' lounge on the other end of the corridor.

For her first men's room experience, Paisley was not particularly impressed.

She walked along the line of stalls, peeking under each one. It was hard to admit, even to herself, but she was actually having a good time at the prom. The decorations were cheesy, and there was a vague wet-basement smell wafting from somewhere, but it was strangely perfect.

She peered under the last stall and saw Henry's sneakers.

Shaking her head, she said, "Henry, I know you're in there. You're the only person at this prom wearing a pair of electric-blue Converse."

There was no answer.

"Please, Henry, at least talk to me."

"Henry's not here. This is the ghost of Henry."

"Oh, come on, Henry, don't make me crawl under this door. You know I'll do it. I have no shame."

"You have no shame because I have all the shame in the whole world. I'm some kind of shame sponge. Why do I feel like garbage for winning something like prom king? Why would this make me want to hide in the bathroom?"

"I don't have answers to those questions," Paisley said, leaning against the white subway tiles across from the stall Henry was in. At least the bathroom was clean. But she really wanted to get back to the prom. She didn't understand the person she'd become over the past hour.

Henry sighed, the sound echoing in the mostly empty room.

"Why don't you come out here and talk to me?" Paisley asked.

"No thanks. That doesn't seem like a good idea."

"Why?" She kept her voice even. The last thing she wanted was for her impatience to get the better of her. He needed a friend and would do the same for her in a heartbeat. Or maybe not exactly the same. She had trouble imagining Henry in a women's bathroom. He would write a supportive and kindly worded note and have someone else bring it to her.

"I can just live in here forever. Someone can bring me food. It'll be great," he insisted.

"Sounds sort of terrible to me. You just have to go out there and dance one dance," Paisley said.

"You say that like it's easy. I can't dance with Amelia. She hates me."

"She doesn't hate you."

"If someone did to me what I did to Amelia, I would hate them."

"Aw, come on, dude. You were in self-preservation mode."

"If anyone else had been crowned queen, I could handle it. But all that attention on top of what I did to her is just way too much. I am not prepared to cope with this. Everyone at school has been talking about it. It's too much scrutiny."

"Who's been talking about you? I'll punch them," Paisley said. "But seriously, you must have realized there was a pretty good chance that she'd be queen."

"I was in denial, Paisley."

Paisley rolled her eyes. "Fine, I know for a fact she doesn't hate you."

"How could you possibly know that?"

Paisley had to think fast. She hadn't mentioned her conversation with Amelia to Henry for several reasons. It wasn't only because of Amelia's threats and her insistence that Paisley follow the girl code. For the record, Paisley didn't even believe in the girl code. But she did believe in karma.

"Um," Paisley said, trying to come up with something logical.

"You have nothing!" Henry yelled.

"Henry, she was obviously interested in you, so she obviously doesn't hate you."

Henry scoffed dramatically.

"She was nice to you, she sent you texts, and she went to your baseball games. She wanted to go to the prom with you, for goodness' sake! And she told people she asked you. All of that adds up to someone who at least sort of likes you. None of that happens on a whim."

"But then I rejected her. So she hates me."

"You rejecting her one time doesn't negate all the nice things she did for you. Maybe you'll be surprised by her niceness."

"You think?"

"Maybe."

"I don't know what to do," Henry said.

"One thing at a time. You just have to come out of the bathroom stall."

The door swung open. "Okay. I can do that."

"Now, I don't want to overwhelm you, but there are only three more steps. Walk back into the ballroom, get your crown, and dance with Amelia. Then we can go home. Exactly like you wanted to all night!" Paisley lifted her hands in a semi-sarcastic cheer. It was hard to be totally un-sarcastic.

Henry banged his forehead against the edge of the bathroom stall.

"Bro, you're gonna hurt yourself, don't do that."

He looked back at Paisley. There was a pink line running down below his hairline. Paisley rubbed at it.

"I'm not good at this stuff, Paisley," he said, walking to the sinks to wash his hands and face.

"You don't have to be good at it; you just have to do it."

"I'm not good at *doing* this stuff," he amended pointedly.

"Look, I don't know what else you need to hear in this moment, but don't you think it's way embarrassing for Amelia to be out there waiting for you in front of everyone? Ms. Huang started announcing the class court, but that's not going to take all that long. And every minute that ticks by it looks like you ditched Amelia alone."

"Ugh," was all Henry said.

"And you know I hate making her look like a victim in all this, but it could potentially mess up her night if you don't go dance with her. This one little dance."

Henry stared at Paisley for a second and then shook his head.

"One dance," Paisley said, holding up her finger for emphasis. "Then home."

"One dance, then home," Henry repeated as they walked out of the bathroom and back to the ballroom.

"You got this, big boy!" Paisley called after him as he walked toward the front of the room.

"Stop calling me big boy!" he shouted over his shoulder before the crowd swept him up and everyone started to clap for their newly elected prom king.

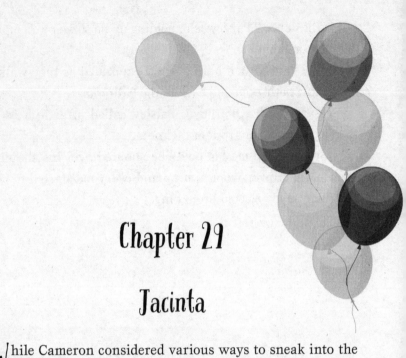

Chapter 29

Jacinta

While Cameron considered various ways to sneak into the prom venue, Jacinta tried to come up with a different plan.

She knew how excited Lizzie was about meeting Mystery Boy. She'd been there the whole year, watching Lizzie smile dreamily at her laptop screen. Jacinta needed to make this right for her friend. There had to be something she could do. They had tried reasoning with Mr. Muehler to no avail, and then tried to sneak in through the front doors of the hotel, but the front desk clerk told them they couldn't get to the prom through the lobby and they had to see the teacher at the side entrance.

At the moment, she and Cameron were standing outside one of the fire exits around the back of the building. He seemed to be considering scaling the wall around the outdoor pool.

"Once you're finished lurking," Jacinta said, "meet me back by my car."

She had a plan formulating, but she needed to get away

from Cameron's anxious energy for a few minutes to really think it through. Her mom was always asking if Jacinta wanted to have people over. She had even offered to have a post-prom pool party at their house. Jacinta always said no, believing that her friends had better things to do.

While that might be true sometimes, it wasn't true tonight.

Tonight she could be the Boss Level Prom Savior just by putting in a call to her mom. She couldn't save her own prom night, but she could damn well save Lizzie and Cameron's night.

Jacinta took a deep breath and called home.

"Jacinta!" her mom said, answering the phone. "I didn't know you still knew how to talk on the phone."

"Very funny, Mom," Jacinta said.

"What can I do for you?"

"Well, remember how you offered to have people over after the prom?"

"Yes, but I thought you were going to the city with Kelsey and your friends."

"I was, but now I don't want to anymore. So there are a few people I might invite over. If that's okay. I know it's last minute."

"Of course it's okay," her mom said. "I'll just go change out of my pajamas."

"Oh, I'm sorry, Mom. I shouldn't have asked. I don't mean to put you out."

"Jacinta! I said yes. Now, what time will your friends be over?"

"Well we're, um, still at the prom," Jacinta said. It wasn't a lie. They were at the prom. It was just that she had never actually gone inside the prom. "So at least a half hour. Probably closer to an hour once we wrap everything up here."

"Oh, that's plenty of time. Don't you worry about a thing. Are you inviting Henry Lai? How many people are you inviting?"

Jacinta took a quick count in her head. Cameron and Lizzie, maybe Madison since she seemed to be wherever Lizzie was. Maybe Jacinta should invite Cora, or maybe not. She probably had something awesome planned after the prom.

"Not too many. Four or five. I don't think I'll be inviting Henry."

"Oh, too bad," her mom said. "Okay, well, see you when you get here."

Jacinta hung up with her mom just as Cameron returned to the car.

He leaned back against the headrest and looked thoroughly dejected. "This sucks."

"It's okay," Jacinta said. "We're going to find you-know-who, and then you guys can come back and hang out at my house. I have a pool."

Cameron looked over at her. "Seriously? Why are you being so nice?"

" 'Cause I know how excited . . ." Jacinta had to stop herself before saying Lizzie's name. "You-know-who was to meet you, and I want to make something good happen on prom night."

"That's awesome," Cameron said. "Thanks, Jacinta."

Jacinta checked her phone again.

"Anything?" he asked.

"Nothing yet, but have faith," Jacinta said, cursing herself internally for not having the number of any of Lizzie's friends. She had texted Kelsey to see if she could help find Lizzie, but hadn't heard anything back. But Jacinta didn't have time now to worry about Kelsey being mad at her for ditching the prom.

She had other things to focus on. She would make this meet up happen for Cameron and Lizzie. No matter what.

Henry

Henry had the worst best luck of anyone on earth. If there was something other people wanted, but he didn't want, it seemed likely that he would get it. Just take for example, becoming starting pitcher of the baseball team, Amelia asking him to the prom, and winning prom king. And these examples had all occurred over the course of the past few months.

Someday he was going to win the lottery and get a Nobel Prize when he least wanted it.

When he got up to the front of the room, he looked at Amelia and she smiled at him.

When Ms. Huang handed him his crown, she said, "Nice of you to join us, Henry." But he could tell she was teasing him. Maybe she thought he had explosive diarrhea; somehow that would be less embarrassing than anyone finding out that he was really just panicking in the men's room.

The room burst into applause as he was crowned. It's a phrase you hear all the time, but that was the only description for the moment, Henry thought.

The DJ queued up the official prom song, and the first few chords of "Sign of the Times" by Harry Styles filled the ballroom. Henry took Amelia's hand and led her to the middle of the floor.

"Sorry I kind of ran off," Henry said, not looking at her. "I'm not really great with attention."

"Paisley explained that to me," Amelia said.

"What? When?"

"I may have cornered her in the bathroom. She never told you?"

"Definitely not," Henry said. He was going to give her a talking-to later.

"Don't be mad at Paisley. I pretty much threatened her not to talk to you about it. But I shouldn't have done that. I'm sorry this whole thing isn't fun for you. I should have noticed sooner that you weren't into it."

"Thanks," Henry said, even though it felt like a weird response to Amelia's sentiment.

"I can tell this is super uncomfortable for you."

She wasn't wrong. Henry felt like his entire body was vibrating with pins and needles.

Amelia rubbed at his arms. "It'll be over in no time."

Henry and Amelia made small talk for a full minute, giving Henry a spurt of confidence. He surprised Amelia with Paisley's twirl move, but her arm went in an awkward direction and the spaghetti strap of her dress popped.

"Oh man," Henry said. "Oh no. I am so sorry!"

She held it together with her fingers and ran from the dance floor with Henry close behind her.

"Come on," Henry said, grabbing her hand. "Ms. Huang has a sewing kit."

"How do you know that Ms. Huang has a sewing kit?" she asked.

"Because I got a big rip in my gym shorts and Coach Stevens sent me to Ms. Huang for help. And she fixed those shorts in no time."

254

"You had a gym shorts emergency?"

"Well, yeah, I didn't want to miss out on badminton day in gym class."

"Boys are so weird."

Amelia and Henry walked down a short hallway. "I know I saw her come this way," Henry said. "She went in this direction after announcing the winners."

They took a left, and there was Ms. Huang, totally making out with the algebra teacher, Ms. Bishop.

"Holy crap!" Amelia said, slapping her hand over her mouth.

"Oh," Ms. Huang said.

"Hey there," Ms. Bishop said.

Henry and Amelia could barely keep it together. Laughter was starting to bubble up in their throats.

"Um," Henry said.

"Um, yes, um," Amelia said.

"Do you need help with something?"

"Oh, we, um, I mean, Amelia, um." Henry snorted. He couldn't keep it in a second longer. "You're like the worst chaperones," he said before doubling over at the waist and bursting into a fit of giggles.

"We really are," agreed Ms. Huang. "Now what can we help you with?"

Amelia showed Ms. Huang her dress strap, and it was fixed in no time thanks to the sewing kit she had in her purse.

"Good as new," Ms. Huang said. She and Ms. Bishop turned around and scurried away from them, probably in search of a new make-out spot.

Amelia turned away and Henry grabbed her hand.

"I have to say." He paused, clearing his throat. "I want to tell you, that I'm sorry about what happened with the prom."

"I get it. You don't have to feel bad."

"But I wanted to thank you for even asking me to the prom."

"You're welcome."

He and Amelia headed back out to the dance floor, but before they got there Amelia started laughing again. "Ms. Huang's face when she saw us."

And then neither of them could stop giggling.

"Oh god, I know we shouldn't tell anyone, but I have to tell someone," Amelia said.

"Maybe we should wait until after graduation at least," Henry said.

"They didn't say we couldn't tell anyone."

"I feel like it's implied when you walk in on the English teacher and the algebra teacher making out."

"Guess I better get back to Drew now," Amelia said with a shrug. "Thanks for the dance, Henry Lai."

"You're welcome, Amelia Vaughn."

Henry practically jogged back to Paisley's side

"Well, that was . . . something," Paisley said.

"It was," Henry agreed. "Maybe not even an entirely bad something." Henry looked around the room, taking in his classmates. A lot of them were slow dancing, but there was a group of girls in the corner belting out the last few lines of the song.

Henry grinned.

"You ready to go, buckaroo?" Paisley asked.

She slipped her arm through his and they moseyed out.

Chapter 30

Cora

On the dance floor, Cora was going through a checklist in her head.

The food had been good. People seemed to enjoy their dinners; no one was complaining.

The DJ was excellent, taking everyone's requests but not talking too much over the music or anything annoying like that.

The coronation drama had people buzzing. Henry Lai never made a scene, so it made the prom just that much more interesting to find that he'd fled elsewhere rather than be crowned prom king. When he came back ten minutes later with his head held high everyone was shocked. They cheered and applauded as he walked up to get his crown. There was just something about an underdog story.

Cora did another scan of the room. The box of keepsake

champagne flutes still needed to be unpacked and put out for people to take. That meant that Henry and Paisley didn't get theirs, so she'd have to be sure to give them to them on Monday.

She nodded to herself, feeling like things were pretty good.

A slow song started, and Jamie came up behind her, wrapping his arms around her waist. "Hey, there. You got time for a dance?"

His mouth brushed against her ear. Not long ago that would have sent shivers down her spine, in a good way. But now. Now it did nothing for her.

She did in fact have time for a dance, though, so she took his hand and they made their way to the center of the floor.

Cora had put her class court crown jauntily on her head.

"It's a good look for you," Jamie said, gesturing with his chin toward the gaudy bejeweled plastic crown.

"Thanks," she said distractedly. She was watching Madison dance in her sparkly jumpsuit on the other side of the room.

"For the record, I didn't really think I'd win king. And good for Henry for winning. He deserved it."

"I agree," she said, moving her hand from one place to another on Jamie's chest. He pulled her in closer.

"You did such an awesome job on prom. Imagine how amazing our wedding is going to be someday."

Cora stopped dancing. "No."

She shook her head and sighed, walking toward the bright lights of the hallway, in need of somewhere to hide. If she didn't get away from him there was no telling what she might do.

Ms. Huang and Ms. Bishop were out there, whispering. For some reason that was a last straw for Cora.

"Who's in the prom chaperoning?" she asked the adults.

They both turned to her, shocked.

"Um, Mr. Muehler?" Ms. Bishop said.

"No one!" Cora said. "No one is in there."

The two women scurried back into the ballroom, and Cora honestly couldn't believe they'd listened to her or that she'd just yelled at her two favorite teachers. This night was something else.

When she turned, Jamie was there. Of course.

"What is it, Cora?" he asked, grabbing her hand as he stepped toward her.

"I love you, Jamie," she said, squeezing his fingers.

He looked so relieved that she almost couldn't finish. "I love you, too."

"But I just . . ." She paused, shaking her head and dropping his hand. "I'm not in love with you. And I want to break up with you."

Her relief was immediate, like all the worry and anxiety she'd been carrying around with her was swept away by saying it out loud to Jamie.

Jamie was shocked; it was etched in the lines of his face. He moved away from her so fast he almost fell over backward.

"You're breaking up with me?" he asked, his eyes flashing with an emotion Cora couldn't quite identify.

"Yes."

"But we're going to the same college. We're going to get married and have kids and open up a little general store in New England."

"We're not getting married, Jamie. I'm so sorry to do this to you here. But I want to break up with you, and I have for a while, and the idea of standing there and agreeing with you about wedding plans felt too much like lying."

"But we're supposed to . . ." He trailed off.

"Are we supposed to?"

"I thought so. I think I'm in shock. Is this what being in shock feels like?" He shook out his hands at his sides.

"Maybe. I'm sorry," she said.

"What the hell, Cora?"

"I'm sorry."

"This really sucks. Couldn't you have at least waited until, I don't know, the prom was over?"

"I have waited!" she said. "I wanted to break up with you weeks ago. But it was always something. I thought I could make it through the prom. But I just couldn't nod and smile through wedding talk. We're eighteen, Jamie."

"I know. I didn't really think we'd get married. I don't know. I like to say stuff like that sometimes."

She crossed her arms.

"And I know how old we are," he said when she didn't respond.

"I need to be on my own. I've been Jamie's girlfriend for too long."

Jamie's hurt expression made Cora want to soften the blow.

"I love you too much not to tell you that I don't love you enough to stay with you forever," she added.

"We could take a break?" he offered. "For the summer? Or even for next year or something?"

Fighting the urge to agree with him, to tell him that maybe someday they'd get back together, was far more difficult than she could have expected. She closed her eyes.

"I don't want to make any promises that I'm not sure I can keep," she said.

Perfect Boyfriend Jamie turned to her with tears in his eyes. He had actual, literal tears in his eyes, and Cora knew in that moment there was no better boyfriend in the world than Jamie. It was good that he was her first. She'd had a good experience.

She gave him a hug, but he didn't hug back.

"I'm so sorry," she said.

"Me too," he whispered, pulling away. "I'm going to go, okay? I'm just. I'm gonna go. I'll find a ride home or whatever. Don't worry about me."

"Okay."

"Of course you won't worry; you broke up with me," he mumbled, shaking his head. He wiped his face. "I gotta go." He was moving sideways so fast away from her that he almost tripped over his own two feet a few times before finally turning his back on her and jogging away toward the front lobby of the hotel.

The urge to follow him was almost as strong as the urge to tell him they could get back together. But she fought it.

She fought it hard.

Luckily Teagan and Josie were right there to stop her.

"We had a feeling something like this might happen," Teagan said.

"So we were sort of lurking around, just in case," Josie said, threading her arm through Cora's.

Cora leaned her head on Josie's shoulder.

"Let's dance," she said.

Otis

Otis was having the BEST NIGHT EVER.

It helped that he'd had quite a bit of Madison's coconut rum. It was the perfect thing to cut the rising panic he felt in his throat every single time he thought about how pissed off his parents probably were. Though the fact that they hadn't stormed the ballroom spoke volumes.

He had only checked his phone once since he left the house and found a single text from his mom. It said, "Have fun tonight. We'll have plenty to talk about tomorrow." He imagined that she had probably thrown his dad's phone into the lake to keep him from yelling at Otis via text, voice mail, Facebook message, FaceTime, or whatever other means he could have come up with.

And really, all that text meant was that they were probably going to cut him off financially and disown him.

"Hey, what are you thinking about?" Luke asked when Otis had been quiet for too long.

"Oh, nothing much. The possibility of my parents disowning me, stuff like that," Otis said as breezily as he could.

"Well, if they disown you, you can come live with me," Luke said.

Otis nodded. Life with the Martinez family didn't sound too bad. And Luke had a car. If they adopted Otis, maybe they would buy him a car, too.

"Are you having fun?" Otis asked.

"Hell, yes," Luke said. "I honestly still can't believe you're here. All because I showed up at your house to throw pebbles and tell you I'd miss you."

"It was too much. I couldn't withstand the pull of prom night. Also I felt completely taunted by your white dinner jacket."

"So fancy, right?" Luke said, brushing a hand down the crisp fabric.

"So fancy," Otis agreed. "I can't believe I'm here, either. I need to drink up these last few hours of freedom before I'm placed in solitary confinement for the foreseeable future."

"Well, we better make this worth your while," Luke said.

Otis danced.

Otis was happy.

Otis danced a lot.

And then he danced a little more.

The leather wing tips that he had stolen from his dad's closet during his rush out of the house crushed his toes and nipped at his heels, but he did his best to ignore it. When they took a quick break for Otis to massage his feet, Luke sighed thoughtfully.

"What are you thinking?" Otis asked.

Luke propped his head in his hand on the edge of the table. "I thought maybe you didn't want to come to this with me, but I guess I was wrong. And I was just thinking that I still don't understand why you were hesitating. Why you seemed like you didn't really want to come when you were willing to totally go against your parents tonight."

Luke didn't look him in the eyes.

"It's kind of a long explanation, but I promise I always

wanted to go to the prom with you. We have all night to talk about the other stuff. I promise."

Luke looked as happy to be sitting there at the table with Otis as he had all night on the dance floor. There was something about how Luke could literally be happy anywhere, anytime that made Otis lean over and kiss him.

"What was that for?" Luke asked.

"Oh, you know, just because," Otis said. Before he could say more, Luke's face wrinkled. He sniffed.

"Do you smell something?" Luke asked.

Otis inhaled sharply, trying to figure out what Luke smelled and doing his best not to make a he-who-smelt-it-dealt-it joke, considering mere seconds ago he was about to maybe tell his boyfriend he loved him.

"Mostly I smell too much cologne and a lot of carpet cleaner. And sweat."

"There's something else," Luke said.

Otis stood up. Now he did smell something, but he couldn't place it.

While he was standing he heard a crack, followed by a whooshing sound from behind him. When he turned back, water was gushing from the wall next to one of the tables. And then another hole opened up, and another, and another, until water was coming from everywhere. Someone started to scream.

"Oh my god," Luke said, standing when he saw the deluge. "What is that?"

"A broken pipe?" Otis offered.

"Why is Amelia Vaughn sitting there screaming instead of getting out of the way?" Luke asked.

Otis hadn't noticed who the screaming person was, but Luke was correct. Amelia sat beneath the spray of water, screaming her head off.

Otis stepped into action, abandoning his shoes under the table and jogging over to Amelia.

He held his hand out. "Come on," he said to her.

"My dress is stuck on the table!" she cried. "This is literally the worst prom ever."

"Oh, for the love," he said, ducking down and finding that yes, her dress was stuck to the table, on a screw, more specifically. He worked the material back around the screw and then yanked.

She stood up and Otis joined her.

"Oh my god, thank you so much!" She grabbed her tiara from the table and ran.

At that point other people, hotel workers and even a police officer, had arrived on the scene and the ballroom was being evacuated.

Otis followed the crowd out of the room and into the parking lot in search of Luke. It was rough seeing as how he was barefoot and he forgot to look for his dad's shoes on the way out the door. He'd just add losing those shoes to the list of reasons he was in big trouble with his parents.

Luke waited for him at the edge of the crowd outside, with the shoes tied together and thrown casually around his neck.

"My hero!" Luke said, giving Otis a kiss on the lips.

"You're my hero for saving those shoes," Otis said, taking them from Luke and sliding them onto his feet.

Chapter 31

Lizzie

Lizzie leaned in to shout-whisper to Madison. "Where are Otis and Luke?"

Madison shrugged and kept dancing. Thank god for Madison. Through the majority of the prom she'd kept Lizzie laughing and dancing and thinking about things besides getting stood up.

She would shake and shimmy her blues away until she got some concrete information about what happened with Mystery Boy. She'd keep dancing for the rest of her life if she had to, just to keep the sad thoughts at bay.

As one song moved into the next, Lizzie heard a crack and a whoosh from somewhere at the perimeter of the dance floor. She tried to stand on her tiptoes to see over the heads of the people around her, but it was no use.

Someone screamed, which seemed odd to Lizzie, that whatever was happening hadn't made more people scream. Lizzie spun in a quick circle but couldn't locate where the sound was coming from.

But then she saw it. There was water gushing from every direction in multiple places along one wall. It was like geysers had spouted from behind the wall and ceiling, and it was raining on one half of the room.

Lizzie ran to their table where she'd left the clutch her mom had lent her with her precious phone inside. It could not drown; that would be one more terrible thing in a night of terrible things.

Madison ran after her, skidding and slipping on the wide legs of her jumpsuit and nearly pulling them both down in a heap. Lizzie grabbed her clutch from the table. It had only gotten dripped on by that point, and she shoved it down the front of her dress just as another geyser broke above her.

This time she did slip, and she and Madison both ended up in a heap on the soaked carpet.

"Did you get your phone?" Madison asked, almost having to yell over the sound of rushing water.

"Yes!" Lizzie said, pointing at her boobs. "Did you?"

Madison shook her head. "It's under the table! I'm gonna crawl over."

Lizzie gave her friend a thumbs-up and watched as Madison crawled over to the table and carefully extracted her purse from underneath. She stood quickly and nearly fell again as she stumbled back to dry land.

Lizzie grabbed Madison's hand and ran for the door with the rest of the crowd, unable to stop laughing even though they were both soaking wet.

After avoiding her phone for hours, Lizzie finally checked it again as she and Madison were being evacuated from the hotel.

She had a missed text from Jacinta.

Jacinta:

> Sorry I didn't make it to the prom.
> But I have a surprise for you.

Lizzie stared at the phone.

The text was from over an hour ago.

What on earth kind of surprise could Jacinta have for Lizzie? What was going on?

Lizzie:

> What kind of surprise?

Lizzie prayed that Jacinta would check her texts sooner than Lizzie had.

Jacinta:

> I can't tell you yet. Is something happening inside the prom?

Lizzie:

> Yes, there are like all these burst pipes.

Jacinta:

> Are you coming outside?

Lizzie:

> Um, yes. I am outside.

Jacinta:

> Cool, let's try to find each other. Walk straight through the parking lot from the main hotel entrance. Because you're really going to love this surprise I have for you.

Lizzie:

> What is it?

The three little dots that indicated someone was writing a message popped up and then went away, popped up and went away.

And then nothing. Jacinta didn't say anything else.

Lizzie showed Madison the texts, and they started looking for Jacinta in the parking lot. They were going to find her.

"Ugh, couldn't she drop a pin or something?" Madison asked. But it was hard to see among the crowd of people being evacuated from the hotel.

And then, to make everything a little more dramatic, the power went out.

"We should split up," Lizzie said, flicking on the flashlight on her phone.

"Yeah, I should probably try to find Otis and Luke, too," Madison said, squinting into the semidarkness around them and walking toward the evacuating crowd.

Lizzie looked back toward the hotel entrance and followed the instructions that Jacinta had texted, walking a perfectly straight line through the parking lot.

Headlights flashed up ahead.

And in front of them stood a boy in perfect silhouette.

Cameron

Cameron stood in front of Jacinta's car and watched the mass of people pour from every set of doors of the hotel. They came from emergency exits, side entrances, and the revolving door at the front of the hotel. There was no way to know which direction Laptop Girl would come from.

"Do you see her?" Cameron asked Jacinta.

She shook her head.

"Can you text her and ask which direction she's coming from?"

If only he could text her himself. If only he could walk into the crowd and find her, but Jacinta had this whole grand reveal planned.

"I did. She didn't respond. It's probably better to stay in one place rather than all of us getting lost in the crowd," she said, as if able to read his thoughts.

Jacinta slipped off her shoes and shimmied onto the roof of her car to get a better look.

"You probably shouldn't stand up there," Cameron said. "You might dent it. And I don't mean that as a dig. Car roofs should not be stood on."

"Excellent point," she said, and then the power went out in the hotel and the parking lot around them.

The streetlight above them flipped off, making it all the more difficult to find anyone, or anything. Jacinta slipped her keys into the ignition and put her headlights on, but all that did was make Cameron feel completely blind.

"Maybe if you would tell me who she is, I'd have a better chance of actually finding her."

"I told her where we were. I'm sure she's coming."

Couples, groups, and families continued to pour from the hotel exits.

"She'll never find us," Cameron muttered.

"Not with that attitude. I'll try to text better instructions."

Before Jacinta could text again, a girl was standing there in her dripping wet prom dress, her shoes in her hands, and her hair falling in her face. She had a lime green ribbon around her neck.

Cameron smiled because he didn't know what else to do. He wasn't even sure she could see him in the brightness of the headlights.

The girl held a hand up to her face. "Jacinta, could you turn off the headlights?"

"Oh god, yeah," Jacinta said, pulling her key from the ignition. "Sorry about that."

"Hey, Cameron," Lizzie said, a smile lighting up her face even in the dark parking lot.

"Hey, Lizzie." Cameron felt shyer than he would have expected. But she knew who he was and didn't run away screaming. That could only bode well for him.

Lizzie stepped up to Cameron. "So, you're Mystery Boy."

"If that's what you call me." His face was growing warm for no particular reason. "I called you Laptop Girl."

"We're, like, generic dollar-store superheroes."

Cameron laughed, a little maniacally thanks to his nerves.

"Like what the heck would Laptop Girl's powers even be? I can leap over laptops in a single bound?"

Cameron shrugged. "Apparently I solve mysteries." He swallowed and tried to ignore the way his heart was thumping in his chest.

"That's cooler than jumping over laptops." She looked at him from head to toe. "I like your lime green shirt."

He looked down at it. "The guy at the tuxedo place called it chartreuse."

"Yeah, that's the same thing."

"I like your, um, thing," he said, reaching up to touch the ribbon at her neck, then pulling his hand away quickly, still unsure of himself.

"Thanks," she said, grinning and touching the same spot he had.

"Why are you so wet?" he asked at the same time she said, "Why didn't you come into the dance?"

"I'm going for a walk," Jacinta said, taking off in the direction that Lizzie just came from. She locked the doors to her car with a surprising *honk* that made both Lizzie and Cameron jump.

"I didn't go into the dance because I ran late at work and Jacinta happened to come in and she yelled at me and drove me here and said we should wait for you out in the parking lot so, now we're here."

"Like every pipe in the entire ballroom burst, and I had to rush into the water to get my purse and my phone," she said, pulling a small black bag out of the top of her dress.

"Wow, that was like magic," he said. "Are you okay? From the harrowing experience?"

"Yeah." She narrowed her eyes at him. "I think I'll recover."

"So," he said.

"What do we do now?" Lizzie asked.

"Um. Well. As it turns out"—he stumbled over his words and then cleared his throat—"Jacinta actually made plans for us. If you're interested."

"I think I am," Lizzie said, a smile spreading across her face.

He smiled back. Maybe this would work out after all.

Chapter 32

Otis

M s. Huang and Ms. Bishop were quickly ushering the students into the corner of the parking lot. There was still technically another hour and a half left of the dance, but that didn't seem particularly important at the moment. Especially now that the power had gone out, it seemed like the prom was effectively over.

As the students stood in the parking lot, Ms. Huang tried to take a head count.

"Why?" Madison asked, coming from the other direction. "In case someone is drowning in there? Wouldn't you notice something like that?"

Madison, Otis, and Luke stood in a group, unsure what to do.

"Where's Lizzie?" Otis asked, but before Madison could answer a firefighter walked past and Luke got his attention.

"Sir, excuse me, I'm sorry to interrupt your work, but my boyfriend and I smelled gas or something right before the pipe burst."

"Yeah," Otis chimed in, not having anything to add but wanting to support Luke's assertion.

The firefighter nodded. "Thanks for the information."

Otis nearly swooned. There was something about firefighters.

As the firefighter walked away, Jacinta approached their little group.

"Hey, I don't know if you guys heard, but I'm having a party," she said. "Bring whoever. Everyone's invited."

"Your mom's cool with having so many people over?" Otis asked.

"Well, I was having a couple people anyway. And then I called her after the whole flood thing to see if I could have more people over." Jacinta shrugged. "I don't know if she realizes just how many I mean this time. But anyway. Bring whoever. I'm going to go see who else is looking for somewhere to go."

After she walked away, Luke turned to Otis.

This was the moment. The deciding moment, where Otis took door number one, a hotel room, or door number two, being a disappointing boyfriend.

He'd felt closer to Luke at the prom than he ever had, nearly saying *I love you* and being so physically close on the dance floor.

Maybe he could explain to Luke when they were alone what all his worries were about. Luke would listen. Luke loved him.

Before Otis could say anything, Luke took the reins.

"Do you maybe want to . . ." He paused, clearing his throat.

"If you still do," Otis said before he could finish, feeling more confident in this decision by the second.

"We kind of have a hotel room," Luke said, taking Otis's hand and turning to Madison.

"Ohhh, right. I remember hearing something about that. I also remember being invited. But I'll allow you to go alone together. If that's what you want," Madison said.

Otis raised an eyebrow at Luke and shook his head in faux exasperation.

"I can't believe you invited Madison to our post-prom hotel room!" Maybe this wasn't the intimate situation that Otis had been envisioning and worrying about all these weeks.

"Only when it seemed like you weren't going to make it to prom! It was too late to cancel the room."

"Well," Otis said. "Sure you can still come if you want to. Obviously."

"Guys!" Madison yelled. "I'm joking. I'm going to Jacinta's. You need some alone time. Have fun, boys. Be careful. Don't do anything I wouldn't do. All that jizz. I mean jazz!"

Otis's eyes went wide and he shook his head at Madison.

She cleared her throat and stifled a laugh. "But you just have to wait a hot second before running off. Because Lizzie and I both have stuff in your car."

Madison followed them over to grab her and Lizzie's things.

"Do you want us to wait until you find her?" Luke asked.

"Definitely not," Madison said. "There's literally a hundred people here who could drive me to Jacinta's. I'm not even a little worried."

Otis and Luke looked at each other.

"Go!" Madison insisted.

And who were they to disagree?

Paisley

Playing video games back at Henry's house was much more Paisley's speed. Though there was a feeling that she couldn't quite shake, like she should have socialized more at the prom.

Being home was definitely more Henry's speed, too. He'd calmed way down after the whole bathroom thing, but it took until he was out of his tuxedo for him to shake off that last edge of anxiety.

"This is so much more comfortable than my dress," Paisley said, gesturing at her T-shirt. She'd changed into one of her *It's not you, it's prom* T-shirts as soon as they'd gotten to Henry's.

Before Henry could respond, his mom came in the room holding her phone. "Did you hear about what happened at the prom?"

Henry and Paisley looked at each other and shook their heads.

Henry's mom gave them the brief version and then continued. "Jacinta's mom called to tell me what happened and to say that she hoped you were okay. I said you've been home for an hour. She said you should come over and join the party."

"Um, no," Henry said. "No thanks."

"Suit yourself," Henry's mom said with a shrug as she turned and left the room.

"Dude," Paisley said. "What is your problem?"

"We can't go. That's a pity invite from Jacinta's mom to my mom. It has nothing to do with Jacinta or me or you. They do this all the time. Jacinta and I have this unspoken agreement to not let our moms interfere."

Paisley looked at him.

"Don't give me that look," he said.

That just made her look at him harder.

"What?"

"We have to go," she said. "Come on. Turn this crap off. We have things to do."

"Nah, not really," Henry said.

"Come on, Henry."

"I thought you hate everyone."

Paisley shrugged. "Turns out I made some snap judgments. Turns out I might miss people. Maybe they're all not terrible."

"Oh. You mean like Amelia?"

"No, she's terrible."

"I mean that you talked to her about me."

"Oh right, right. I did that. But she yelled at me to never tell you. I can't believe she brought it up. That's a little bit two-faced, come to think of it."

"See? People are the worst. You're right to be wary of them."

Paisley thought about that for a second. "They are. They can be. But I bet Amelia will not be at Jacinta's house, and I think we should go. And maybe prom wasn't as terrible as I thought, and I kind of want to have one last hurrah with a bunch of crazy, maybe slightly drunk, soaking-wet people who I might not ever see again after graduation."

Paisley looked at her friend and did her best to read his

mind. But then she looked away. Maybe she didn't really want to go too deep into the mind of an eighteen-year-old boy. Even if that boy was Henry.

"Fine," he said without any further prodding. "But this feels pathetic. Going to a party thrown by someone only because their mom invited us."

"You're not pathetic. You're with me."

Henry rolled his eyes. "My mom will force us to take something with us, like soda or Rice Krispies Treats, and we'll look dumb."

"I won't look dumb. I never look dumb. And I love Rice Krispies Treats."

He crossed his arms.

"This is pretty much our last chance to hang out with everyone like this. Let's not skip it."

"Yeah, but there's still the problem that her mom invited me through my mom. Jacinta didn't invite us."

His phone pinged at that moment. He looked at it.

"It's a text from Jacinta."

"Oh, that's weird."

"Kind of feels like a sign," Henry said.

"Well, don't just sit there staring at it, read the message."

He unlocked his phone. He was taking for-freaking-ever, so Paisley lunged at him and grabbed it.

"Hey, what are you up to?" Paisley read, leaning away from Henry as he ineffectively tried to grab his phone back. "Everyone is coming over to my house. You should, too. I think we might go swimming if it's not too cold. Bring Paisley, too!"

Paisley swatted Henry's hand away. "Totally. Can't wait," she texted back, saying the words out loud. "And send."

Henry buried his face in his hands. "This is the worst!"

"It's not. I promise it's not. This is the best."

"Do I really have to go?"

"Well, no. You don't. I just think it's good to push your boundaries sometimes. And that you might have fun. Jacinta's house shouldn't be too far out of your comfort zone. And I'll be there."

"It's still the worst," Henry said.

"It really isn't. Now stop being dramatic, go get your bathing suit, take me home to get mine, and let's get our asses over to Jacinta's house."

"Fine," Henry grumbled. He pretty much grumbled the entire way there.

"This is going to be fun. I promise," Paisley said, patting him on the back while also dragging him in the direction of the Ramoses' backyard. She had super strength when she needed it. It came in handy when she had to force Henry to do things he didn't want to do.

The yard was already pretty crowded. At least half their class was there. Paisley was impressed.

"Cam's here," he said, surprised.

"You should talk to him."

"Maybe."

"Well, talk to someone," Paisley said. "Besides me. That's your assignment for the evening."

"Okay. I will talk to Cam. And I will talk to . . ." He paused, looking around the yard. "Jacinta, obviously. And then I'm allowed to leave."

"That's entirely fair." Paisley extended her hand to shake on it, and Henry took it, giving one firm pump.

And with that, she left him to fend for himself. Though she did check on him a few times. He seemed to actually be having a good time.

Paisley talked to everyone at the party, one by one. People that she hadn't talked to in years. People she hadn't even wanted to talk to in years. She got an unexpected number of compliments on her *It's not you, it's prom* shirt.

High school was ending, and she might never see them again. She was okay with that, but she liked the idea of closure. One last conversation, one last laugh, and one last night together before the end of the year.

And eventually, she decided, she might even miss these people.

Eventually.

Chapter 33

Cameron

Lizzie and Cameron were quiet on the way to Jacinta's house, and quiet when they got there, quiet as they helped her mom set up a table for snacks and drinks, and then they were quiet while waiting for everyone else to arrive.

And then they separated for a while so Lizzie could change out of her dress. When they found each other a little later on, it was like seeing each other again for the first time. At least, that's how it felt to Cameron.

"Hey," he said.

"Hey," she said.

They stood there mostly looking at the ground, but sometimes sneaking glances at each other.

"I liked your dress," Cameron finally said. "I'm sorry it got soaked." Lizzie had a bag in Luke's car, prepared for the hotel room slumber party, so at least she had clothes to change into after her dress got soaked. Cameron had changed back into the jeans and T-shirt he'd had on for work earlier.

"Thanks," Lizzie said.

"I'm sorry I didn't show up," Cameron said. "I know I said it earlier, but I really just want to say it again, slower this time. I don't even really have a great excuse, but I was working, and it got later and later. I should have tried harder to get a message to you or something. I shouldn't have stood you up. That was very not cool of me."

"I mean, you did get a message to me, through Jacinta."

"Right, yeah."

"Did you know who I was?"

He looked at her, finally meeting her eye. "Definitely not. Jacinta didn't even tell me who you were. She made me wait in the parking lot while you found us."

Cameron looked around and realized that the backyard had been slowly filling up around them. The news of the after-prom party had spread with the demise of the prom. He tried to find Jacinta, to catch her eye, to smile, to thank her for putting this together.

"I was worried when you didn't show up it was because you knew who I was."

He shook his head. "I really did try. We just couldn't get in after eight. I couldn't leave the pizza place without getting fired, and time just got away from me."

Lizzie nodded. "I get it."

"God, I'm so freaking nervous," Cameron said, wiping his forehead.

This time Lizzie laughed. "Why?"

"I just want to make a good impression. And I already

messed up so bad by not showing up to the prom. I figure I'm working from like down here," he said, then he gestured with his hand, down at floor level. "And I want you to, like, not hate me."

"I don't hate you."

"I'm so sorry I didn't show up. I know I could apologize like a million times."

She put her hand on his arm. "It's okay. I'm really not mad."

"How?" he asked.

"I wanted you to be there, of course. I was disappointed and pretty bummed out. But, like, you didn't do anything that bad. Hearing you explain yourself, it's not like you purposefully skipped out. You worked late, you got held up."

He blinked hard a couple of times and shook his head.

"Next time you'll have my number, and you can let me know if you have to work late," she said.

He broke into a huge grin. "You'll give me another chance?"

"Of course! Why wouldn't I? God, you made this whole year bearable, you realize that, right? Like I'm not just going on what I know about you from tonight. You were like my saving grace half the time. Coming in at the end of long days at school to make me laugh last period."

"Oh, last period," he said. "I had English first period."

"I'm really surprised it's you," Lizzie said. They had finally moved out of the center of the patio and found a pair of seats in the corner, away from the action where they could talk.

"I'm sorry. Did you hear that I deal drugs behind the pizza place?"

"No, I did not hear that," she said. "Who said that?"

"Somebody heard it somewhere, I guess," he said.

"I never heard it."

"Okay, cool. Good. I feel better." He wiped his hands on his pants.

"This was really awesome of Jacinta's parents to let everyone come here like this."

"Yeah, it's super awesome of them. We should send them flowers or an Edible Arrangement or something."

"Me and you?" she asked, clarifying.

"Me and you," he said, taking her hand and squeezing.

Jacinta

Jacinta felt like the belle of the ball. Everyone kept coming up to her and thanking her for putting together such a great last-minute party.

Otis's friend Tag approached. She wasn't sure she'd ever actually spoken to Tag before, but he hooked his arm around her neck.

"Bro," he said. "Thank you so much for this. I had like zero after-prom plans, and when the walls exploded I figured my night was over. Which is just so dumb, you know?"

"Totally." She pulled away because damn, his arm was heavy.

"Turned out you had my back," he said, holding his fist up.

She bumped it with hers, feeling awkward. "Uh, you're welcome."

"I grabbed the box of plastic cups from the hotel," he said.

"I don't know what that means," Jacinta said.

"You know, the prom-to-remember cups."

"Oh, the keepsakes."

"Yeah, I rescued them. So you could give them out here. 'Cause, dude, it was definitely a prom to remember, right?"

"Totally," Jacinta said, the irony not lost on her that she was going to get stuck with hundreds of champagne flute keepsakes for a prom she didn't even attend. Maybe she'd return them to school on Monday, or maybe she'd make them disappear so one less class would have to use the aging theme.

He pulled an airplane bottle of vodka out of his pocket. "A gift for the hostess."

"Oh, no thanks. My parents are actually home, and they will be super pissed if they find out we were drinking. So you should probably put that away."

He raised his eyebrows and shoved it back in his pocket. As he turned away, he held a finger to his lips, a silent promise that he wouldn't tell anyone about his own liquor, she assumed.

After that bizarre exchange, Jacinta couldn't stop smiling. For once she was the main character in her own life; she'd finally found a leading role that she felt good about.

Kelsey and Landon walked in around eleven with their dates after having gone home to change and grab their bathing suits. When they heard about Jacinta's party, they had decided not to go to the city.

Kelsey walked right up to Jacinta. "Thank you, again, for doing this. And I'm so sorry about the prom."

"You don't have to be sorry. I didn't want to go."

"No, I totally understand. I kind of forgot that you might not have fun at the dance. And holy crap! I can't believe you helped with the surprise for Landon! How could you keep that a secret from me?"

As if on cue, Landon popped up in the middle of their conversation. He hugged Jacinta hard.

"Thank you so much," Landon said. "Emma told me that you made sure she'd be able to go to the prom with me, and I totally appreciate it. It wouldn't have been the same without her."

Jacinta worked hard to keep her nostrils from flaring. Even though she felt totally over the Emma issue, apparently she couldn't stop involuntary physical reactions. Her nostrils might flare at the mention of the name Emma, any Emma, for the rest of her life.

"You're so welcome."

But it was hard to hold on to whatever was left of her hurt feelings when Emma swooped in and hugged her just as tight as Landon had. Jacinta had done a good thing, no matter how much it annoyed her. She had helped people and made them happy.

And that's what a good supporting character is supposed to do, but sometimes you need to be the one in the spotlight. For once, Jacinta had chosen herself, and it was good to know that things didn't fall apart just because she didn't go with the flow. It was better than good, it was relieving, it meant that maybe she'd be able to do this again in the future, to leave her comfort zone and say no to events that didn't interest her.

Landon, Mike, and Emma wandered away to find some drinks.

"This is a really good party," Kelsey said.

"I know, right?" Jacinta said. "Kind of shocking. Sucks that it took me until senior year of high school to realize I'm kind of good at planning stuff. Maybe I would have spoken up more during prom committee."

Jacinta's conversation with Kelsey was followed by what felt like a million more. Madison, Paisley, Margie Showalter, Cora, Josie, and Teagan. The sheer number of people who'd shown up at her house shocked Jacinta.

The highest echelon of popular kids seemed to have opted out. Amelia Vaughn and her lackeys weren't there, for example, and neither were many of the guys from the football team.

But aside from that, it seemed like everyone had decided to go to Jacinta's.

She hadn't just saved prom for herself, she'd saved it for her graduating class.

That's not something a background character does.

That's the move of a Boss Level Prom Savior.

And Jacinta couldn't stop smiling.

Chapter 34

Henry

After Paisley wandered off, Henry made a beeline for Cameron. Henry was holding a tray of Rice Krispies Treats that his mom had somehow managed to throw together in the ten minutes that Henry had spent looking for his bathing suit.

"Oh man. Can I get one of those?" Cam asked, gesturing toward the tray.

Henry grabbed one and handed it to Cameron.

Cam sighed contentedly. "I haven't eaten all night. Thanks for this."

"You're welcome."

The two boys stood in silence for a minute while Cameron's jaws were glued shut by marshmallow-y goodness.

"I'm so sorry I didn't make it to the prom," Cam said. "I know I said I'd be there to cheer you on with the prom king stuff."

"It's cool," Henry said. "I was wondering where you were."

"Yeah, I probably should have texted or something. But I had like the craziest night."

"Oh yeah? Did you meet the girl from the laptop thing?" Henry asked.

"I did. It was Lizzie Hausner. She's inside changing out of her dress."

"Huh," Henry said. "I didn't have a guess who it was. But I feel like Lizzie makes sense."

Cameron nodded. "Anyway. I hope it wasn't too terrible."

"Confession. I may have hidden in the bathroom when Ms. Huang announced my name."

"That sounds about right for you. Like when you hid under the table while everyone sang "Happy Birthday" at your seventh birthday party."

"You remember that? Man, I still want to hide under the table when people sing "Happy Birthday." Guess that's something I'm not going to grow out of."

Cam shrugged. "It's all part of the Henry Lai experience."

As Lizzie came out of the house, Henry smiled at her before fist bumping Cameron and moving on. He didn't need to play third wheel to anyone tonight.

After his conversation with Cameron went so well, Henry decided to track down Jacinta. It took longer to find her than he would have guessed. As he walked around the yard in search of Jacinta, he handed out Rice Krispies Treats along the way, interacting with more people than the two he had promised Paisley. Even if he did kind of feel like a cater-waiter.

Finally Henry found Jacinta in a gaggle of girls in the far corner of the yard. He lurked around for a few minutes and almost decided to try again later, but then Jacinta caught his eye.

"Hey, Henry," she said. "I wasn't sure if you would come." The group around her dispersed.

"Yeah, Paisley talked me into it."

"I had a feeling she might."

"My mom made me bring these, but I passed most of them around already."

"Thanks. We could always use more food." Jacinta took the tray from him and stuck it on a nearby table where a few people quickly descended on the remaining squares.

Jacinta and Henry chatted for a while about what happened at the prom, about how and why they both missed the big flood.

"I thought you should know that before you texted, your mom called my mom to invite me over."

Jacinta sighed and put a hand over her eyes. "They're monsters. They're never going to let this go."

"It's very possible that they never will." He shoved his hands in his pockets. "I just wanted to thank you for having everyone over."

"You're welcome."

He scanned the yard, watching his classmates have fun together. "It's a really good party."

"Thanks. Turns out I'm not half-bad at this kind of thing."

"I think you're probably not half-bad at all kinds of things." He shook his head. "That was a really awkward sentence."

Jacinta shrugged. "I appreciate the sentiment."

"Well, just so you know, you have a standing invitation to come hang out with Paisley and me whenever. No mom interfering necessary."

"Cool."

"I'll let you get back to your guests," Henry said.

"Make sure you take one of the champagne glasses from the prom!" Jacinta said. "Please don't leave me with two hundred plastic champagne flutes emblazoned with the phrase 'A Prom to Remember'."

Henry smiled and gave her a thumbs-up.

She waved and Henry walked off in search of Paisley, and the aforementioned champagne glasses, only to find her in the middle of a game of pool volleyball. She hopped out of the pool to talk to him when he called her over.

"You do know that you hate volleyball, right? Like when we play volleyball in phys ed all you do is complain and try to get out of it."

"Maybe I like any pool-related version of sports."

"I would like to watch you play water polo someday."

"Maybe in college. I have a feeling college-Paisley is going to be a fascinating individual."

"Well, does high school–Paisley want to leave? 'Cause it's been an hour. And high school–Henry is seriously ready to go."

She wrinkled her nose. "Would you hate me if I stayed?"

"Of course not."

"I'm gonna stay, then. I think I might even sleep over. A bunch of girls are, and it sounds kind of fun."

"I don't even recognize you anymore."

"I don't even recognize myself," Paisley said, jumping back in the pool. "I'll text you in the morning."

With that Henry took one more look around the yard, taking a mental picture of this bizarre night.

When he got home, he took a shower and crawled into bed,

exhausted from not only the long day but also all that socializing. He needed several weeks of alone time to recharge.

When he checked his phone one last time, he had a message
from Amelia.

"Is there really a party at Jacinta Ramos's house tonight?"
it said.

Instead of answering, Henry rolled over and fell asleep.

He'd text her in the morning.

Maybe.

If he felt like it.

Otis

"I can't believe we're here," Otis said, lying next to Luke on the
bed. They were still mostly clothed and had only just gotten in
a few minutes ago, having had to wait until Luke's cousin took
over his shift at the front desk. Otis had only shed his wet jacket
and Luke had done the same.

"I can't believe it, either," Luke agreed.

Otis flipped on his side to look at Luke. "I was really scared
to come here with you when you first mentioned it because I
didn't know what you wanted from me."

"Wanted from you?"

Otis rolled his eyes. "Like we've only gone so far, and I was
scared of, like, what a hotel room meant to you. I wasn't sure
what I was ready for."

"You could have told me that!"

"You were so confident!" Otis shot back. "I felt weird and
wrong for not being as confident as you."

"You are weird. But you're not wrong. You're never wrong for how you feel. I mean, nobody talks about this," Luke said. "We don't talk about this stuff. But I definitely can't imagine my dad having a gay sex talk with me. So of course it's kind of scary and unknown. They barely cover straight sex in school."

"And even then everyone knows what straight sex entails, but like gay sex is so completely taboo."

"Which inherently makes it more scary. I get it. But you could have talked to me about it. You could have said, 'Yo, Luke, dude, my man. I am scared shitless about all the sweet gay loving.'"

"That doesn't sound like me."

"It sounds like you a little bit."

Otis grinned.

"There are those teeth I love," Luke said, touching Otis's chin. "Anyway, we don't have to do anything you don't want to do. Tonight or ever. Obviously. Of course. Always."

"Obviously. Of course. Always," Otis repeated. "So now what?"

"Whatever you want."

"Maybe a little TV might be nice," Otis said.

"Sure." Luke turned on the TV and flipped through the channels, stopping for a minute here or a minute there. Otis rolled over and leaned his head on Luke's shoulder, enjoying the domesticity.

After fifteen or twenty minutes, when Otis's pulse had calmed down and his brain felt less fuzzy from the adrenaline of the whole night, Otis said, "Or maybe no TV."

Luke looked at him.

"It seems kind of silly to have this room and only use it to watch TV."

Luke clicked off the set. "Good point. Very fiscally responsible."

"I think I need a shower. I feel like there was gross soot and dust in all that water at the hotel."

"Go for it. There are extra towels on the shelf in there," Luke said as he picked the remote back up.

Otis pressed his hand on Luke's chest. "Or, I mean, it might be fun if you came with me or something."

Luke sat up. "Oh. I could do that. I could totally do that. I know how to shower."

Otis grabbed Luke's hand and pulled him toward the bathroom as Luke shucked his shirt off along the way.

The door closed behind them with a snick.

Chapter 35

Cora

Much later on that night, Cora was camped out on the floor of Jacinta's family room. Pretty much everyone had left except for her, Teagan, Josie, Madison, Paisley, and Kelsey. And Jacinta obviously.

The conversation had turned to online dating and how Madison had recently tried it out. Cora was sitting next to Madison and hung on every word she said.

"Are we even allowed on dating websites?" Jacinta asked, as if the idea had never even occurred to her before. It had never occurred to Cora, either.

"I'm eighteen," Madison said, as if that solved the whole problem. "I figured I might as well give it a shot. There are zero interesting girls at our school. Zero interesting out girls at least. I have a feeling there are a few hidden pockets of lesbianism, but I'm kind of still working on my gaydar."

"Does that really exist?" Josie asked.

"I don't know," Madison said, her voice less confident. "I'm pretty new to all this dating stuff. I've known I liked girls since probably sixth grade, but I only recently got into the idea of doing something about it."

"Isn't that young?" Kelsey asked, but her voice wasn't judgmental, just curious. Cora hoped that Madison could hear her tone and not be offended.

"You know, I've thought about this, and people act like there's a magical age where the switch flips and you know your sexuality. But if Cora and Perfect Boyfriend Jamie started liking each other in seventh grade, then why is it so unbelievable that I realized I was into girls around then?"

"I guess the gossip hasn't made it all the way around," Cora said, rolling her eyes. "But I broke up with Perfect Boyfriend Jamie."

Everyone turned to stare at her, except for Jacinta, who she'd confessed this tidbit to in the middle of the parking lot, and Josie and Teagan, who were there when it happened.

"I wondered where he was all night," Madison said. "Well, my point still stands. And now I need to know why you broke up with him, because I am nosy."

"We were just different. We wanted different things. We've been together for so long I don't even know what it's like to not be Cora and Jamie, which is so stupid when you think about it," Cora said. Then she took a deep breath. "And honestly, lately I've been kind of wondering if I was bi. And if I stay with Perfect Boyfriend Jamie forever, I might not get to explore that part of myself."

Madison's eyes went wide for a brief second, and then she nodded. "That's cool."

"I don't know if it is or not," Cora said. "I only started talking about it, and it kind of feels like I'm lying since I'm not sure. I'm still trying to figure it out."

"You're questioning," Kelsey said. "Isn't that part of what the *Q* is for in LGBTQ?" She turned to Madison like she was the guru.

"Yeah, queer or questioning," Madison agreed. "That's allowed."

Everyone else in the room nodded and voiced their support of the idea.

"Questioning," Cora said. "I like that."

Lizzie

It had been a long night.

A long day.

A long week.

A long year.

But somehow it all led to Lizzie and Cameron in the town park in the middle of the night.

He offered to drive her home as the party wound down, but first they had to walk back to his car at the pizza place, which luckily wasn't too far from where Jacinta lived. Lizzie wasn't ready for the night to end yet anyway. She didn't want the magic to be over before she had inhaled every last bit of it. So that's what she did as they walked along the path by the pond.

She took a picture in her mind of the evening and did her best to document it via all five senses.

"What are you thinking about?" Cameron asked.

"About how we got here."

"Jacinta," he said with a grin. "It's mostly Jacinta's fault from what I can gather."

"Thanks, smart-ass," she said, swatting him in the side.

He grabbed her hand and they continued their walk. Technically the park was closed between dusk and dawn, but they were feeling rebellious.

"It is kind of amazing that we went to school together forever and this is how we ended up," Lizzie said.

"It's amazing that we never talked, at all, ever."

"Life is weird."

"I was so worried we wouldn't like each other when we met in real life."

"Me too," Lizzie said. "I thought for sure you'd take one look at me and head for the hills."

"I would never do that," he said simply. He didn't ask why she thought he'd head for the hills. She liked him for not asking why.

They paused in the path.

"Thanks for showing up in the end," Lizzie said as they sat down on a bench near the pond. It was so quiet, like they were the only people in the world.

"Thanks for not being mad." He chewed his lip for a second, staring out into the pond and then looking back at her. "I guess we really should get out of here before someone calls the cops on us or something."

Cameron stood and extended his hand to help Lizzie off the

bench. Her heart raced even though they'd been holding hands all night. This time it felt different. She looked at Cam's lips.

The moment was too perfect. The pond, the moonlight, the soft breeze teasing at the back of her neck, it was like everything was telling her to take a chance.

She closed her eyes and leaned in, just brushing her lips to his at first. But then he responded in kind and they kissed.

It was perfect.

Cameron wrapped his arms around her waist, and it felt so good to be close to him. She moved her arms up around his neck and drew him in a little closer.

It was like something out of a dream.

Exactly the way Lizzie had expected prom night to be, if she'd let herself get her hopes up.

She didn't want it to end. But then Cameron inhaled and pulled back.

"Sorry, I hope that was okay," he said.

"Okay? Didn't I start that?" she asked with a grin.

"Guess it was a mutual thing," he said.

"You should probably take me home before I decide to make out with you all night long," Lizzie said, grabbing his hand and pulling him in the direction of Main Street and the pizzeria.

"But we could make out all night long," he insisted.

"Or we could go home and sleep and do something tomorrow."

"I like that idea."

So did Lizzie.

Epilogue

Jacinta to Cora

I know you just left, but any chance you're hungry? I'm thinking about getting people together for brunch. Or really more like lunch. Or maybe at this point it's really just early dinner, considering how late it is.

Cora to Jacinta

I honestly have no idea what time it is.
I think I slept-drove home.
But yeah, I could definitely be down for some diner food.

Jacinta to Cora

Awesome.

Jacinta to Cora

I'll bring along all the "A Prom to Remember" keepsake glasses so everyone can drink their orange juice out of them.

Cora to Jacinta

I still can't believe they showed up at your house.

Jacinta to Cora

Seriously. Thanks for nothing, Tag. Everyone in my family is going to be living that Prom to Remember lifestyle, drinking out of those glasses for years to come. Maybe I could convince my sister to use it as her wedding theme.

Cora to Jacinta

Good luck with that.
I'll see you at the diner in like an hour?

Jacinta to Cora

Sounds good! I'll see who else is around.

Cora to Jacinta

Me too.

Jacinta to Cora

Cora to Madison

So I know we just spent eight million years together, but Jacinta and other people are going to the diner in about an hour. Want to come?

Madison to Cora

Hell yeah! I'll see what Otis & co are up to.

Cora to Madison

Can't wait ☺

Madison to Otis

Cora broke up with Perfect Boyfriend Jamie last night, and I'm going to make her fall in love with me this summer. Mark my words. Also are you hungry?

Otis to Madison

I'm imagining you accidentally texting that to Cora and then you dying of embarrassment. I could eat. Then I have to get home and face the music. But I might as well have a last meal beforehand.

Madison to Otis

Good. I need a third-party observer to tell me if it's worth it to pursue Cora.

Otis to Madison

OH! Cora's going to be there!
That makes so much sense now.

Madison to Otis

Be there or be square.
See you in an hour.
I'm gonna go shower. Ask Luke
to text Lizzie.

Otis to Lizzie

Hi. It's Otis from Luke's phone. Luke is
in the shower and so is Madison.

Lizzie to Otis

Together? In the shower?

Otis to Lizzie

No. Sorry. I see how that's confusing.
I was just trying to explain why I'm
texting you and not them.

Lizzie to Otis

Got it.
What's up?

Otis to Lizzie

Everyone is going to the diner in like an hour.
And I mean, like pretty much everyone.

Lizzie to Otis

Oh cool. Can you guys pick me up?

Otis to Lizzie

I'm sure we can manage that.

Lizzie to Paisley

Hey hey. Want to go to the diner?
Also who's working today? I didn't forget
to go in or something did I?

Paisley to Lizzie

I always want to go to the diner. Also I'm still
sitting around Jacinta's because I'm too lazy
to go home and she's too gracious to kick me
out, so I heard about the diner plan and
was going to text you about it. But again.
The laziness got the better of me.
And I think John is working pretty much
all weekend so we could have off.

Lizzie to Paisley

Oh right. That guy is a great boss.

Paisley to Lizzie

He really is.
I'll text Henry and see you guys over there.

Lizzie to Paisley

Excellent.

Paisley to Henry

Are you hungry?

Henry to Paisley

I like food.

Paisley to Henry

There will be people there, too.

Henry to Paisley

Hmm. Yes. I see the issue. I like
people less than I like food.
But! I learned something last night. I don't
have to stay forever in social situations that
I'm not into. So if the diner sucks, I'll eat and
then leave. I can do that!

Paisley to Henry

Yes! You can! I'm so proud of you, buckaroo.

Henry to Paisley

Paisley to Henry

You should text Cameron.
See if he wants to come.

Henry to Paisley

That's a very good idea.

Paisley to Henry

I am full to the brim with very good ideas.

Henry to Cameron

Hey. Want to go to the diner with . . .
people?
I don't actually know who all is going,
but Paisley just invited me.

Cameron to Henry

Hey, sure. Do you know if Lizzie will be there?

Henry to Cameron

I'm not actually privy to that information,
but you should totally invite her.

Cameron to Lizzie

Hi.

Lizzie to Cameron

Hi.
What are you up to?

Cameron to Lizzie

Um. Nothing much. I was just about
to ask you if you're busy.

Lizzie to Cameron

Want to go to the diner with
a variety of people?

Cameron to Lizzie

Will you be there?

Lizzie to Cameron

Yes. Yes, I will.

Cameron to Lizzie

Then I'm definitely in.

Lizzie to Cameron

Cool.

Cameron to Lizzie

I'll pick you up.

Lizzie to Cameron

Cool.

I wish we had met sooner.

Cameron to Lizzie

We have all summer.

Lizzie to Cameron

Then I can't wait for summer to start. ♥

Acknowledgments

The first and biggest heap of gratitude goes to the Swoon Reads family, because without them there would be no book.

A gigantic thank-you to Jean Feiwel for entrusting me with the idea of "The Prom meets *Love Actually*." A supersized thank-you to Holly West for everything. I honestly don't know what I would do without her. She's like my security blanket in the big, scary world. Further thanks to Lauren Scobell and Rachel Diebel for their incredibly helpful and motivating thoughts and comments as we drafted this book.

Many thanks to my library girls, Katie Haake, Kate Jaggers, Melanie Moffitt, Michelle Petrasek, and Chelsea Reichert, for spending one hilariously awesome evening trying to come up with titles. "Promomatopoeia" lives forever in my heart.

Thanks to Shayla Flournoy for giving Paisley a much deserved story line of her own and for being a receptacle for complaints on a daily basis. Thanks, of course, to Lauren Velella, for the draft reading and for loving everything I write to the point where I don't even really trust her opinions anymore.

Thanks to my family, especially my mom, for all of their love and support.

Last but not least, thanks to my readers who stick around from book to book and always come back for more. Thank you from the very bottom of my heart.

FEELING BOOKISH?

Turn the page for some

Swoonworthy **EXTRAS**

Sandy Hall's **PROM** Playlist

Shut Up and Dance
Walk the Moon

Can't Stop the Feeling!
Justin Timberlake

I Gotta Feeling
The Black Eyed Peas

Brand New
Ben Rector

We Are Young
fun.

Sign of the Times
Harry Styles

Happy
Pharrell Williams

Just the Way You Are
Bruno Mars

Every Single Night
Computer Games

Long Live
Taylor Swift

We Found Love
Rihanna

This Town
Niall Horan

A Coffee Date

between author Sandy Hall and her editor, Holly West

Holly West (HW): If you could be a character from any book ever written, who would you be and why?

Sandy Hall (SH): When I was a kid, I would have told you Dicey Tillerman from *Homecoming* by Cynthia Voigt. I thought she was amazing and so brave. As an adult, that sounds like a lot of hard work, all that walking and minding younger siblings. I think at this point I wouldn't mind being a townsperson in an Elin Hilderbrand novel that takes place somewhere on Cape Cod. That sounds like a nice, drama-free life to me.

HW: When you were a kid what did you want to be when you grew up?

SH: Definitely a teacher.

HW: What was the wackiest/strangest dream job you had as a kid?

SH: I had a lot of imagination as a kid, but I was strangely aware of my own limitations, so I never wanted to join the circus or be an astronaut. I think the weirdest dream job I had was when I got glasses in first grade and became obsessed with wanting to be an ophthalmologist.

HW: Can you tell us about your own senior prom?

SH: The dance part of my senior prom was fairly ho-hum in the scheme of things. It was fun, but I only remember little snippets. But tradition in my town was that all the seniors went away to the Jersey Shore for the weekend after the prom and even took Monday off from school. Like everyone just turned a blind eye to the fact that 90 percent of the senior class didn't show up to school that day. That weekend was a LOT of fun. Probably the most fun I'd ever had up to that point.

HW: What is your favorite thing about the Swoon Reads community?

SH: Without a doubt it's the support, the kind comments, and the enthusiasm of everyone in the community, from readers to my fellow authors to the Swoon staff.

HW: What is the best part about seeing your finished book on shelves?

SH: That it never gets old! I get the same thrill every time. I particularly love seeing it on library shelves.

HW: What advice do you have for writers who are in that first stage of submitting their manuscript to Swoon Reads?

SH: Read the comments on all the manuscripts. It's easier to read constructive criticism of someone else's work than of your own. Also there are useful nuggets of information to be found everywhere on the site. Be sure to interact, make friends, and read the blog!

HW: You have such amazing characters. What is your character creation process like?

SH: My characters have a lot of conversations together in my head. Long before I ever write the story, the characters start chatting each other up, and that's how I learn about them.

HW: Once you settle on a story idea, what's the next step? Are you an outliner or a pantser?

SH: I outline EVERYTHING. From chapters to scenes to every little beat. I would never finish anything without my outline. I'm super flexible when it comes to deviating from it, like if things need to be changed or skipped or added, I go with the flow. But before I can start the first draft, I need to have a very distinct picture of what I'm writing toward or else I end up flailing about and get nothing done.

HW: What is your favorite part of being a writer?

SH: The beginning of an idea, right as it crystallizes, when it has all the potential and it hasn't yet become work. I just love the possibility that one little spark of an idea can have.

HW: The most challenging?

SH: Rereading drafts. Literally any draft besides the final. I end up skimming even though I know it needs a full reread, but I just can't bring myself to look at the words for even one more second.

HW: If you could visit your pre-publication self, what advice would you give her?

SH: I'd go back to my young self, like teenage Sandy, and explain that she has this in her, but she needs to stop being a lazy bum. That high school was easy, but college will be challenging, and the number one thing she needs to do is not fail her first-year writing course! That one failure stalled my interest in writing for nearly a decade. Also I'd tell her to be nicer to her mom because someday she'll be very supportive of her dreams.

College was supposed to be Paisley's fresh start. But will old enmities get in the way of new love?

Keep reading for a sneak peek.

CHAPTER ONE

-*Paisley*-

Record scratch.

Freeze frame.

Yup, that's me. Paisley Turner. Making out with a random guy at my first college party. You're probably wondering how I got into this situation.

Not that it really matters at the moment, seeing as how all I can think about is this guy's hand on my waist and his fingers in my hair and, oh my god, there's his tongue in my mouth.

WE HAVE TONGUE, PEOPLE.

This is the weirdest, most wonderful thing that has ever happened to me.

Should I be thinking so much?

I turn my brain to silent mode and concentrate on the kissing.

When that doesn't work, I take to cataloging the moment, so I can remember it always. The way his fingers lightly brush my neck and send a chill down my spine. How the pulsing bass seems to beat along with my heart. The way the dark basement around us fades from existence. The light minty flavor on his lips that makes me wish I had brushed my teeth before leaving my dorm room.

But I wasn't thinking about making out when I left my dorm! I was thinking, "I've never had beer before, and I don't want the first time I taste it to be tainted by toothpaste breath."

Is this how college is going to be? Walking into parties and being swept away in a kiss?

This was not in the brochure.

Did I even get a brochure?

Focus, Paisley!

All too soon he pulls away from me. I want to chase his lips with my own, but I realize I'm breathless and a bit dazed and could probably use a break. I look up at his face. He's so tall I want to climb him like a tree. Just scamper up and perch on his shoulder and hang out there in his sandy-brown hair. But then I wouldn't be able to see his eyes, which are dark brown, at least in the dim light of the basement.

I am the whitest white person, there's no denying that, but my hand on his neck practically glows white because he's got this tan that's like something you'd see in a teen drama that takes place near the beach.

"That was . . . ," I say.

"Yeah," he responds when I don't finish my sentence.

I lean back and try to ignore the way the damp of the wall immediately seeps into my shirt.

"I could use a beer," Mystery Boy says. "You want a beer?"

I nod and almost as soon as he walks away, my new roommate, Stef, ambushes me.

"What the hell is going on?" she asks. Her voice isn't accusing, more intensely curious. Which I understand. This is a very curious situation.

"I don't know!" I stage whisper, glancing over at The Boy. He's standing in the beer line, waiting for a new keg to be tapped. I turn my back to him because I don't want him to be able to read my lips. I start talking. Fast. I need to get this full story relayed before he comes back over.

"So, I'm standing here in the corner, playing with my phone, trying to talk myself out of begging you to leave early. Then that guy comes up to me and he was like, 'Remember me?' And I was like, 'Yeah, totally!' Because I didn't want to admit to not knowing him. I figure he's probably one of the guys who was in our group at the choosing-a-major thing earlier."

"Yeah, maybe. I don't remember him either," Stef says. "But I'm following you so far."

"But then! Then!" I say, gesturing wildly to emphasize how completely unexpected this situation is. "Then he's like, 'I've always wanted to kiss you.' And I was like, 'Huh?' But I didn't say 'Huh,' because honestly, all I could think about was that literally on the walk here we were talking about how I'd never kissed anyone and this was, like, too good to be true."

Stef is watching him, observing him. I can tell she's going to be a really good roommate. "I wish I could place him," she says. "We've been inseparable for the past three days. Maybe he was sitting behind us at the welcome convocation yesterday?"

"I don't know. But the thing is, who cares? He's a really good kisser, and I can play along."

She grins. "Well, I'm glad to hear he wasn't harassing you. When I looked over and saw this big dude all over you, I was worried for a minute. I was this close to interrupting." She holds her fingers a hair's width apart.

"I like and appreciate those instincts," I say.

"But then I saw your arms wrap around his neck, and you seemed relaxed and into it. This makes me think we should have a sign for a time when you aren't into it. Or when I'm not into it, for that matter."

I nod along even though what I'm really thinking about is kissing this boy some more, right away. Stef is going to be a great roommate, but there's a chance that I'm going to be a terrible one.

"He's coming back over!" Stef says in a whisper yell. "Try to find out who he is! I'm going to talk to that girl over there, the one playing beer pong. You can't be the only one of us who gets to make out at our first college party."

She slides away just as The Boy returns with two red Solo cups of beer.

"Here," he says. He smiles a sort of tight-lipped smile that might not be attractive on most people, but on this guy, it really works.

"Thanks," I say.

He shuffles in place, looking as awkward as I feel. Possibly even more awkward.

I wish we could go back to making out immediately. I suppose we can't enjoy our beer and make out at the same time.

All I know is that I am not the same person I was when I walked into this damp, slightly gross basement a little over an hour ago.

"I like your T-shirt," he says, his cheeks pinking up. I might actually be in love with him. "Pilot episode," he reads out loud, gesturing toward my boobs. He quickly puts his hand down when he realizes where he's pointing.

I want nothing more than to assuage his embarrassment. That is my only goal.

"You should know that the way to my heart is through complimenting my T-shirts. I make them myself. I got really into screen printing a few months ago. It's like my hobby." Oh god, that's so unbelievably weird. Why did I say that?

"You're really into screen printing T-shirts?" he asks, a bemused expression crossing his features.

"It's a long story," I say.

"You'll have to make me one sometime."

"I could definitely do that." Okay, that's a little more like it. Maybe he's not totally turned off by my bizarre, nerdy hobby.

"So why 'pilot episode'?"

"Well, I figure if my life were a TV show, this party would be featured in the pilot episode."

He laughs.

"Though I have to say," I continue. "I feel like they really distort college parties on TV, unless this isn't a fair representation of one to begin with. I'm pretty sure we're currently being exposed to asbestos." I point up toward the world's saddest disco ball hanging from one of the exposed pipes.

"My roommate, Ray, his brother Luis lives here," The Boy explains even though I don't technically know who any of these people are. He gestures toward the corner where there are two boys with their heads bent over the keg, laughing about something; their dark hair is nearly black and their golden skin is like something from a teen telenovela that takes place near the beach. I don't get a good look at their faces, but I can tell they're brothers even from across the room.

"That's how I got invited," he continues. "I have to admit this seems pretty spot-on to me."

"I must watch too many shows about rich kids," I say.

He laughs again. I'm beginning to really like his laugh.

-Carter-

This is unbelievable! This is amazing! How is this even happening?

Paisley Turner is right here in front of me, chatting away, making me laugh, and acting like nothing happened five years ago. And we're bonding. At least I think we're bonding.

I saw her a couple of times in passing over the past few days. But we weren't in the same orientation group, so I never got close enough to talk to her.

I'm not sure how I got up the nerve to tell her that I always wanted to kiss her or why it was the second thing that came out of my mouth. I guess I'll blame the sip of vodka I had with Ray while we were pregaming in our room.

When Ray invited me to a party at his brother's house, I expected a dank, dim basement. That's how my older sister Thea always described college parties. I was prepared for that. I was not prepared for Paisley Turner to wander in.

She takes a sip from her cup and turns away for a minute, giving me the chance to really look at her. She hasn't changed much since eighth grade. Same brown hair, same short haircut, same inquisitive green eyes.

"So are you on the swim team?" I ask.

"No," she says. "But my roommate, Stef, is."

I nod and take a sip of beer. It's really not great.

She takes another sip and wrinkles her nose.

"Is this supposed to be good?" she asks.

"I was thinking the same thing! The way people go on and on about beer, I always expect more from it."

"Right? I've never tried it before, and I was expecting much better." She pauses, shaking her head as she takes another sip. "This might be the worst thing I've ever tasted."

I swirl the liquid in my glass and sniff at it. "I'm detecting swamp water and something else. Something earthier," I say in a snobby tone.

She laughs. "It has a bouquet of skunk."

"Ah yes. Organic, I'm sure." I take another sip. "It's medium-bodied with a whisper of backwash."

"And the finish," she says. "The finish is something heretofore unknown to me. Something like butts with a hint of ass."

We can't stop laughing now.

Somehow in the midst of this conversation, I've actually finished my beer.

I stare down at the empty cup. "I guess making fun of it makes it go down easier. Maybe that's the trick that no one tells you about."

She takes a last gulp from her cup. "Guess so," she says.

This time we go over to the keg together, little bursts of giggles bubbling up as we think of something new and funny to add.

"There really must be some kind of beer industry conspiracy. I don't know how so many people can like it when it tastes like this," I say, taking another gulp.

"We should really get to the bottom of this. Maybe start a podcast about the beer industry conspiracy."

"We need to start with beer industry propaganda."

"You mean, the commercials with the scantily clad women and the endless summer fun?" she asks.

"Exactly."

Anytime I think we're about to lose steam in this conversation, one of us says something else funny, insightful, or both. I'm not sure I've ever actually laughed this hard before. Hours seem to pass like minutes. I've heard people use that phrase before but had never personally experienced it in real life.

"Okay, so aside from hating beer, what else do you hate?" I ask. I have a feeling that anything Paisley says is going to be enormously entertaining. "Like what are your pet peeves?"

"Hmm," she says, eyes going wide. "I have so many, starting with people who walk more than two across on a sidewalk and won't get out of the way when you need to pass them. Also, when the fitted sheet comes off one corner of the bed, chewed pen caps, and people who use radar sounds for their cell phone ringtone."

"That's quite the list," I say.

"I could go on and on," she says. "What are yours?"

"I hate excuses," I say. "I hate people who make excuses and I hate making them myself." This is the truth, but I didn't expect to share such a serious truth at the moment. But might as well be up-front from the beginning.

"Wow. That's very specific and makes my pet peeves seem petty."

"Nah, I've just thought about this a lot."

"Obviously. And duly noted, I will never make excuses to you."

A yell erupts from the beer pong table.

"Dammit, Bart!" someone yells, and I look over.

I glance at Paisley, and she's looking at me. "What?" she asks.

"I thought I heard someone call my name."

"Oh, okay," she says, and giggles. I think she might be getting drunk.

On our third or fourth beer—I'm not sure because I'm definitely drunk at this point—Paisley takes a long sip and ends up with some froth on her nose. My life has become a goddamned romantic comedy tonight.

"You've got a little something," I say, pointing at my own nose.

She tries to brush it away and misses it, so of course I have no choice but to brush it away myself.

"Thanks," she says, her eyes lingering on mine.

This is the moment to kiss her again. This is the time to make my move. I don't want to be greedy, but I want more.

As I'm about to lean in, a human blur runs past us toward the stairs and out the back door. Paisley pulls back and away from the moment.

"I think that was my roommate," she says.

"You think?" I ask, trying to get Paisley's focus back on me.

She stands. "I know it was my roommate."

Abandoning her empty cup, she runs up the stairs and out the back door in pursuit.

I figure I might as well follow. Couldn't hurt, might even be seen as chivalrous.

I find them in the corner of the tiny backyard. It's mostly full of garbage. College kids have no pride in a place. There's a perfectly good bicycle in the corner with two popped tires and a rusted chain.

Paisley's roommate is standing near that bicycle, bent at the waist with her hands on her knees, breathing heavily, her long, dark hair creating a curtain around her face.

"What's up?" I ask Paisley.

"Stef doesn't feel well, so I think we're going to head back to the dorm."

"What dorm do you live in?"

"Robinson."

"Oh, me too! I'll walk back with you."

We head out to the street, leaving the depressing backyard behind, and Stef walks a few feet in front of us, swaying a little.

"I don't think she can really hold her alcohol," Paisley says.

"Oh right, yes, not like us."

"No, you and I are obviously seasoned drinkers." She lets out a loud belch and giggles.

"This is probably the most I've ever drank in one night," I admit.

"Same," she says. "I just feel so full." She rubs her stomach.

"Maybe this is why people do shots. So they don't feel so full," I suggest.

Stef stands at the corner, waiting for the light to turn in our favor. There's not a lot of traffic out in the wee hours of the morning on the roads surrounding our campus, but it's good to know that even though she's drunk, she still remembers to follow the rules of the road.

"I am Estefania Gomez! And I am here to have fun!" she yells into the street.

"Sure you are, Stef!" Paisley calls back to her.

"I'm sorry I interrupted your time with the cute boy," Stef says over her shoulder as a lone car passes.

"I'm cute?" I ask Paisley.

"Don't be coy. You know you're cute."

"I really don't know that. It's nice to hear," I say, my neck heating up.

She gives me a sidelong glance and steps in front of me to link arms with

Stef as the walk sign lights up. I stay a few paces behind them, realizing that I probably should have told Ray I was leaving the party. We don't have each other's numbers yet, so I can't text him.

Hopefully, he'll realize I left and come back to the dorm on his own. Or maybe he's staying at his brother's tonight. I don't know his life.

Either way, I doubt he'll be worrying about me. I make a mental note to exchange numbers with him tomorrow, though.

When we get to the dorm, Stef tries to use her card to get in, but she's holding it backward. She's basically the cartoon stereotype of a drunk person. Paisley helps her out, and we enter the building. I stand and wait for the elevator with them.

"Um, so this was fun," I say.

"It really was," Paisley says. Stef tugs on her arm, pulling her into the elevator.

"Good night," I say.

"Night, Bart," she says as the doors slide shut.

It takes me a second to process, and when I do, I almost hit the up button to stop the elevator.

"Did she just call me Bart?" I ask the empty hallway.

Check out more books
chosen for publication
by readers like you.